An aspiring dressmaker, orphaned Starling Smith is accustomed to fighting for her own survival. But when she's offered a year's wages to temporarily pose as a wealthy man's bride, she suspects ulterior motives. She can't lose the chance to open her own shop, but she won't be any man's lover, not even handsome, infuriating Alisdair Seymour's…

To prevent his visiting sister from parading potential brides in front of him, Alisdair has decided to present a fake wife. He lost his heart once, and had it broken—he doesn't intend to do it again. But stubborn, spirited Starling is more alluring than he bargained for, and Alisdair will risk everything he has to prove his love is true…

Set against the sweeping backdrop of 1866 South Australia, Starling is a novel of cherished dreams and powerful desires, and the young woman bold enough to claim them both…

Visit us at www.kensingtonbooks.com

I0677337

Books by Virginia Taylor

Starling

Published by Kensington Publishing Corporation

Starling

Virginia Taylor

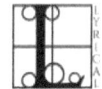

LYRICAL PRESS
Kensington Publishing Corp.
www.kensingtonbooks.com

RJT, all my love forever.

Acknowledgements

Thanks to my author friend, C. S. Harris, for leading the way.

Chapter 1

Adelaide, South Australia, 1866

"Straighten your collar, girl," said the sharp-faced clerk guarding the office door. His olive jacket faded into the green-papered walls of the anteroom. "Mr. Seymour don't like to see his employees looking scruffy."

Starling Smith fingered the starched white cotton around her throat. She didn't look scruffy in the Seymour's Emporium uniform she had worn with pride for the past two weeks. She looked neat and anonymous in the plain gray. Any female lucky enough to be employed selling fabrics should be nothing less than tidy—and diligent, too.

Yesterday, when the owner, Mr. Alasdair Seymour, had toured the emporium he stopped to inspect the materials she had ranked using the rainbow color scale, a new idea of her own. He had taken her name from the department manager, and now he possibly meant to commend her.

His office door opened. "Miss Smith?"

Remembering her place, she leapt to her feet.

He glanced at his clerk. "I'm not to be disturbed. Come into my office, Miss Smith." Broad shouldered and tall, he looked younger than he had the day before, under thirty and handsome enough to deserve those sighs from the shopgirls.

Starling's knees wobbled as she hastened past him through the doorway.

"Take a seat," he said, taking his own. He wore his dark hair fashionably collar-length.

She perched on a carved chair upholstered in dark green brocade. The hovering red of sunset shone through the tall windows dressed with swags of yellow-striped silk. Sparkling motes floated to his desk where he sat, picked up a pen, and tapped the end on his blotter. His forehead was smooth, his nose precisely chiseled, and his jaw firm.

"Do you enjoy your job?" He looked straight at her. His eyes, an assessing luminous gray, sent a shimmer of panic through her.

She quickly lowered her gaze, trying to regain her breath. "I do." Her voice sounded embarrassingly husky. "I like working with fabrics."

"You worked in a hotel before you came here." He scrutinized a page lying on his desk. "They gave you no reference."

She had thrown away the crumpled piece of paper that described her as "a good worker," hoping she could gloss over the six weeks she had been employed at the Star Inn, mentioned in the South Australian police records as a site of gambling and prostitution. "I didn't think a temporary job would matter when I was waiting on the Seymour's list for more than a year."

He glanced up, his gaze again causing a strange jumble inside her. "You've had a small amount of education? That is, you can read and write?"

"Yes, sir. Or I wouldn't have applied here."

"Unfortunately, you've been annoying my customers." He set down his pen.

She drew a surprised breath. "I sell them what they want, sir."

"You sell them what you think they should have."

Shaking her head, she stared at her fingers knotted in her lap. "I sell them what they need. It wouldn't be right to sell fabrics not strong enough for their purpose or too heavy or the wrong color."

"And it seems you have decided on the colors they should have."

"I advise them on what might...suit."

"I don't pay you to advise my customers to buy cheaper fabrics than those they choose or less material. I pay you to make money for me."

"I do, sir." She leaned forward. "Just the other day, a young lady came back to buy more fabric. She said I'd given her just the right material for her ball gown, and she wanted me to help her again."

"Mr. Porter thinks the fabric department can cope without female staff."

"Female staff?" she queried, shaken. "But he told me I'm a quick learner."

He shrugged. "I'm sorry but I am not going to keep you at the emporium."

"You're going to get rid of me? Oh, no, you don't mean that. I get twice as many sales as Mr. Porter."

He shook his head, placing his pen in the holder. "I can, however, offer you a different position." He aligned his blotter with the edge of the desk. "In my home."

A quick shake of her head dealt with his offer of a maid's job. "I won't advise your customers about colors. I was wrong, and I'm sorry." Her voice rose with hope. "I would accept a position in any other of your departments."

"I don't have a position in any other department. I *do* have a list a mile long of women wanting to work in the emporium, as you know." He evaded her gaze.

Focusing on her weary black shoes, she exhaled her last hope. She'd loved measuring the soft fabrics, feeling the quality, and sliding the sharp scissors across the width. She'd loved working out the profits. She stood, not caring that her shoulders drooped.

He pushed out his chair and stood, facing her. "You could earn quite a bit of money if you accept my alternative. I'm much in need of a woman like you."

She straightened. *A woman like her?* "If you don't want me, I will get a job at Harris's."

"Unlikely, given that they don't employ females *with* or with*out* references. I won't beat around the bush." Pausing, he eased his black cravat with a forefinger. "You look respectable. I need a woman to pose as my wife for a couple of weeks."

Aghast, she took a step back. He didn't want a maid. He wanted to tup her. "I don't know what gave you the impression that I might do that, but—"

"Money." His lips tilted cynically. "Now, what would you say to five pounds for the two weeks?"

"No." Her jaw tense, she backed to the door. "I worked as a laundress at the inn. Not a prostitute."

He raised his eyebrows. "You only have to *pretend* to be my wife."

"I'm not good at pretending. I never have been." She opened the door and walked out.

Cheeks hot with humiliation, she strode past the clerk and down to the fabric department where, with shaking hands, she grabbed the cloth bag holding an apple, a clean pair of cuffs, a handkerchief, and a few pennies. Tying her shawl across her shoulders, she took the staff exit leading to a narrow alley off Rundle Street. She didn't have time to weep.

First, she would need to retrieve her belongings from the emporium's boardinghouse and next find accommodation for the night. The Star Inn might let her use the laundry room. If not, her friend Meg would find her a safe place.

Starling's chest hurt and her eyes prickled. As she pulled the heavy door, she noticed the purple haze hovering over the sunset. She stood staring, her dreams shattered and her life in pieces. Gathering her bag under her arm, she hurried down the cobbled alley, chased by the aroma of fresh horse manure and settling smoke. A hot wind whipped her hair across her face, forcing her to pause. Blinking hard, she tucked the strands behind her ears.

Dashing the back of her wrist over her eyes, she cornered into Rundle Street. Mr. Seymour stepped in front of her. His high-crowned hat cast a shadow across his features.

"This way." He seized her elbow.

She wrenched her arm out of his grip. "Let me be. I don't want your money or you."

"I have to have you tonight." He drew a deep breath. "I'll give you six pounds."

She backed away, disgusted. "I know at least three women who would accept your proposition. Go to the Star Inn and see which you would prefer."

He shook his head. "I wouldn't be standing here with you if I hadn't already tried that. None could pass as a lady."

"So, now you want a lady? I thought you said a wife."

"My wife would, of course, be a lady. I spent the last two weeks interviewing whores and actresses. Then I looked at my staff yesterday, and there you were with your careful speech, your background at the Star Inn, and your neat and plain appearance."

"Neat and plain." She firmed her lips.

"Good Lord, girl." His voice softened. "I'm offering you real money, far more than the fourteen shillings a week you earned here, to live a life of luxury for two weeks. You don't need to look at me as if I'm Satan. I'm giving you the greatest opportunity of your life."

"I had the greatest opportunity of my life—a job as a shopgirl." She blinked hard. "And for reasons of your own, you've taken my best chance from me."

His brow creased. "I'm offering you a better one."

"I have plans that don't include being anyone's wife, real or not."

"Two weeks, that's all I ask," he said in a long-suffering tone. With a sweep of his hand, he indicated she could move in the direction he wanted her to go.

She folded her arms.

He gave her a sideways glint. "I'll pay you *twenty* pounds."

"No." She wet her mouth.

"Perhaps you *won't* suit," he said, shrugging. "Mr. Porter said you were intelligent, but you are acting like a simpleton. I have offered you more than half a year's wages, and all you can do is persist in your belief that I want to bed you."

"Mr. Porter said I was intelligent?" Her voice rose with hope.

He raised his eyebrows.

"So, why can't you put me back in the fabric department?" She brushed down her sleeves, stalling while she thought. "I'm good at selling materials because I like selling materials."

He didn't want her as a maid, and he didn't want to tup her? She didn't understand what he wanted.

He heaved a monumental sigh. "And I'm sure you'll like pretending to be my wife because if you make a convincing job of it, I'll give you *forty pounds*."

Her mouth dried. Forty pounds! That was double twenty. For twenty pounds she could hire a little shop of her own. For forty pounds, she could not only buy stock, but also employ at least two other *Birds* from the orphanage. Robin and Nightingale would be her first choice.

Her breath fluttered. "You don't want to bed me?"

He looked her up and down. "Do you think you're my type?"

She put her hand to her hair and, blushing, quickly brought her arm down again. A gentleman who owned a number of emporiums, proving a head for business, wouldn't invest more than a few shillings in an untried, drab bed partner. He could take his pick of women.

"Well, what would the job entail *exactly*?"

"Just doing whatever wives do. Having breakfast with me in the morning, arranging flowers, eating cakes, drinking tea, sitting in the drawing room doing whatever you please until I tell you otherwise."

"What might 'otherwise' be?" She eyed him narrowly.

"Standing by my side and agreeing with every word I say while smiling pleasantly at my guests. You can smile, I suppose?"

"I'm not sure."

He gave her a suspicious glance.

"The job can't be as easy as you say." For forty pounds, there had to be a catch.

"It's as easy as you want to make it. I have a household that runs perfectly already."

"Then why do you want a wife? Other than to idle away the day."

Pushing aside his unbuttoned jacket, he slid his hands into the pockets of his biscuit-colored trousers. How he maintained a fit, broad-shouldered physique while sitting behind a desk all day was a mystery to Starling. Although she'd met no other rich men, she had assumed they were those with barrel bellies. "Last week my sister notified me she is bringing a lady with her, a lady she is sure I would like to see. She arrives from Victoria tomorrow."

"I don't understand."

"I don't like my sister's plan. She has tried this matchmaking before." His mouth tightened. "I told her I wouldn't marry any of her hopefuls."

"You don't need to marry the lady simply because your sister knows her."

"Nor do I need to have prospective brides presented to me so often that I give in out of sheer self-defense."

"Life is hard for rich men," she said sweetly.

"Exactly." He nodded for emphasis. "If I present you as a *fait accompli,* I will stop my sister in her tracks. So, are we agreed?"

She caught her bottom lip between her teeth.

"My deadline is today. I need to present a wife to my household by tonight. And, since I doubt you own suitable clothing," he said, averting his gaze, "we'll pick out a couple of gowns and, er, the trimmings before the emporium closes."

She deliberated. "I only have to smile, idle the day away, and agree with you?"

He nodded. "I want you to be as meek, quiet, and respectful as a good wife should be."

"And I will be a wife in name only?"

"That is our agreement."

Growing hope straightened her shoulders. Perhaps her dream was not lost.

He began to herd her along North Terrace. "I expect it will be worth forty pounds to prove my point," he muttered.

"That you won't ever marry? Are you a lady-man?"

His eyes widened momentarily. "A lady-man? Do you mean...? You do. Don't use gutter terms around my guests, or you'll be out of the house without a penny before you can sneeze. Of course I'm not bent. I simply want only one woman."

She could but wish. If she'd thought he only liked men, she could relax. "But isn't that a reason to marry?"

"I'm not sure intelligent and smart are the same thing. Enough. You have agreed to our bargain. The lady I want is already married, and it's time you became the sort of wife I require."

Starling nodded. He had specified a wife with a neat, plain appearance. She was neat and plain. Ordinary. Her body was slender, her skin was sallow, and she had brown hair and eyes. No male had ever glanced at her twice. At the inn, her plainness had been her best protection. Meg had told her she could be pretty if she tried, but she had no need to be pretty. She didn't want or need a man. In fact, her plan depended on her remaining single. No husband would let her follow through with her business idea. Married, she would blight more lives than her own.

She had nothing to lose by doing as he asked and had gained instead an opportunity to earn a great deal of money. She would obey Mr. Seymour's every edict. Opportunity had knocked, and Starling Smith only had to widen the door to reach her goal.

Half a pace behind Mr. Seymour, she passed the lawyer's offices, the pastry shop, the tailor, and a saddlery. The main commercial thoroughfare of Adelaide was familiar to her: the old wooden sheds, the new Georgian buildings, the constant grind of carriage wheels, the thump-thump of hooves, the bustle of people, and the push of their presence. Not only had she worked in the city, she'd lived nearby her whole nineteen years, watching the adornment of the newest constructions with ornate pillars and pretty plastered curlicues. She couldn't imagine living elsewhere.

Mr. Seymour pushed open the front door of his emporium. Dimly lit, the shop was preparing to close. He led the way to the ready-mades area upstairs and stood waiting for attention. The floor manager bowed from the waist.

"Miss Smith needs assistance," Mr. Seymour said.

The manager clicked his fingers for a shopgirl, who hastened forward. Starling knew Jinny, the red-haired assistant, from the boardinghouse.

"Three new gowns. Nothing gaudy. Help Miss Smith choose. I'll be back in half an hour." With that, Mr. Seymour strode away.

Jinny widened her eyes at Starling, who smiled and shrugged. Jinny moistened her lips and bustled about finding ready-made gowns while Starling stood by her left shoulder, pointing out those she wanted. Brown, being the cheapest dye, had been the color for the foundlings. She had worn brown her whole life until two weeks ago, when she'd exchanged that color for the gray of the Seymour uniform. Knowing neither flattered her, she decided that because this handsome man had chosen a plain woman for his bride, she should not try to change her appearance.

She kept on the last gown she tried. Patterned in a jaundiced green and brown, the high-buttoned fit was as unflattering as the other two she'd chosen. Continuing her disapproving silence, Jinny parceled them and Starling's uniform. When Mr. Seymour returned, he took the purchases, cramming them with a few other parcels into a new holdall. Next, he let Starling choose a plain brown hat. She wore that, too, certain she looked even more thin faced wearing a flat-brimmed poke with a long ribbon tie.

Finally, he took her to the jeweler's shop and bought her a plain gold ring. Keeping her face expressionless, she slid on the circlet. How she would pass as the wife of a gentleman, she didn't know. Nor did she know why he thought she might. She could only hope that the colors she had chosen to wear would merge her into the background, as she didn't plan to lose the forty pounds before she'd seen a single penny.

When he marched her outside the shop again, she totaled his purchases: one pound for the ring and more good money for a hat and gowns. He had shelled out a tidy sum to deceive a sister who merely wanted to see him happily married. Starling hoped she could play her unworthy role.

She kept pace with him, her bonnet ribbons fluttering as she moved closer to her goal. Eagles might soar. Starlings took chances when they saw them.

Chapter 2

Mr. Seymour's carriage smelled of new leather. Starling stepped in, taking as little space as possible on the dark blue seat. "What should I call you?"

He sat beside her, placing his hat on the space between them. "Mr. Seymour. Perhaps Alasdair. Yes, that would be more convincing."

Starling mulled using his first name as the carriage trundled through the dark whispery parklands and turned onto a street off the park road, not five minutes out of the city. The wall in front was red brick with one arched entrance to the front of the house and another larger one to the coach house, where the conveyance headed as soon as Mr. Seymour assisted Starling out of the carriage and into the warm night air.

Through the heavy gate, a façade fronted by two white pillars glowed in the lamplight. Heart racing, about to take a role for which she had no experience, she breathed in the night-time scents from his garden and followed him up a flight of four marble stairs to the front door, which was opened by a lace-capped, upright lady in black.

"The bride." She smiled. "Welcome to your new home, Mrs. Seymour." Her expression didn't slip even when she saw Starling in the light of the marble-tiled hall.

"She'll want a bath, Mrs. Brighton," Mr. Seymour said, handing her his hat. "She's been traveling for days."

"I'll organize one immediately." Mrs. Brighton didn't need to snap her fingers for a pretty maid to appear. "This is Ellen."

Starling glanced at the girl. Ellen, a young, round-faced female of medium height, bobbed a curtsy, took the holdall from Mr. Seymour, and whisked Starling up the main stairs. Reaching the last room around the landing, Ellen opened the door to reveal a huge bedroom, dominated by a tester bed covered in gold and blue brocade. Windows were positioned at the side and back of the room. A polished table and two blue velvet chairs sat in front of closed gold curtains.

Starling entered the room practically holding her breath. An arrangement of ferns sat in the marble fireplace, the mantelpiece set either end with a gilded horn held by a barely draped lady.

"You must be so tired." Ellen placed Starling's gowns into the bottom drawer of the tallboy. "It's a long journey from Ballarat. Mrs. Brighton thought I oughta bring you a meal and tuck you into bed after your bath. She said she'd show you the house and introduce you to the rest of the servants tomorrow." She pulled the brown paper wrapping off Mr. Seymour's parcels and put them in a drawer above Starling's gowns. Then she began to set up a bath behind a screen painted with bright, exotically swirled flowers.

Starling would have given the world to have worn a uniform as becoming as Ellen's—dark blue, beautifully cut, and embellished with a white linen cap and apron. "Who is Mrs. Brighton?"

"The housekeeper." Ellen giggled. "Me and the other servants're glad that the master finally has what he needs."

Starling stared at the maid.

"A wife." Ellen put a palm on her blushing cheek. The first two fingers of that hand were missing. "He should'a got you from Ballarat in his coach, though, rather than leaving you to travel all alone on the rattler." She shook her head as if in rebuke. "I better get the water."

Within ten minutes, Starling was sitting up to her neck in the first hot bath she'd had in a week. She let her head drift under the water, enjoying the gurgling block to everyday sounds that allowed her to hum and assume she was tuneful. Finally, she washed, and then she soaked, dreaming about being someone's daughter, loved and cherished. But like the Starling she'd been named for, she had no uncommon attributes. Perhaps her sense of the ridiculous was too highly developed, but she kept that well under control. She saw herself as practical and diligent, perhaps a little obstinate with her opinions. That would be why, when the whores had listened to her advice on colors, her head had swelled and she had thought herself an expert. She now knew the folly of overconfidence.

The bath water cooled. She wrapped herself in a thick white towel and ate her apple, never one to waste good food. Ellen had whisked away her discarded underclothing and put her gown in the long drawer. Not prepared to be tucked into bed naked, she inspected the drawer in which Ellen had placed Mr. Seymour's trimmings.

Her eyes widened. On top sat three new sets of underwear. Nightwear, too. Not silk or satin, just plain linen, though much finer than her usual calico. The realization that Mr. Seymour had handled her underwear sent a rush of embarrassment through her body. Closing her eyes against her fantastical thoughts, she slipped on a nightgown that covered her from her neck to her toes, and she wished she also could cover her hands. The damage done by the lye soap at the inn would likely never heal. Clean and cozy, she tugged the bellpull beside the fireplace as Ellen had asked her to do.

Almost instantly, the maid arrived and began emptying the water. "Mrs. Brighton wants to know if you'd prefer wine or tea with your supper?"

"Tea, please."

She stared at the maid's retreating back while she combed her hair with her fingers. Mr. Do-As-I-Tell-You Seymour hadn't let her get her belongings, among which was a new comb. She glanced around the room and spotted a silver-backed brush in front of the tallboy mirror. The rich provided every kind of luxury.

Luckily, her hair was easily managed. She brushed her locks through and fluffed her curls to dry, then she went back to the bed and sat cross-legged. She sank inches deep in the down-filled mattress.

Ellen arrived within moments bearing a heavy silver tray. Efficiently, she set the table, uncovering the food dishes with pride. "Cook's been preparing most of the day." She pulled out the velvet-covered chair for Starling. "We're all that excited. She wanted to do something special for you. She hopes you like the food."

Starling sat, her disappointment in Mr. Seymour making her chest ache. He'd prepared his obliging servants for his bride, and instead he'd presented them with a shopgirl, a former laundress. How used they would feel when the charade ended. Mr. Seymour wouldn't have thought of that, nor would he have cared. He lacked respect for them and his sister, too. A man like him didn't deserve a sister.

Ellen put a white linen napkin on Starling's lap.

"Soup and pie. Lovely. And cream. My favorites. Thank you."

The maid beamed. "Cook'll be glad to hear that. Ring when you've finished, and I'll clear up. Then you can pop into bed."

Starling doubted that she'd ever tasted a meal as good. The vegetable soup slid smoothly down her throat. The meat in the pie hardly needed chewing. She also devoured a rich custard covered with cream and decorated with tiny sugared violets. Had everything tasted rancid, she still would have enjoyed the prettiest meal she'd seen.

After Ellen had cleaned up and said good night, Starling turned down the gas lamp and sank into the luxurious bed. She could have been dead and floating to heaven on a cloud. Her hands supporting her head, she gazed at the ornately decorated ceiling. Surely through the gloom she could see gold paint on some of the leaves. She sighed contentedly. Heaven.

This was her night, the best night of her life. She'd had hours of pampering and kindness. *And the bed, the bed, the bed,* she thought, turning over on her face and breathing the freshly laundered smell of the sheets. A girl would do anything for a bed like this, huge and unshared. She turned down the lamp and snuggled into a guiltless sleep.

* * * *

Starling didn't wake suddenly. At first she felt an awareness of someone in the room. Before opening her eyes, she caressed the linen sheet and let her head roll on the feather pillow. She remembered the night before and luxuriated in the safety and comfort. Inside, she smiled. The unmistakable smell of a lit candle made her realize that darkness surrounded her, not the morning light. She opened one eye.

The rotten, dishonest dog turd! Mr. Seymour had lied to her. Everyone had lied to her.

She squeezed her eyes tight again, hoping she'd been dreaming. But she knew she hadn't been. The candle smell was as easily recognizable as the perfumed soap on her skin. Her welcome had been a trick. The servants had connived with their master to lull her into bathing, perfuming, and climbing into bed. A lamb for the slaughter, a sacrificial offering for this man's foul lusts. She'd seen him, almost completely undressed.

Through her slitted lids, she absorbed his wide, straight shoulders, bunched with muscle; his tapered waist; and his hard, tight bottom. He had a powerful, dangerous body. She remembered her last thought before she'd gone to sleep. *A girl would do anything for this bed.* She feared the words might be true.

She eased the sheet to her nose, squinting at him in the candlelight while not wanting to see his hard body, not wanting to see his lustful face. She stayed completely still. If she moved or tried to escape before she had to, she might warn him of her intentions.

With her heart beating in her throat, almost choking her with its rhythmic thundering, she waited, stiff with fear.

He turned. She saw his pecker. Not a little pointed thing as she thought a pecker might be, but a blunted rod of flesh. As he slid a white robe over his head, she quickly closed her eyes.

She heard his approach—the whisper of his feet on the carpet. Her breathing halted. The blankets lifted. The bedsprings sagged. If he took her, she would scream the walls down.

He moved. He sighed. The acrid smoke of a candle assaulted her nose. The sheet was tugged a little from her body. Then nothing. When she resumed breathing, her chest ached.

Naked or clothed, he was the most magnificent man she'd ever seen. The man with everything except principles. He'd said he didn't plan to tup her. Why, then, did he share her bed?

* * * *

Breezes sent leaves scurrying in the street. A night bird chirruped. In the distance, a dog barked. Alasdair closed his eyes, too aware of the fresh aroma emanating from the body beside his. With nowhere else to bathe tonight, he had conceded his daily luxury to her, regrettable but imperative. The working classes were called "the great unwashed," and he knew why, having had a limited income himself until seven years ago.

These days, now rich, he saw being clean as symbolic. Each lathering removed the years of poverty, and in his case, the clinging dirt of the mines. With each bath, he cleansed himself of his past.

He eased out a breath as he relaxed for sleep, hoping his fake marriage would thwart his sister long enough for her to understand that he was no eligible bachelor needing help to find a bride. Marriage was definitely off his agenda. Telling Mary so was like fighting a curtain. He'd suffered her two previous aspirants, pretty enough and well connected, but neither had inspired in him anything other than a desire to lie face down in a stagnant puddle.

Because he would never love any woman but Lavender, he did not contemplate a life sentence with another. He had always known Lavender's parents would not consent to her marrying a man in trade. He had always known he was not gently born; yet when she'd told him both, he took her rejection like an angry child...until sanity rescued him. He had nothing to offer the well-bred beauty, nothing but a head full of dreams and a home he shared with his mother and young sister, nothing but love and the will to better himself, both of which she had spurned.

Soon after, she'd married a wealthy banker.

Determined to prove himself good enough for anyone or die trying, he left for the goldfields in Ballarat. Within the next two years, he'd earned enough money to leave his parents' dilapidated warehouse and begin the empire he now owned. However, no amount of money could replace the haughty beauty whose smile had brightened the dreariest winter, whose body had warmed the coldest bed.

And nothing could make him trust another woman with his dreams.

* * * *

"Water's hot, Mr. Seymour."

Alasdair grunted. He rolled onto his back as the bedroom door closed behind Ellen. As always, he raised his arms, stretching and lacing his fingers together, turning his palms uppermost. Then he eased each arm to the side, connecting on his right with a fleshed presence.

"Sorry. I forgot you were there."

"I shouldn't be," said the shopgirl, the supposedly ex-laundress, the assuredly ex-whore, her expression guarded. "In a house this size, no one needs to share a bed."

"To convince the servants of our hasty marriage, we do." He yawned. "That's why I needed a female like you. I could hardly ask an *innocent* to sleep with me."

"You let me think—"

"I don't enjoy sharing any more than you do. I'm used to sleeping in the middle." He sat up and glanced at her. "What happened to your hair?"

Her assessing eyes examined his face. "Lice," she said finally, sliding out of bed. "Little crawly things. When they breed in your hair, you get your head shaved."

"I wasn't wondering why you don't have long hair. I meant your hair looked..." He could hardly say "pretty." In this forced bed-sharing situation, a compliment could be misconstrued. "Softer." He scratched his neck, hoping the itch wasn't due to a bite.

She pressed her lips together and averted her gaze. "What should I do today?" she asked in a casual voice.

"Stand beside me. Smile when you meet my sister." He swung out of bed, tangled in the nightshirt. Normally, he slept naked. "For the next two weeks, you're my dutiful wife." He walked over to the hot water, hauling the blasted nightshirt over his head. After tying a clean towel from the rack around his waist, he picked up his hairbrush, which had snagged a few long, curly, brown hairs. He put the brush down again.

As he stropped his razor, his conscience pricked him. "Perhaps you ought to use the water before I shave."

"I had a bath last night."

"And you'll wash every morning, too. Hurry. I don't want to stand around half-naked." In the future, he would get Ellen to fill two basins.

He turned toward the window. Low brick walls and paths sectioned the back area into herb, vegetable, and flower gardens, with fruit trees along the sidewall of the coach house and stables, from behind which the sun was emerging. From where he stood, he could see straight ahead to the trickling river.

Derry, the gardener, had begun to weed. The housemaid, Ellen, walked up to him and tapped him on the shoulder. She smiled. Derry stood, shading his eyes and grinning back. The two were clearly smitten, although no betrothal had been announced as yet.

After a little splashing, Starling said, "Thank you for the new underclothes."

"I said I'd buy the trimmings."

"The trimmings are pretty. With ribbons."

"Good."

She splashed without speaking, then she said, after clearing her throat, "Need the chamber pot."

He turned to face her. "*I* need the chamber pot."

"After you." She tilted her head to the side, like a big-eyed bird hoping for a morsel.

He crossed his arms. "Don't throw orders at me. If you want the chamber pot, say, 'I want the chamber pot,' and if you expect me to listen to you, say 'please.'"

"I need the chamber pot, please."

"I don't have one." Fortunately. As her employer, he was already forced into more intimacy with her than he wanted. "There's a privy room near the stairs. I'll show you where if you'll just wait for me to put my trousers on."

"Be pleased."

"*I'd* be pleased."

Her eyes widened. "Well, then, you should've put them on before."

He laughed, surprised by her neat trap.

After her trip down the passage, she didn't dress, and she showed no signs of preparing to do so before Ellen entered bearing the best silver to set his table for breakfast.

"Was the bed comfortable, Mrs. Seymour?" Ellen asked.

"Lovely."

"I hope the master—"

"Careful," Alasdair warned. "It might be safer if you brought in breakfast without speaking."

"I was just going to say that I hope that the master enjoyed—"

"Ellen!"

"Supper last night, by himself. I thought he shoulda—"

"For God's sake, bring breakfast!"

Ellen scuttled out of the room.

Alasdair couldn't imagine why he'd assumed Ellen was asking about his wedding night. Maybe she had meant to. She could be scurrilous at times.

His "wife" sat silently while the maid served breakfast. Alasdair watched in amazement while Ellen set a slab of butter beside Starling, a full toast rack, and three eggs. He was left with one slice of toast and one egg. Ellen left the room with her nose in the air.

He rested his hands in his lap. Starling waited. He cleared his throat. She stared at him.

"Use the butter. The toast is getting soggy."

"I was waitin' f'you."

He wondered why she had suddenly developed a strange accent when he had hired her because she spoke well. Or was she trying him again? If she continued, he would simply make sure she kept that rather lush mouth of hers closed most of the time. "Perhaps you don't know that ladies begin first."

She picked up her knife, cut off a portion of butter, and began to spread it on her toast. Fortunately, she had graceful movements. She would pass as respectably born should she behave with the modesty and decorum he expected.

When she reached for a second piece of toast, he noticed her chapped hands and ragged fingernails. He lifted his eyebrows. At least their work-worn condition showed that she could do something other than spread her legs.

She piled her butter high, her shoulders lifted with expectation. "The food 'ere's good. Do the cook serve lunch'n, too?"

"Yes. Ladies have luncheon, gentlemen have a midday repast, and we all have dinner at eight."

"Will I be 'avin' my lunch'n in the bedroom, too?"

"I find it strange that you've suddenly lost your aitches and your gees. Unless you pick them up again, I'm going to find it mighty difficult to let you out of here." He dropped his napkin on the table and stood.

She stared at him, her top teeth clipped on her bottom lip and her eyes gleaming.

Determined not to show a chink in his armor, he exaggerated the sternness of his expression and rearranged his neckcloth. "My sister will arrive sometime this afternoon." He checked his appearance in the cheval mirror as he buttoned his jacket.

She began eating her third piece of toast. "Is she older than you?"

"Four years younger. Mary is twenty-three."

"Is she pretty?"

"She's tall and dark. Personally, I admire shapely blondes."

The slender-framed woman nodded and, assuming he had put her back into her place, he turned and strode out of the room, meaning to catch up with his paperwork. In a matter of hours, his sister would see his choice of bride as the final irony, being the antithesis of Lavender.

"Mrs. Brighton," he called as he paced down the hall. "Come and see me in the library." He would send the housekeeper off to Seymour's to get a suitable dressing set for Starling Smith.

That would stop the wretch using his brush.

Chapter 3

"The Elliots's carriage has just arrived." Ellen's pretty face edged around the doorway. "Let me take those plates."

Starling stood as the maid came into the morning room and began to pack up the dishes from the luncheon Starling had been served.

She had enjoyed the idleness of the past few hours. After being escorted by Mrs. Brighton downstairs to the roomy kitchen at the back of the house, Starling had thanked the cook, Mrs. Trelevan, for her meals. She had then been introduced to the kitchen maid, Ellen's sister, Freda, who was slightly younger and with darker hair. Next, Mrs. Brighton had taken her to meet the boot boy, Will, who'd bowed from the waist. She'd also met the women who managed the various daily cleaning jobs and the good-looking young gardener, Derry, who lived in a room off the stables.

Left to her own devices and ignorant of the role of a wife in this efficient household, she'd let herself be directed to the morning room, and there she'd stayed. With idling to do, she had stared out of the window at the pretty garden, counted varieties of birds, plumped a few cushions on the comfortable sofa, and pondered exploring the house. Just as she had decided to wander, Ellen had delivered the cook's list of the week's meals, which had occupied her until now. She couldn't wait to taste salmon poached in wine. Mousse confused her. She thought it might be a game meat.

"Do you know what mousse is, Ellen?" Starling smoothed the brown-striped skirts of her gown.

"Just a custard. I think it's French."

"French." Musing on the vagaries of the rich, Starling turned to check her appearance in the mirror above the marbled fireplace. Wearing the corset Mr. Seymour had bought for her gave her a shape, at least, but the mustard-yellow bodice of the gown reflected on her skin. Mr. Seymour had hired her and not someone striking for good reason, but perhaps she could have looked pretty in a clearer color. She couldn't tell. She only knew that while she wore warm muddy tones, no guest of his would remember her name.

"You'll want to be with Mr. Seymour in the drawing room to greet his sister," Ellen said. Behind the maid, through the window, the leaves on the fruit trees shifted restlessly. Clouds had begun to gather.

Starling patted her hair to make sure none escaped her neat scraping back. She drew a deep breath. "To the drawing room."

The time had come to smile and earn her wages.

* * * *

Alasdair turned. Against the fashionable background of the gilded wallpaper, Starling Smith looked like a waning moth. He moved from the window of the drawing room where, over the high wall, he could see the top of the traveling carriage outside.

Her head tilted slightly, Starling stopped to examine a large gilt-framed painting of a hunting scene, looking for all the world as if art interested her. He jammed his hands in his pockets. "So, you finally decided to join me?"

Her lips opened, but her words were stopped by the sound of a female voice in the hallway, directing the placement of her trunks.

"Remember, don't speak unless you are addressed," he said in a low voice. "I'll do the talking."

On his last word, Mary, dressed in red and white, appeared in the doorway. She looked as elegant as usual. With a laugh of happiness, she dashed across the room and flung herself at him. "We've had such a trip! You wouldn't believe the condition of the roads. So many potholes. Seven days, it took. Seven days! Could you believe that?"

"Yes, Mary. It always takes you seven days. Now, how is my mother?"

"Happily spoiling your two-year-old nephew, who has been left with her and, of course, his dear nanny. Mama's in her element..." Her voice faded as she noticed Starling behind the armchairs. She shot a questioning smile at him.

He held out his hand to Starling and slid his arm around her waist when she moved to his side, easing her closer. She stiffened, and he loosened his grip. He gave her a loving-husband smile. "My wife, Starling," he said, assuming he looked suitably fatuous. "Starling, this is my sister, Mary Elliot."

"Your wife?" Mary said, wide-eyed. "Oh, dear! I don't mean 'oh, dear.' I mean, oh, how do you *do*, my dear? So you're my brother's wife.

How delightful." Her expression somewhat fixed, she reached out and shook Starling's hand.

Starling smiled brightly but quickly took that hand behind her back with the other.

"Starling. What an unusual name."

"A pretty name," said her husband, Paul Elliot, the handsome, good-natured gentleman who had married Alasdair's loyal, if not misguided sister. The only son of a wealthy landowner, Paul had always been a fashion plate. His shirt was a dazzling white and his waistcoat a red patterned silk. A beautifully curved blonde dressed in a pale lilac gown clung to his arm. Alasdair stared at Lavender...lovely Lavender.

Paul shook Alasdair's flaccid hand, took up a position beside Mary, and bid Starling a good afternoon.

Lavender gave a throaty laugh. She reached out and placed her gloved fingers in Alasdair's. "Dare. How wonderful to see you again," she said in a low voice. "How long has it been? Three years?"

"Seven," Alasdair managed to say.

"*Seven*," Mary emphasized in a precise tone to Starling. "I expect Alasdair told you we would be bringing a mystery guest. He and Lavender have known each other since, oh, years and years. And, because her mourning period is over, she thought she should look up her old friends. And since we were coming here for a visit..."

"Mourning?" said Alasdair, his brain still not quite functioning. He discovered he was clutching at Lavender's hand.

Lavender lowered her fanlike lashes. "Indeed. Mary tells me your business is very successful—"

"You're a widow?"

"Richard died two years ago." Her gaze met his and her lips softened.

"Lavender, before you catch up on too much history, I would like to introduce you to Starling, Alasdair's *wife*." Mary's voice sounded a little high. "Mrs. Seymour, Mrs. Lavender Frost. And, Starling, this is my dear husband, Paul." She tilted her head towards her poker-faced husband.

"Mrs. Frost. Mr. Elliot," Starling said, her pasted smile extending from ear to ear.

"Paul. Call me Paul. We're related now, Starling."

"Your wife?" Lavender fixed two stunned amethyst eyes on Alasdair. She directed a quick glance at Starling's waist. "You married recently?"

To save his life, Alasdair couldn't have spoken at that moment.

Starling glanced at him. "Yesterday." She kept smiling.

"You must wish us elsewhere in that case." Lavender removed her hand from his. She turned her back on him and picked up a porcelain ornament from the nearest side table. "Exquisite," she said, her lashes covering her expression as she glanced at the bottom. "Your taste seems to have...changed." Her incredible eyes flickered back to Starling.

"Indeed," said Paul with a short laugh. "He has hidden depths. No doubt he will tell us later why he couldn't remain a bachelor for one more day."

"He knew we would be arriving today," Mary said in an off-hand tone. "And since he married yesterday, he must have wanted us to celebrate his marriage with him." She shot Alasdair a dangerous smile.

"Though perhaps not today," Lavender said, running her fingers delicately across her forehead. "I, for one, am far too tired after our tedious journey. Every night a new hotel and every night a more uncomfortable bed. My sheets were damp in the first."

"I'm sorry you were given poor service," Mary said, a crease between her eyebrows. "You should have let us know and we would have insisted on better."

"Well-trained servants are rare and I should never have said a word. You and Paul have been very gracious to me."

Alasdair at last found a voice, albeit strained. "As Mary said, I knew guests would be arriving today. I think you will find my servants polite and efficient and my home amply prepared for your stay. Lavender..." He stopped. Until he knew the purpose of her visit, he would not explain his ruse. From her, he had learned not to make assumptions.

She gave him her profile, a straight delicate nose and a perfectly rounded chin. "I'm sure I'll be looked after while I'm here...tonight." She directed her glance at Starling. "You would be very pleased with this lovely house, Mrs. Seymour. You must have at least twenty rooms."

"Rooms?" Starling said, holding her smile as if it was the only expression she had ever known. "I don't know the number. Until not long ago, I'd seen little more than the bedroom. Not that that was a punishment," she added after a quick glance at Alasdair. "The bed is wonderful and—"

"Eighteen rooms," Alasdair relaxed his shoulders. The shopgirl was proving her worth. The implication that he and she had made much of their married life was not lost on Lavender, who straightened, her eyes clouding.

Mary made an impish purse of her mouth. "Perhaps we should go to our rooms and rest before we hear Alasdair's plans for us this week. I, for one, need a nap. I doubt I slept a wink last night."

"Nor I." Paul gave his wife a grin. "I'll nap with you." Although always a gentleman, Paul could be mischievous. Perhaps the plan to withhold Lavender's identity had been his.

Taking Paul with her, Mary left the room, calling over her shoulder, "I'll see you at dinner tonight, Starling, my dear." Paul echoed her from the hallway.

Alasdair glanced at Lavender, who'd moved to a large painting of the English countryside. Her figure was as graceful and curved, and her body was as breathtaking as ever. "A Ross Anderson," she said with a glance at Alasdair. "One would know his style anywhere. The soft leaves, the shafts of color. Do you admire this painting, Mrs. Seymour?"

Starling nodded. "Should we offer you refreshment?"

Lavender shook her head. "Perhaps someone could show me to my bedroom. I'll need to supervise the unpacking."

His pulse thundering in his throat, Alasdair said, "If I may? Starling is new to the house."

Lavender slowly pulled the ribbons of her silk-flowered hat undone. "Call for a maid, Alasdair. I'm sure you would prefer to stay with your new bride." Her voice and expression conflicted, but in the past, she had constantly confused him.

Now older and wiser, he tugged the call-bell. After giving his orders to Ellen, he went through to the billiard room and paced. He couldn't let Lavender entangle him again. The shopgirl had been an inspired choice.

Lavender deserved to see how happy he was without her.

* * * *

The drawing room darkened and thunder rumbled in the distance. Starling plumped down on the low, dark-gold velvet sofa, fidgeting, picking at her fingernails. Again, she'd been left alone in a strange room and again she had no idea what was expected of her. Lightning flickered outside. She glanced at the window, wishing she had kept her mouth shut, as ordered.

Although she had not hesitated to try Mr. Seymour's patience this morning, her tiny payback was for his lack of an explanation regarding the sleeping arrangements. She hadn't deliberately annoyed him this afternoon. Her words about the bed had been meant well and offered because of his unexplained silence. Though, as a married couple... She lifted her chin. His sister had taken no offence at the accidental implication, and her belief in Mr. Seymour's story had been bolstered.

At least Starling could now understand why Mr. Seymour wanted to be protected from matchmaking. His old acquaintance, Mrs. Frost, was a cold woman despite her incredible beauty. Not even lilac, a color that made her look like a scented pastille, took attention from her huge blue eyes and her soft, pale hair.

Mrs. Elliot, too, was a beautiful woman, with a hand as smooth and cool as silk and skin the texture of white rose-petals. She knew how to dress to complement her coloring. The red and white patterned gown with the fashionable fullness at the back flattered her dark hair and light eyes.

With reluctance, after examining each painting, smelling each scented rose in each vase, and examining the bottom of each porcelain figurine and finding nothing but minute crossed swords, Starling decided the time had come to investigate the rest of the house. She could idle tomorrow instead. If the beautiful Mrs. Frost asked her about other rooms, she would need to know the answer.

She crossed the marble-tiled hall and opened the opposite set of doors, finding a room the size of a meeting hall arranged with seating around the walls. At the back corner stood a rostrum with a red curtain on either side. She stepped across the parquet floor to adjoining double doors leading to a vast dining room, which displayed at least twenty delicately carved chairs placed around a long gleaming table. The carpet was flat-piled and multi-patterned. The room next to the drawing room was a library.

"Oh, my," Starling said, walking into the insulated silence. Shelves of books reached to the picture rail. Her nose tickled with the smell of wood polish and ink. Comfortable chairs upholstered in dark blue surrounded another white marble fireplace. A massive table, holding various stacks of papers, stood in the center of the room. Barely two steps inside, she reached reverently for a book named *The Silk Routes* with a spine embossed in gold.

"Mrs. Seymour!"

Heart leaping, she turned to face her accuser. "I didn't—"

"Sorry for startling you, ma'am." Ellen's face looked flushed and anxious, and she pressed one hand to her breastbone, as if trying to calm herself. "I can't find Mr. Seymour. Tammy Burdon's fallen in the well. They need him. They can't get her out. When Derry tried, the bucket rope broke—"

"Who is Tammy?"

"The daughter of a neighbor." Ellen's eyes glistened and her mouth trembled. "She's only six years old. She's wedged, jammed, and the men can't get down to her because the shaft's too narrow."

"Where is the well?"

"There." Ellen pointed to the back of the house, in the direction of the river.

"Mr. Seymour went into the billiard room. He might still be there."

"I'll see. Thank you, ma'am," Ellen spun on her heel. She ran off in a twirl of white petticoats, sprinting across the hallway.

Starling heard her calling Mr. Seymour. She heard more than one set of footsteps thudding on the marble flooring. A faint voice shouted. Thunder rumbled. The curtains lifted with a gust of wind. Lightning flickered frantically.

They need him.

Pity help them. They needed a child dug out of a well. Although Mr. Seymour had shoulders like a blacksmith and a tall, strong frame, he had white elegant fingers that did nothing more strenuous all day but ink his pen.

She hoped they could use a man who could issue high-handed orders, for that would be Mr. Seymour's only true skill.

Chapter 4

Being an idle wife wasn't as easy as it sounded. After her scare, Starling wasn't brave enough to touch another book and so, straightening her shoulders, she followed the aroma of roasting meat to the kitchen.

"May I help?" she asked Mrs. Trelevan, who was possibly five feet tall and five feet wide. She had gray-streaked hair and round red cheeks.

"Bless you," Mrs. Trelevan answered, aiming twinkling pale eyes at Starling. She rinsed her knives in the reticulated water piped to the sink. No luxury had been overlooked in this house.

"I could wash those dishes."

Mrs. Trelevan glanced at Starling's hands. "I'll give you a job, right enough. Freda!"

"I'm getting the flowers ready for tonight," a voice answered from an arched alcove.

"Run upstairs and get Mrs. Seymour's gloves."

"My things haven't arrived yet." Starling reddened with discomfort.

"No gloves? Well, then, we'll make do. See this-here ointment." Mrs. Trelevan lifted a jar from a shelf above the sink. "I use it every day. Comes from sheep's wool. Smells like it, too." She opened the jar and dug her fingers in, and before Starling realized what she meant to do, she dabbed an unpleasant-smelling cream on Starling's hands, back and front. "Rub it in," she said with an encouraging smile. "You need to keep those hands of yours protected while you work."

The cream was sticky at first but melted when smoothed on, leaving a shiny glaze on Starling's skin. "Bless you," she said in wonder to Mrs. Trelevan. She glanced at the bowl of peas that Mrs. Trelevan had begun to shell. "There's enough here to feed the starving hordes. Let me help."

Mrs. Trelevan laughed. "You'll be wanting to dress for dinner."

Starling glanced at her bodice. "I'm already dressed."

"The other ladies will be changin' into evening gowns."

"I don't have an evening gown. My things haven't been collected yet."

"Freda, come in here. What do you think, girl? Can you spare the time to do a little fancyin' up of one of Mrs. Seymour's day gowns?"

"No offense," said the kitchen maid, who had a smiling mouth and wide eyes like her sister. "But there's not much I can do with the one she has on. Do you have anything a little...plainer, Mrs. Seymour?"

"Plainer than this?" Starling raised her eyebrows. "Only a gray gown. I don't think it could be fancied up, though. It is, um, very like your uniform, except for the color."

Mrs. Trelevan grinned. "Freda is a wonder with the needle. You shoulda seen what she done with my Sunday best. A very elegant creation now, it is."

"I'll need to see what you've got." Freda washed her hands in the sink. "There's a roll of patterned silk in the store room, water-stained along the length. Mr. Seymour brought it home from the emporium, thinking Mrs. Brighton could make use of it. Might be, I can use it for you...if you can arrange the flowers while I sew."

"Thought she might manage," Mrs. Trelevan said smugly. "Do anythin' to get out of arrangin' flowers, Freda would."

Starling would do almost anything to be allowed to arrange flowers, and along with idling, Mr. Seymour had told her to do that task. However, she doubted he would like Freda being taken from her job to sew for one of his shopgirls. He'd definitely ordered Starling to have no gaudy gowns. "I'm not sure Mr. Seymour would approve."

"We'd ask him, wouldn't we, Mrs. Trelevan, but he's outside helping the Burdons." Freda chewed at her lip.

"Oh, he'd approve." Mrs. Trelevan nodded confidently. "He wouldn't've thought of Mrs. Seymour bein' embarrassed without her trunk. He'd want us to help where we can."

"I'd need to get the alterations done quick because I'll have to run out food to the rescue team."

Mrs. Trelevan tutted. "Bless you for thinkin' of that. I don't know where my head is. Mrs. Burdon will be too worried to feed the men."

Starling cleared her throat. "Mrs. Burdon is the child's mother?"

Mrs. Trelevan nodded. "Miss Tammy's the sweetest little six year old you've ever seen, but such a one for gettin' into things. No point in bein' negative. If anyone can get her out of that well, Mr. Seymour can."

"Course he can." Freda nodded for emphasis. "Never gives in once he's set his mind to helping."

"So, they will dig the child out?" Starling reached for the pea bowl and began, mechanically, to split and open the pods.

"The well's too narrow for anyone to get down, and Tammy's wedged. They're just afraid that..."

"Go on."

"Looks like rain. If that happens...there's a seepage problem. They think the well might fill before they can get her out."

"Shouldn't we help?" Starling's fingers stilled.

"Four men there already. We'd only be in the way. Best if we take out drinks and food. They want us to do anything else, they'll soon tell us."

"I want to help if there's anything for me to do."

"Bless you," Mrs. Trelevan said. "Mr. Seymour made a fine choice of a wife. Indeed he did."

* * * *

Starling stood by the window in Mr. Seymour's splendid blue and gold bedroom and stared out. The expected rain sheeted down. She could barely see the gathering of people down by the river. Umbrellas sheltered some. The trees along the banks threshed in the wind.

At the polished table, Freda sat squinting at her sewing. Starling wasn't sure what the maid meant to do with the gray uniform, but the gown had been buttoned and unbuttoned and pinned. The roll of silk, patterned with pink and purple flowers on a blue background, had been partly unwound and cut into.

"I have to go out and see how...how my husband is." Starling walked to the door.

Freda glanced up. "We keep the waterproofs by the back door. And the umbrellas. Follow the path to the back gate."

After she'd donned the suggested coat, she headed outside. Rain sliced down, making visibility low. Starling came upon the huddled men near the wind-whipped trees some distance from the back gate. She stared at the flow of the river, but the depth was summer low. The water ran fast and dirty.

She glanced at an area covered by a makeshift canvas roof. Only a few stones edged a hole. Apparently, the well had been unused for years and was not easy to spot, which might explain how the child had fallen in. The diggers ignored Starling, which gave her the opportunity to assess the situation. A pale-faced young woman covered by a black cloak stood just under the canvas calling the child's name. No answer came. Starling's throat thickened.

"I'm Starling, from..." She indicated Mr. Seymour's house. "You must be Mrs. Burdon."

"Yes," the woman answered distractedly. "Jane Burdon." She covered her quivering mouth with one gloved hand. "Do you think Mr. Seymour will get her out? He's over there."

Starling narrowed her eyes at the three dirt-streaked men who were peering into another hole mounded on one side with soil, but she didn't spot Mr. Seymour. A few minutes later, she saw him emerge from the hole, shirtless and muddy.

"We'll need strong shoring," he said to the men. "The sides are beginning to move. Take the wagon to the timber yard, Derry, and tell Joe I sent you. Grab every piece of planking you can find. Don't take more than half an hour. We can't wait any longer than that, or the work we've done will be a waste of time." He hauled a bag of dirt out of the hole and dumped the weight on the slippery verges. His big shoulders strained.

"Need spelling yet, Seymour?" A stout man emptied the soil and handed the limp sack back to him.

"Not until it's safe. I'll go on until the shoring arrives." Mr. Seymour wiped a stained hand through his dirt-plastered hair.

This morning, while he'd wandered around more than half-naked, Starling's only reaction had been embarrassment. She'd never seen a bare man before him. Now she gazed at his manly form, wishing he wasn't quite so physically attractive. She would hate to see such a fine body injured, and she was scared for him, but as he stood with the rain sluicing over his skin, he looked insoluble, like a great stone monument.

Within moments, and not even glancing at her, he disappeared headfirst back into his hole.

Starling held her umbrella over Mrs. Burdon. "He'll get her out," she said, repeating the words the servants had told her. "He never gives in once he's made up his mind to help."

"I wish I could see Tammy. I can't even hear her. Mr. Seymour says he knows how far down she's wedged." Mrs. Burdon's face creased with worry.

Starling reached out a tentative hand. Mrs. Burdon grasped her fingers. The men continued to empty the bags of soil while Mr. Seymour filled them. The hole looked tiny, not much wider than a man's shoulders, yet the earth being removed seemed never-ending.

When the shoring arrived, Mr. Seymour widened the hole, and then the heavy-set, older man, who Starling had identified as Mr. Burdon, took over. Mr. Seymour paced. Not wanting to be noticed by him, certain he would not be bolstered by her presence, Starling pulled the waterproof farther over her head, left the umbrella with Mrs. Burdon, and squelched in her waterlogged boots back to the house.

"May I have something sustaining to take out to the men?" Starling's hands trembled as she spoke to Mrs. Trelevan. Perhaps after her poor night's sleep, she was tired. She had no reason to be frightened. No one had been hurt and the little girl would likely be rescued.

"Bless you." Mrs. Trelevan poured boiling water from her kettle and filled a bottle with hot, sweet tea. "We can make cake if the men want sustaining. I've got nothing prepared but dinner."

Within a quarter of an hour, Starling had returned to the well. She poured the tea into mugs and passed them around. Mr. Seymour took his with both hands. Dirt ingrained his fingernails and mud clung up his arms to his elbows. His once cared-for hands were blistered and covered with small cuts, as damaged as hers had been by the laundering.

"Your hands are very dirty. If you would like, you can use this first." She offered him the towel from the bottle, but in his lordly way, he held out his hands for her to clean. Adopting her role as an obedient wife far too easily, she wiped them, dabbing the cuts and trying not to touch the blisters. The intimate contact shortened her breath. The man was strong and handsome, and she would share a chaste bed with him again tonight.

The rain continued to drizzle. The men continued to dispose of the soil Mr. Seymour dug from the hole. Mr. Elliot arrived, discussed the work with the men, and after a jaunty tipping of his rain-soaked hat to Starling, returned to the house. Likely he'd only wanted news. Although tall and broad-shouldered, he was clearly a gentleman unused to outdoor labor. She'd thought the same about Mr. Seymour, who had surprised her, but she knew Mr. Elliot wasn't needed. Only one man could tunnel at a time.

Other than nodding thanks to her when she passed food or poured tea, the rescuers kept their concentration entirely on their task. Twice more she went back to the house, ferrying hot tea and, later, the big brown cake Mrs. Trelevan had made. Ginger, she called the taste. Hourly, Starling learned more about the luxuries in life.

Dusk began to shade the sky. The hole, angled to a depth of six feet, had now been changed to intercept the well. Mr. Seymour seemed to be digging faster as the day waned. Finally, he called, "We've hit the stone wall. I should be able to tunnel through in no more than an hour or two."

Mrs. Burdon gasped and put her soft, white hand to her throat. "He's found the edge of the well. He's almost reached her."

The men above ground showed a tense satisfaction. Mr. Burdon clapped Derry on the back, grinning.

Mr. Seymour came up for a chiseling tool. He noticed Starling and frowned. "You're still here? Why?"

"In case you need me."

"You should be indoors with the others."

Mr. Burdon came over and put his arm around his wife's waist, and she rested her head on his shoulder. "You've been wonderful," he said to Starling. "But I can take care of Jane now that Seymour has finished the worst. You ought to get back to the house. You look as though you could do with a good coddling."

"Thank you, Starling," Mrs. Burdon clung to her husband's coat lapels. "I agree. I shouldn't have insisted you stay out here in the rain with me."

"You didn't ins—"

"Mrs. Trelevan serves dinner at eight," Mr. Seymour interrupted with a distracted expression on his face.

Mr. Burdon glanced at his fob watch. "It's not much after seven."

"Go."

Rebuked, Starling left. Despite his attitude toward her, she had relented hers toward him. He'd worked long and hard. She might be wary of him, but she had to admit to a grudging respect.

She had accepted his bargain. From now on, she would, to the best of her ability, do the job for which he had hired her.

* * * *

Alasdair crashed the mallet onto the stone chisel. The well walls were thicker than he'd expected and better built. His plan was to dig beneath Tammy and bear her out along the new shaft. Some years had passed since he had last tunneled, and he ached in a way he could never forget. Each beat of his hammer on the chisel brought back memories of being confined in a dark and airless space. He coughed, clearing his lungs.

The rain hampered the digging and the shoring hampered the tunneling. If he couldn't get the child out within a couple more hours, he doubted she would live. No one had heard a cry from her since his hired wife had begun impressing the diggers with her selflessness.

He struck the stone, hard. His hand was wet and slippery, whether from the damp or his perspiration he couldn't tell, and the chisel flew out of his grip. He sought the tool in the dark, grimly determined to break through the rock by sheer persistence, if necessary. Persistence had served him well the last time he had mined and would again. The word applied to Starling, too. Unwillingly, he remembered her readiness to stay out in the pelting rain despite the blue of her hands and the pinched white of her face.

He struck the stone again with more force. Insisting on sharing his bedroom with her had been an inspired move. Not for a second had his servants queried the hasty marriage, nor had Lavender. His lips stretched hard over his teeth. He would not disabuse her of that idea too soon.

A rock dropped on his shoulder—a rock as hard as Lavender's final words to him seven years ago. He shoved the impediment aside, fully intending to use Starling to make Lavender regret trampling on his heart.

He inched forward. First, he had to rescue Tammy.

Chapter 5

Starling sat, rearranging her newly refurbished skirts. While the others settled themselves into their dining chairs, she examined the rose arrangement between a pair of silver candelabras on the polished dining table. She knew now she should have cut some inches from the stems. The blooms sat at eye height, which made seeing past a matter of leaning sideways. In the future she would be more careful—that is, if anyone let her do the flowers again.

However, the ladies praised the roses and the paintings on the wall while Mr. Elliot filled the wineglasses. Starling sipped her wine. The taste hit the side of her cheeks and puckered her mouth.

"It's a shame Dare is not here for dinner." Mrs. Frost wore shades of violet again. Diamond teardrops shivered on her ears. "We need a man at the head of the table."

"Not half as much, I expect, as he is needed outside. I'm sure he's tired and..." Starling stopped, appalled that she had contradicted a lady.

Mrs. Frost took a spoonful of soup. "The accident was most unfortunate, of course, but he should leave the digging to the others. Gentlemen don't perform manual labor."

"True." Mrs. Elliot wore emerald green, frogged with black braid down the front. "But he's never been one to leave the dirty work to others."

Mr. Elliot grinned. "I'm content to let him dig for hours in a muddy hole while I spend time with my dear wife instead."

"Too, too flattering of you," Mrs. Elliot said, her expression droll. "But only when you were told you were not needed outside."

"But I am, of course, an Elliot of Bellamie Hall." He leaned back, his eyebrows aimed with expectation at Mrs. Frost. "A gentleman born and bred."

Mrs. Elliot rapped a finger on the back of his hand. "Don't give Starling the wrong impression of you. She is your new sister-in-law and married to my favorite brother. Where did you two meet, Starling?"

Starling swallowed a spoonful of the green soup made from the peas she had shelled. "Ballarat," she said, remembering Ellen telling her she'd had a long journey from a place she'd never been.

"Were you born in Ballarat?" Mrs. Frost blotted her mouth with her napkin.

Starling took a bigger sip of wine. That seemed to be the way to get used to the foggy taste. "No. I was born in Adelaide."

"What was your single name?"

"Smith." Starling drank down the rest of her wine. The second half tasted better than the first, rather like sugared rhubarb.

"I've never met a Smith. What did your people do?"

Starling wished Mrs. Frost would stop interrogating her. She cleared her throat. "My people's main concern was with charity. I learnt business matters from Mr. Seymour, if that is what you are asking. He is an amazing teacher."

"There speaks a loyal bride," said Mr. Elliot. "As an old friend of Alasdair's, Lavender was just making certain he had chosen the right wife."

"If I don't suit, he'll put me off without a reference."

The Elliots laughed. "I suspect you have him twisted around your little finger," Mary said. "He could have chosen a wife from any amount of women, but he chose one fresh and sweet and unpretentious. There's hope for him yet."

Mrs. Frost raised her chin. "I was seventeen when I met him. Mama wanted new curtains for our formal rooms, and he came with samples. I was very struck by his looks. Such a handsome young man. But for my parents..." She shrugged. "I may well have married him, eventually."

"It turned out for the best," Paul said, finishing his soup. "I'm sure you were perfect for Richard Frost."

Starling glanced at him. She'd thought his tone cynical, but Mrs. Frost appeared to take his words as congratulatory. "His father was a banker in England."

"And Alasdair will always be in trade," Paul said, leaning back and staring at the lady. "Despite making a fortune."

"This is old history." Mary raised her glass. "We should be toasting the new bride. To Starling."

Mr. Elliot refilled Starling's glass and everyone drank, though Mrs. Frost took the tiniest sip. Starling finished that glassful, then she noted the others also took only a sip. She realized she needed to copy their behavior to be the sort of woman Mr. Seymour would have married.

After Freda took the soup plates and brought in the next courses, Starling waited for Mary or Mrs. Frost to give her a clue as to which of her four pairs of knives and forks she should use. In the home, they'd never had more than one. She remembered Mr. Seymour saying ladies start first.

When the other two ladies didn't appear to know Mr. Seymour's rule, she steeled herself, chose the outer pair and began her poached salmon. She knew she had made the right choice when the others picked up their outer pair, too.

"Do you come from a large family, Starling?" Mary left her implements on the plate while she chewed.

Starling did the same. At the home, the only rule during meals was to eat quickly. The tables needed to be cleared for the mending of the laundered linen. "Very large. Lots of sisters."

"How many?" Mrs. Frost asked in a cool voice.

"Eighteen at last count."

Mrs. Frost gasped. "Incredible. I'm an only child."

"There was just Alasdair and me. As I'm sure he told you."

"He hasn't been too forthcoming about his life," Starling said with truth to Mary.

"That's so like him." Mary shook her head. "He doesn't talk about himself, but I'm quite happy to talk about him."

"Make yourself comfortable." Paul raised his eyebrows at Starling. "This could be a long night."

Mary cast a reproachful glance at her husband. "Alasdair was sixteen when Papa died. I was twelve. For the next four years, and without a word of complaint, he added to the warehouse in Melbourne and managed to send me to a boarding school. Then, he employed a manager for the business and left for Ballarat...to take advantage of the gold rush." She flickered a look at Mrs. Frost.

Paul lifted his glass to the light and inspected the color of the wine. "He made good enough money in the first year to expand farther."

Mary smiled. "Alasdair isn't just lucky. He is also very smart." She glanced at Lavender. "Usually."

Mrs. Frost nodded. "He found gold," she said, her tone regretful. "Unfortunate. Diamonds are worth so much more."

Mary stared at her.

Mrs. Frost reached for the buttered asparagus. "Is it accepted that he worked in a mine?"

"Oh, he didn't work in a mine," Mary said in a casual voice. "He owned the land. I expect he had quite a few men digging for him."

"He could be termed a mine *owner*." Paul glanced at Mary.

"Yes," Mary said firmly. She gave Starling a complicit stare. "Alasdair wouldn't, of course, have been mining himself. Not when he was in Ballarat to consolidate our markets."

Starling stared at the table, wondering about this story. She had seen Mr. Seymour dig. Apparently, rich gentlemen could only dig tunnels for altruistic purposes.

"In the second year, his mine struck gold and he made a fortune. Fifty thousand pounds!" Mary stared wide-eyed at Starling. "In the meantime, the business here was running at a great enough profit to buy Mama a grand new house and to send me to a finishing school. I met Paul's sister there and..." She spread her hands.

"And how many retail establishments does Dare now own?" Mrs. Frost smiled as if not truly interested in the answer.

"Four. The original in Ballarat, the next in Adelaide, another in Prospect, and the latest in Kapunda. He sold the warehouse in Melbourne when he moved here. By the way, Starling, that's a lovely gown. It's the very thing, I swear. Where did you find it?"

"It came from Seymour's." Starling touched the ruffled floral edging around the lowered neck of her gray uniform. "The fabric department has everything a person could want. Silk, wool, velvet, satin, muslin, or lace and embroidered, netted, or woven—fabrics from all over the world in the most wonderful colors." She stopped, knowing she sounded far too passionate.

"Do you shop at Seymour's?" Mrs. Frost sounded curious.

"I used to work for Mr. Seymour."

Mary gave a spurt of laughter. "At his store in Ballarat! He said he planned to have a female choose his fabrics. He so loves his little mysteries. I shall tease him about falling in love with one of his employees, don't doubt it."

Mrs. Frost clicked her tongue. "Oh, you're being too romantic. I wasn't in love with Richard when I married him. My Papa thought of marriage as a business proposition, and if Starling knew the workings of Alasdair's businesses... Was yours a love match, Mrs. Seymour?"

Starling blushed. "I shouldn't say. Really."

Mary widened her eyes. "It's obvious Alasdair adores you. He needed to marry for no other reason."

Mrs. Frost inclined her head, ending the subject. "Mary, what color is your bedroom?"

"Green. Such a soothing color, and I like the placement because the window overlooks the side garden. You have the yellow room next to ours, I believe. A view of the front street."

"Yellow. Yes." Mrs. Frost tightened her lips.

"You would look quite lovely in yellow," Starling said, concentrating. The blonde had skin the color of a white peach. "It would be perfect on you, that or any other warm color."

Mrs. Frost gave her a glance of affront. "I never wear anything but shades of lavender. Never. I dislike warm colors. Perhaps this headache was brought on by resting all afternoon in a yellow room."

"More than likely from traveling for days. I would think yellow would brighten one's mood rather than cause a headache," Starling said without thinking.

"Perhaps I ought to go to my yellow room and dance for joy?"

"Dancing might be difficult with a headache," Starling said with sympathy. Her head, too, seemed heavier than usual and her tongue had taken on thoughts of its own. She didn't object to being meek. She just couldn't seem to keep her mouth closed tonight.

"With your permission, then, I shall retire instantly. Could you add to your goodness and send me a cold compress?"

Starling blinked. "Of course."

"How delightful it is not to have a fuss made over my headache." Mrs. Frost rose, placing her napkin carefully on the table. With an uptilted chin, she left.

Paul grinned. "The journey here lost her two years of her life. She was nineteen when she met Alasdair, not seventeen. In a couple of days, she'll be your age," he said to Mary, who looked rueful.

Starling said, "I assume I've been a lax wife. Should I have offered her something else?"

"A left to the jaw," said Paul.

"Don't listen to him. I expect the long journey made her tired and headachy. Perhaps you could send up the rest of her meal on a tray. She likes to pick at her food."

Starling giggled, then she covered her mouth with her hand. "How strange. Likely, she has never gone hungry."

"Her parents were very rich and doted on her. Her father died just after her husband, and her mother died recently. In a few short years, she's been left with no one. That would be dreadful. I think she should be allowed some leeway. It's just hard to bear when she talks of Alasdair as her property. I'm sure you don't like to hear that, either."

Strangely, Starling didn't, but she assumed that was because Mrs. Frost seemed to be a woman who didn't like other women. Brought up by females and associating only with females most her life, Starling had a great deal of respect for her own sex. Perhaps she would like Mrs. Frost tomorrow. She liked Mary and Paul already.

She hoped she had acted out her part as well as Mr. Seymour would have wished. Rather than being told to act meekly, to be believable she should have been asked to make an effort to speak to his relatives. Now that she had, in her opinion the evening had been a mild success, except for not knowing her role well enough to ask a servant to assist Mrs. Frost.

Had the little girl not fallen in the well and Mr. Seymour not been put in the dangerous position of trying to get her out, Starling would be quietly triumphant. Mr. Seymour's sister had accepted her without a blink, including the fact that she had worked for Mr. Seymour. Starling had to assume she was adequately managing the job he had asked of her.

With a smile that kept coming, she ate a big serving of jellied fruit.

* * * *

After removing his mud-caked shoes in the laundry, Alasdair strode through the dimly lit house to his bedroom. Light gleamed under his door. He moved across the threshold, almost surprised to see Starling asleep in his bed. Such was his preoccupation with getting Tammy safely in her parents' arms, he had forgotten about the woman who shared his room. Her hair curled around a young face etched with weariness. Bearing in mind the to and fro-ing she'd done in the rain today, she had earned her rest.

He dropped his dirty clothes behind the dressing screen; washed as quietly as he could; and, chilled, slid into bed. With an ironic smile, he turned down the bedside lamp, remembering that until the rigors of Ballarat had left him with too little energy to waste, he'd agonized over Lavender sleeping with Richard Frost. He hoped she thought about him with his "wife."

Starling stirred. "Did you get Tammy out?" Her voice was husky.

"About ten minutes ago."

"I'm glad. Mrs. Burdon must be the happiest woman in the world right now." Her arm moved, lightly resting against his turned back.

He tried to quell his reaction to the warm skin contact, but the truth was he was as horny as a goat. Thoughts of Lavender had been stirring him for hours. His body had been ripe and ready since he had walked into the house. "Don't encourage me," he said. "I'm too tired." Pulling the sheet to his ears, he tried to will the ardor between his legs to disappear.

"You're cold." She sounded slurred. "I'll warm you so that you can sleep."

His toes curled and his body tightened. Doubtless, after going without for a while, she was as ready as he. "We agreed that you would be a wife in name only, remember?"

"Shh," she said, as if trying to quiet an unruly child.

Her body curled against him. Her knees pressed into the backs of his. Feet like hot bricks rested on his calves. His breath grew forced. She spread her palm on his back.

"I think you're bare," she said in a surprised voice.

"You'd be right." He tried to ignore his erection.

Her soft breath tickled the skin of his back. "Are you relaxed now?"

"Have you heard the term, 'propagate or perish'?"

"No."

"Of course not." In the past, during times of stress or danger, he had known irresistible urges to have a woman, any woman. Although the danger from the collapse of the tunnel was over, the urge remained.

"It can't have been easy in that muddy hole, and I'm sure you must have worried about losing Tammy when you were so close."

"The tunneling was uncomfortable, I'll admit. I didn't think a lot about Tammy. More about the task."

"But you would much rather have been here with your guests."

"No." He made a rueful mouth in the darkness. "I would rather have been tunneling. At home, I had an unsolved problem."

"Nevertheless, you performed a brave deed. Are you warm enough now?"

"More than warm enough," he said in a voice that even he could hear sounded ungrateful.

Her hand dropped from his back. "Good. I have a headache." She sighed and rolled away from him.

"Good night, then." He cleared his throat. "Thank you. Your support outside was...surprising."

He closed his eyes and his weariness overcame him.

* * * *

Starling woke with a start when Ellen brought in the hot water. She attempted to moisten the inside of her mouth. Head pounding, she tried to sit up, but with Mr. Seymour's arm lying heavily across her chest, she couldn't move.

Mr. Seymour had threshed around most of the night. She didn't mind the bristled chin resting on her shoulder, the nose pressed into her throat, or the crumpled dark hair against her jaw. Nor did she mind the leg between hers or the faint snoring sounds. She was glad he finally slept.

He'd been a hero. She had questioned his moral integrity, which seemed to shift with the tides, but he had kept his side of the bargain last night after he had taken her offer to warm him the wrong way. If he hadn't, she would have screamed, of course, and he would have had to explain the situation to his family, but they would have no sympathy for a woman who shared a bed with a man for money. And she would have lost the promised money, no doubt of it.

Now he no longer made her nervous. She could think of him as a trustworthy employer. That was, when she didn't think of him as a self-seeking, sinfully attractive, untouchable male.

Ellen filled the basin, looked at Starling, and mouthed quite clearly, "Breakfast?"

Starling shook her head and pointed at the dark head snuggled against her neck. "We should let him sleep as long as he needs," she whispered.

Ellen nodded and left.

Starling tried to slide from the bed, but her arm, beneath Mr. Seymour, was numb. The useless appendage wouldn't obey her will. As she wriggled, his snoring stopped. His lips pressed against her neck. This small movement freed her. She flicked her fingers to regain feeling.

Suddenly the one knee between hers became two and his hand slid to her covered bottom. He lifted her closer to him and pressed his hips against the junction between her legs.

Her face heated and her breath shortened. Embarrassingly, she wanted to shift her legs to feel the hardness of his pecker there. Perhaps Meg had been right. Women had been made to fit with men. This one hadn't even woken, yet he was ready to rut.

He moved his lips from her neck to her jaw and kissed her there. She jerked away.

He blinked his beautiful gray eyes once or twice. "Who are you?" he asked in a fuzzy voice.

"Your wife," she answered, annoyed by his handsome face, his demanding maleness, and her treacherous body.

"Good," he said. "I can fuck you."

His mouth covered hers and, stunned, she let his lips sweep hers and his tongue caress inside. His lower body urged at her. As suddenly as he had begun, he stopped.

He groaned. "Sorry," he murmured in a gruff morning voice, "I wasn't quite awake." He rolled off her onto his back on the other side of the bed. "Don't take any notice. I really am asleep." He lifted one heavily muscled arm to cover his eyes.

Within a minute, he made his last statement true.

* * * *

Starling shifted the screen to hide behind while she washed, and she quickly dressed in her new mold-green gown. With her hair scraped up into the usual tight knot, she made her way to the kitchen. As she passed the dining room, she heard voices.

"You're up early, Starling," Paul said from the table. "I thought after the bottles of wine you consumed last night, you'd be confined to bed all day with a headache."

"The wine," Starling said, aghast. "Is that what happened to my head?"

"She didn't drink as much as you did," Mary said in a chiding voice. "Don't tease her, you brute. It's nice to see you here, my dear. Alasdair never joins us for breakfast. I imagine Lavender won't, either."

"Is there enough food? Or should I go to the kitchen to ask for more?"

"There's plenty. I'll ring for more hot water for the tea." Paul arose and tugged the bellpull near the fireplace.

Starling examined the silver lids lined along the sideboard. She lifted the nearest and saw sliced ham. The next bore cold roast beef. In the next was a sliced cake, and a board held sliced bread. A bowl contained stewed plums. She helped herself to beef and bread and sat in the seat she'd occupied the evening before.

"What are our plans for the day?" Mary asked.

"I thought I'd idle around eating cake," Starling answered. "Like every other wife."

Paul and Mary laughed. "I can see you're going to lead Alasdair a merry dance," Mary said. "How is he this morning?"

"He's tired and his hands are cut and swollen. Other than that, I'm sure he's very pleased with himself. The child was rescued before she came to any harm. I'm sure Mr.... Alasdair will want to know how she is, and so I'll make inquiries later."

"Not too much later. I'll need you to go shopping with me this morning," Mary said. "You can show me around Seymour's."

Starling's heart skipped a beat. "I don't think Mr....Alasdair would like me to do that. He wouldn't expect me to...flaunt our marriage."

Paul reached for the butter. "Of course not. Do you even know the Adelaide store? If not, it would be better if you avoided Seymour's, in my view. Perhaps if you simply avoided shopping altogether..."

"Very clever." Mary nodded encouragingly. "But I intend to buy fabric for gowns for myself and you know that. I should also buy a wedding present for Starling and Alasdair. I expect you'd rather stay at home."

Paul gave her a look of wariness, overlying his calm amusement. "Nothing will drag me off on an expedition to buy fabrics. Nothing. Unless Lavender decides to stay home, too. Then I'll have to leave the house for some reason or another."

"Lavender wouldn't miss a chance to show off her extensive wardrobe. Oh, dear. I shouldn't have said that."

Ellen entered the room.

"Fresh tea, please, for Mrs. Seymour," Paul said.

Ellen glanced at Starling, who nodded. "Don't take up breakfast for Mr. Seymour. Leave him to set his own pace today."

"Yes, ma'am." Ellen took the used plates from Paul and Mary, balancing the second neatly along her arm. Her missing fingers made carrying two separate plates difficult. "When will you be wantin' me to do your hair?"

Starling glanced at the maid in surprise. "I'm going shopping with Mrs. Elliot. My hair won't be seen under my hat."

After a disappointed glance at Starling, Ellen left the room.

Mary gurgled with laughter. "She needn't worry. Lavender will keep her occupied."

Starling lowered her gaze. Naturally, the maid would rather style hair than be used in the kitchen. Better, though, that she did Mrs. Frost's hair. The refurbishment of Starling's gown last night hadn't mattered because Mr. Seymour hadn't been at home to see her. While he was around, she couldn't consider being primped or prettified.

At this early stage, she didn't plan to lose her job.

Chapter 6

Alasdair washed and shaved. Dressed in a shirt, gray trousers, and a gray waistcoat, he went to the kitchen to beg for a bite. "A midday repast will be served in the dining room," Mrs. Trelevan said, her attention on the large lettuce in front of her. "Mr. Elliot will join you."

He found Paul in the sitting room.

"The ladies must be gallivanting," he said, seating himself in his favorite chair.

"The ladies are shopping." Paul's black cravat held his chin at a lofty angle as he lowered *The Gazette*. He peered over. "They'll be here later this afternoon."

Alasdair stretched his legs and eased back. His whole body ached from being cramped in the tunnel yesterday. The only exercise he seemed to manage these days was his daily walk upstairs to his office. He glanced at his bruised hands. "I hope they won't be too late. I need to speak to Lavender."

Paul grinned. "She'll want placating. Starling's adorable. She kept us, well, Mary and I, entertained in grand style last night." He winked at Alasdair. "I imagine you know what a clever lass she is. Pity about the wine. I assumed she had a harder head than she did."

"Don't tell me you got her pie-eyed?" Alasdair raised his eyebrows.

"Merely relaxed."

Alarmed, Alasdair sat up. "I hope she behaved herself. If she said anything indiscreet..."

"Not a bit. She's a sweet thing. You're a lucky man. Few new brides would put up with Lavender's—"

"If she tangled with Lavender..." Alasdair tried not to sound annoyed.

"Not at all, though I'd say Lavender was trying to upset her, talking about you and her and your previous...um..."

"Lavender talked about me?"

"About old times, about how she might have married you instead of Frost. Tragic thing, that, being widowed and orphaned in the same year. It's been hard on her and her nose is somewhat out of joint to find her former suitor, whom Mary led her to believe still, ah, thought of her, has now changed his mind. Fired up the old competitive spirit. Do her good. She couldn't have expected you to pine after her for a lifetime, despite what you told Mary. The woman needs a shake-up."

Alasdair held his gaze. "Jealous, you think?"

"Draw your own conclusions. On the way here, she said that husband of hers didn't treat her well, gambling, other women, et cetera. She said she'd likely not marry again. Only came to keep Mary company, or so she said."

Alasdair pressed his palm to the side of his neck, massaging his fingers into the bones of his upper spine. Lavender was the one love in his life. If her first marriage had been so bad, she may have been turned off marriage. "Mary should have told me she'd contacted Lavender. If that wife of yours was wanting to do me a favor, she should have said so."

"She wanted to surprise you. And what do you mean, do you a favor?"

"Perhaps I wouldn't have married Starling."

Paul didn't respond immediately. "Lavender isn't to my taste," he finally said.

Alasdair creaked to his feet. "I'll go to the Burdons' to see how Tammy is."

"She's doing well. Starling was there earlier for an hour. She says Tammy has a broken collarbone and she's still a little shocked, but there doesn't appear to be any sign of pneumonia, which was the doctor's main concern."

"I'll see the child, regardless."

"According to Starling, they want to award you some sort of medal."

"I won't go then." Alasdair clamped his lips.

"Only joking. The medal was Starling's idea. She thinks you're a hero."

"Fortunately, I have a tall stack of paperwork to catch up on," Alasdair said, walking to the doorway. Starling should never have met the Burdons. Who asked her to go outside yesterday? He'd specifically told her to... stay by his side. If she had told them she was his wife, he might have to explain why he'd hired an ex-whore not only to Mary, Paul and Lavender, but also to everyone he knew.

"Coward," Paul said with a rustle of his newspaper.

"And fool," Alasdair added to himself as he left the room. With Lavender in his house, he felt nothing but guilt about his physical reaction to Starling last night. Before Lavender had arrived, thinking about fucking a woman or even taking one into his bed would be nothing other than a normal, healthy pastime. Now that normal, healthy pastime seemed sinful, though Lavender was no more his than before.

He strode into the library, knowing that if he had complied with Mary's plans, he would have had the opportunity to rekindle a relationship with Lavender. However, he'd formerly had her body without being granted the ultimate prize, her hand. He dropped his ledgers on the table. Because his lesson to Mary had rebounded, fate led him in a more promising direction. Since he could fire up Lavender's jealousy with this charade, he might grab the chance he'd not been given before.

He rearranged the papers on his desk until he had found the precise order.

* * * *

By prearrangement with Starling, the brougham drew up outside the Seymour house. Like a military man, the driver swung down and marched to the front door, using the brass lion's head for two sharp raps. He returned and let down the steps.

Mrs. Frost rose to her feet, her face creased with a polite smile. She turned, swiftly picked up her parcels and, with her chin aloft, she waited for the driver's aid. Within moments and ignoring Mary and Starling, she glided up the path to the veranda, her parcels dangling by the strings. The bootboy came rushing out and almost cannoned into her. She stepped aside and disappeared into the house.

"She's very miffed," Mary said, giving Starling a complicit glance. "She hardly bought a thing. What a shame she couldn't have two or three new gowns."

"I'm sure my husband wouldn't have minded her using his account."

"That may be, but she was dishonest to imply that she was his wife."

Starling stood, not wishing to have this conversation. "I think it was assumed because she's so...eye-catching."

"Well, I'm glad I put the matter straight." Mary grinned while wrinkling her nose. "I thought being confined in a carriage with her for seven days was the worst experience of my life, but I hadn't yet been shopping with her." She reached for her nearest parcel.

The bootboy arrived at the brougham's open door, wiping his hands down the side of his trousers. He wore a high starched collar and a dark jacket, which he had apparently just donned, judging by the adjustments he made to his shirtsleeves. He glanced at the front door of the house. "She shoulda waited for me. It's my job to carry them parcels."

"Here, then. Have this." Mary handed Starling's biggest parcel to the lad. "Oh, and these. Take them all up to Mrs. Seymour's room." She gave half her own purchases to Starling and stepped out of the carriage.

Starling followed with Mary's parcels and the brougham trundled off to the coach house.

The bootboy led the way to the bedroom wing, scarcely able to peer over the top of the load he bore. Even Starling and Mary, only half burdened, staggered up the stairs. Mary stopped at her door, jiggled the handle with one elbow, and stood aside waiting for Starling to enter.

"Where shall I put your things?" Starling glanced around the room, which wasn't quite as large as Mr. Seymour's but was every bit as luxurious with a big bed, satin topped, and two velvet-covered chairs.

"On the bed. Don't leave. We haven't had a moment alone yet."

Starling carefully placed Mary's purchases on her bed and stood with nothing to say. She liked Mary, but Mary had a tendency to question her and Starling didn't know the answers to most of the questions Mr. Seymour's sister asked, or at least not the answers he would have wanted from her.

"I have never thought of myself as unattractive," Mary said, unwrapping her smallest parcel. "But Lavender...she only had to step out of the carriage to make people stop and stare. When we walked into the shops, all activity ceased so that every single person, male or female, could stare at her. After being with her for days, I can only see the shallow mind that lies beneath the glorious exterior. I forgot how she actually looks." She stared at the three pairs of gloves she had bought as if she had never seen them before. "People fell over themselves to please her. You and I only existed to carry her parcels. And the worst of it is that she expects that kind of notice."

"Beautiful people do," Starling said prosaically.

Mary considered, then she nodded. "Unlike her, you're a darling girl. Too darling. While she was trying to buy everything in town with Alasdair's name, you were trying not to cost him a penny. You shouldn't have bought those mean little gloves. Alasdair would want you to have the best quality."

"Truly. He doesn't want me to buy more things."

"He knows women *always* buy more things."

"He said he doesn't want me to look showy or gaudy."

"Well, he's not the brother I know. He has excellent taste, and so do you. I don't understand why you wear... No matter." Mary averted her eyes for a moment, then she took a breath. "I saw what you meant by

Lavender looking quite lovely in warm colors because when she held that roll of peach fabric under her chin, she looked so breathtaking that even I stared."

Starling's eyes widened with surprise. "You told her it did nothing for her."

"I don't see why she should look even better than she does." Mary tilted her chin.

Starling stifled a laugh with a cough.

Mary plumped down on her dressing table stool, her blue eyes gleaming. "So, I'm glad I bought that pale blue evening gown for you."

Starling chewed at her thumbnail. She had never wanted anything so much in her life, but she would never have need of a gown made from a fabric that couldn't be washed. She moistened her lips. "It was very generous of you but surely not a suitable wedding present. My husband might insist on you returning it."

"He wouldn't return a gift," Mary said casually. "It would be very ungracious. And you look so beautiful in it that his hard heart will melt in a moment."

Starling did her best to look modestly thrilled but the best part about owning the glorious gown for a moment in time was that Lavender didn't. The gown looked truly awful with the other woman's coloring. Unknowingly, Mary had done Lavender a favor.

"I'd best get to my unpacking, too." She backed to the door, hearing the bootboy hurry down the passage.

"I can't wait to see Alasdair's face when he sees you in that gown."

Starling gave a weak smile. She didn't plan to give him the opportunity. "You've been so generous. Thank you for today."

When she stepped out of the room, she heard Lavender's door latch click.

* * * *

Alasdair stepped inside Lavender's room.

Slowly straightening, she looked up from the parcels she was unwrapping on her bed. "Dare," she said in a voice of surprise.

He shut the door, trying to remember his prepared speech but his head emptied as her expression changed to the seductive pout that had broken the class barriers seven years ago. No longer an eighteen-year-old salesman desperate for wealthy customers, he held her expression long enough for her to drop her parcel and slowly approach him.

"You don't love her," she said in a low voice, all glinting eyes. "Tell me you don't love her."

He shook his head, unable to speak. She was scented, glossed, and curved, but he steeled himself not to reach out and take her into his arms.

"Thank you for not lying," she said, placing a pale hand on the lapel of his jacket. "You can't look at me like that and tell me you love another."

"Look at you like what?" He could barely breathe.

Her mouth lifted and her gaze held his. "Exactly the same way you did on the day we met. You look just as young and just as ardent."

"Ardent," he repeated, his smile twisted. She didn't look the same. If anything, she looked more beautiful, more perfect, but saying so would be comparable to complimenting the sun for the light.

"You've always been mine. Make love to me, Dare." She slid her arms around his neck.

He should have stepped back. Instead, he moved forward and found his hands on her hips. "Make love to you? Surely that would be overextending a host's duties," he said in a voice he couldn't quite control.

Her laugh sounded contented and her body melted into his. "It's accepted in the best of houses." She raised her face and found his lips.

Lost in a heart-thudding moment, he groaned when her hand slipped between them. With aching reluctance, he stayed her clever fingers.

"Let me. Your cock is as willing as ever."

"My mind is less so."

"Then why else did you come to my room?"

"I wanted to make sure you were comfortable," he said into her soft hair.

She gave a breathy laugh. A light tap sounded at the door, which opened the distance of the step he had unwisely yielded.

He stared into Ellen's shocked eyes. Although she couldn't possibly have seen Lavender's hand, the maid's thin lips and glare told him that he should be neither in Lavender's room nor her embrace.

"Don't ever again enter a bedroom in this house without being invited," he said, guilt icing his tone.

The maid closed the door in a hurry.

"She didn't see anything." Lavender's mouth sought his.

He turned his face. "Damn. What if she did?"

"She's only a maid. Why would you care?"

"What if that had been Mary at the door?"

"Or your wife. What could anyone do? You are the man of this house. Don't be so..."

"Lower class?"

She dropped her arms from his neck. "You pleasured me once in our stables, when anyone could have seen us at any time, remember?

Even after I was married... I don't see why it should be any different just because *you're* married."

"Why the hell do you think I left Melbourne?"

"To make your fortune. You didn't leave because of Richard. You knew I'd come to you whenever you wanted. I can't live without you."

"You managed well enough for seven years," he said grimly.

"You gave me no choice."

"*Choice!*" He backed out and slammed the door of her bedroom behind him. She still didn't see the difference between *coming to him* and *going with him*. When something hard hit the door, he knew *his* "marriage" hadn't changed her any more than *hers* had. She was still content to conduct a hidden liaison with a man she had seen as impossible to marry.

He strode down the passage to his own room, which he should have done in the first place. He was a married man who Lavender couldn't inveigle into an affair, a married man who needed to change for dinner. He jerked open the door to his bedroom.

Starling sat on the edge of his bed, surrounded by brown-paper-wrapped parcels. She lifted a rueful gaze to his face. "I'll pay for everything, I promise."

He didn't answer. Wrenching at the handle on the cupboard door, he pulled out his evening jacket and tossed that and his black waistcoat onto the bed. He began to undo his cravat.

"I can take everything back. Almost everything," she said. "This one was a wedding present from Mary, and so I can't return it until she leaves."

"You're not married."

"Did you want me to tell her that?"

He turned from the contemplation of his face in the mirror to the brown-haired female whose tilted eyebrows challenged him. The light had begun to fade. Soon he would have to light the lamp. In the dusk, her skin looked pale. Her severely scraped back bun did nothing for the shape of her face. As a child with that thick, rich, curly hair of hers let loose and tumbling around her shoulders, she would have looked quite pretty. Her eyes were huge.

"Do you think you should?"

She shrugged. "I agreed to your bargain."

"What if I want to end it?"

"I don't mind, as long as I get the money you promised me."

He sat on the bed. If Starling left, he would be at Lavender's mercy again. She said he was hers, always had been. More than likely she had only missed having a young, impressionable lover. To lure her into marriage he had to refuse to be her lover.

As he turned to Starling, he noticed the gape in his flies and accordingly dealt with the buttons. Lavender had been more efficient than he thought.

"That looks neater," Starling said in her prosaic voice.

"I went to talk to Lavender. She and I were lovers years ago. And so..." He shrugged, relieved he didn't have to censor his words for her.

"Lovers? Should you tell me that?" She stared into his eyes.

"I want to marry her."

She watched his face. "I thought you were set against marriage?"

"Only because I couldn't have her. She is the woman I have always wanted."

Her mouth opened and closed, and she dropped her gaze. "So you'll tell her you hired me?"

"She doesn't want marriage, not with me." He squeezed the bridge of his nose. "She never did. She wants me, and she admits that, but I'm not about to be used for her pleasure."

"My. There's a turnabout. I've never heard of a man holding out for marriage. Though I'm sure if you tell her you are not married and exactly how much money you have, she will marry you in an instant."

"Her family has more money than I will ever make."

"In that case, she can marry where she chooses."

"Exactly. That's why I can't give in to her until she realizes she loves me."

"I don't understand what business this is of mine."

"Be her competition. While she knows she only has to snap her fingers, she won't consider making an honest man of me. Think of yourself as an altruist. She's never had to compete for a man. You'll be giving her an opportunity to experience, firsthand, the pleasure of earning something she wants."

"What exactly do you want me to do?"

"At this stage, I merely have to smell her perfume and I'm a horny eighteen year old again. This puts me at her mercy every time she brushes by me." He picked up her hand. "If you could possibly look interested in me, rather than shifting away every time I come near, I might be able to convince her that I'm not so easily distracted."

Chapter 7

Starling's hand froze.

"I don't think flirting with you was part of our bargain," she answered, thudding with curiosity or perhaps a wayward interest.

"This is simply a request." He averted his eyes, clear and thick-lashed. "I won't beg you," he said, moving his hand to the bedspread, "if you don't want me to touch you."

She glanced at his bruised knuckles and the cut on the back of his hand. While greatly admiring him because of his deeds yesterday, she also respected him because he kept his promises. Unfortunately, he also physically attracted her. Lying beneath him in bed had been the most sensuous experience of her life. All too tempted to relax around him, touch his hand, or let him hold hers, she couldn't afford to let down her guard. Her side of the bargain was as important to her as his was to him.

She shook her head. "Ours is a monetary transaction, not one of affection."

"A monetary transaction?" His laugh sounded wry. "Making me no different from every other man you had at the inn? Trust me. I'm not about to throw you on your back while I'm dreaming of Lavender."

"I can't."

"You must have faked affection hundreds of times before."

"No, never." She twisted her fingers together.

He brought one knee to his chest, propping his forearm. "You can't kiss me, but you can fuck for money." His chin dropped onto the curve of his elbow.

"No. I can't." She wrapped her shaking hands in her skirts.

"I'm no worse than any other man."

"As far as I can see, all men are the same."

He shifted, took his arm around behind her, and lifted back, settling his bent leg behind her back. Encircled by him, her cheeks warmed. She could hear him breathe.

"Were you hurt by one of your customers at the inn?"

"A few men annoyed me, and a couple disgusted me, but I haven't been hurt by a man. The thing is, I don't need to earn my living by selling myself. At four shillings a time, why would I, especially now? You've promised me forty pounds to fool your sister. To earn that same money as a whore, I'd have to do something horrible too many times to count." She wanted to move away, but she wanted to stay.

"Something horrible?" One of his hands lifted to her chin, which he took between his thumb and forefinger, turning her face toward him. "Fucking shouldn't be horrible, Starling. Haven't you ever been pleasured?"

She could have told him she wasn't the whore he thought her, but she doubted he'd believe her any more the second time than the first. Aside from that, if he did, he wouldn't let her share his bed, being a respectable woman; then she would be of no use to him. She would lose her money. She shook her head.

He tugged a curl that had loosened around her face and focused on her as if noticing her features for the first time. She stared back. The moment seemed fraught and her heart began to race.

He broke the silence. "What did you buy?" He lifted one of her brown paper parcels and rattled the insides.

"You *do* still want me here, don't you?"

He sucked in his cheeks, as if thinking. Finally, he sighed out a breath. "I still want you to pretend to be my wife for two weeks."

With a tug of relief, she reached for the topmost parcel. "I didn't unwrap these in case I had to return them. Mary said I could charge everything to you because I don't have a penny, you know. You didn't pay me for my last week at Seymour's and I spent my wages from the inn on a jacket, which I left at the boardinghouse. I hope I can go there tomorrow to get my things."

"I'll send for them."

She hauled out a pair of gloves. "Mrs. Trelevan thought I ought to have these."

"And this?" He shifted another parcel toward her.

"A hat. It will go with the jacket I have at the boardinghouse. The last is a gown that Mary insisted on giving to me as a wedding present. I won't wear it. You can return it after I leave, but I can pay you for these other things."

"Let me see the gown."

"No. She gave it to me because I lied and so I don't deserve it."

"I said we were married and so the lie is mine."

"I said my things hadn't arrived yet from Ballarat. You told the servants I came from Ballarat. Mary said I can't keep wearing the same evening gown night after night, especially when Lavender...well, when Lavender looks so lovely."

The tips of his fingers tapped on his chin. "She's right. You need to dress as my wife."

"I told Mary you wouldn't like me to have this gown."

"Open the parcel," he growled.

"I won't pay for this. When I leave here, I'll have no use for it."

"Consider it my property, on loan," he said, sounding exasperated.

Carefully, she untied the string. "You won't want me to keep the gown." With reverence, she drew out the pale blue silk.

"Hold it in front of you."

Standing, she did as he asked. In the dressmaker's shop, she'd looked serene and pearly skinned in this gown, an expensive version of the one she'd dreamed of owning for years. She thought the color would suit her. However, Alasdair had chosen her because she looked plain and drab. He would frown when he saw she looked nice and make her pack up the gown again.

"I'd have to see the color next to your skin. Expose your shoulders and hold the gown up again."

She pulled at the neck of her gown but only managed to constrict her shoulders. When she made a helpless face, he rose to his feet and unbuttoned the back for her. She held the blue gown against her skin, and he took the garment from her, slowly sliding both necklines lower. Lightly clasping her upper arms, he drew her toward him and touched her mouth lingeringly with his.

"That's to show you that kisses are given for many reasons," he murmured. "Not all of them as a prelude." With a steady smile, he put her gown back into her hands and began changing his clothes for dinner.

Striving for composure, she covered her shoulders with her brown gown. "Should I wear the blue tonight? For dinner?"

Turning his back, he put on a black waistcoat and a white cravat. "Do so if you wish. I've made my decision. You have a right to make yours." Shrugging into his black jacket, he left the room.

Starling put away her new hat and gloves. Alasdair had admitted that he'd been rutting with Lavender. Apparently, the beauty didn't see a wife as any impediment to her needs.

A knock sounded at the door. Thinking she must have misheard when no one entered, she began to fold the tissue paper around the blue evening gown. The knock rapped out again, a little louder. "Yes," she called.

"It's Freda, ma'am."

"Come in, Freda."

Freda sidled into the room, head down. "Shall I bring in a bath now?"

"Please. Is Ellen ill? Shouldn't you be in the kitchen at this time of night?"

"We've changed jobs for a while." Freda took a deep breath. "Mrs. Frost says that Ellen isn't a real ladies' maid. She said El takes too long to button her gowns." She jutted her jaw.

Starling frowned. "Perhaps Mrs. Frost is simply used to a maid who works another way entirely. Ellen is very fast with me."

"She can do everything just as good as me. She learnt to manage without them fingers, and it's not fair."

"Is that why Mrs. Frost says she is slow?"

Freda nodded. "El lost her fingers barely a year ago. We was piece-workers." She spoke as she set up a bath and draped towels over the screen. "We did beading and embroidery. Seymour's bought from us."

"How did Ellen lose her fingers?"

"The thread dispenser. She got her fingers caught. Then she got an infection and she near died." Freda walked to the door. "I stayed home to look after her while she was sick, and so our manager put us *both* off. When Mr. Seymour found out he took us on as maids, though we'd never been in service before. Conditions is much better here."

Starling put her thumbnail to her mouth and chewed. "Mrs. Frost might be gone in a few weeks. If she hasn't, she'll soon see what a fine worker Ellen is."

"Will you tell Mrs. Frost?"

"I'll tell her." Starling squared her shoulders.

"El might have been tactless. She had a small amount of trouble lacing Mrs. Frost's stays and Mrs. Frost thought she said she was fat. Silly, really, when anyone can see Mrs. Frost is as beautiful as a princess." Freda opened the door.

"Before you fetch the water, I wonder if you'd mind... I need Ellen to style my hair again. Could you tell her I can't manage without her?"

"Yes, ma'am. And she's sorry she came in this morning without being asked. We know things has changed around here, what with the marriage and all, and neither of us will do it again."

"Is that why you didn't enter until I answered?"

"We can't walk into rooms just because we've knocked. Mr. Seymour said."

"He wasn't awake when Ellen came in this morning."

Freda lowered her gaze and turned to leave the room.

"When did he say that, Freda?"

Freda shook her head. "It's Mrs. Frost's fault. She's makin' everything awful, just awful. I wish she'd go away."

Starling raised her chin, looking the maid in the eyes. "Mr. Seymour likes her. He wouldn't like someone bad, would he?"

"No, ma'am." Freda bobbed her head. "I'll get El for you."

* * * *

Alasdair sipped his predinner sherry with Paul, Mary, and Starling all companionably conversing. Starling had an amazing ability to fit in, which surprised him. He wasn't surprised that Lavender hadn't yet arrived. After his apparent rejection of her advances, she would be likely to punish him and sulk for a while.

When she finally entered the sitting room, he rose to his feet. Her primpings had been worth the effort. As usual, she looked breathtaking. The sparkling amethyst necklace she wore matched her beautiful eyes.

"I'm not late, I hope?" she asked with a sweet smile.

Alasdair did not intend to come to heel instantly. "Certainly not," he said, keeping his expression purposely bland. "Too late for a glass of sherry, though. Now you're here, we'll go into dinner."

"Oh, I did keep you waiting. I'm so sorry." She put her hand on his arm.

He patted her fingers in an avuncular way, leaving her and moving toward Starling, whose arm he took instead. "Our first formal dinner," he said to her, trying to sound doting, while leading her into the dining room.

"Come, ladies." Paul scooped up both Lavender and Mary. "Our newlyweds must be allowed their indulgences. Their first formal dinner, eh? I'd never thought Alasdair such a romantic fellow. Course, I've never seen him married before."

With almost a pettish flounce, Lavender sat at her designated place. "Such a pretty gown," she said, inclining her head toward Starling. "When you wore that floral last night, I forgot to say how much I admired the colors. Perhaps I should have worn the same gown I wore last night, too, but my gowns have spent days packed and so I need to give each an airing in turn."

Alasdair filled Starling's glass. "Yes, my wife looks very lovely." The slender bird looked softer in the frills, paler skinned and with lustrous eyes. And her hair looked better, softer and fuller around her face.

Not wholly to madden Lavender he kept his gaze on Starling's every move, noting her enjoyment of food. She ate everything with smiling pleasure after savoring first, which fascinated him. Her table manners were faultless. Nor did her conversation shame him. She didn't talk too much or gossip. She simply added content.

"I'll be as fat as a pig when I leave here." Paul finally leaned back, eyeing his last mouthful of Queen pudding with regret. "Has your cook always served food as rich as this, Alasdair?"

Mary laughed. "You don't have to scrape your plate. Look at Lavender. She only ever eats half her servings."

"I've always had the appetite of a sparrow," Lavender said, peeking under her long lashes at Alasdair.

He quickly jerked his attention back to Starling. "And our little bird has the appetite of...?"

"An eagle, I expect. I'm always hungry. We were never given much to eat in the foundling home."

"Are you an orphan?" Mary asked, eyes wide. "I almost can't believe that. You speak so well. You must have been brought up in a very superior establishment."

Starling gave a faint smile. "One of the nuns was a gentlewoman. She taught us to speak like her."

"The orphanage explains the eighteen sisters. I assume they are not all related to you by blood?"

"As far as I know, no one is."

"Were you orphaned very young? Poor thing."

Lavender offered a polite smile. "Paul, do you admire the architecture of Sir Henry Delaine's new country house in Ivanhoe?"

"Very much."

"And you know the Delaines. Yes? Sir Henry was a great friend of my father and after Mama died, he was a good friend to me, too." She lowered her gaze. "A very good friend."

"That was kind of him, Lavender," Mary said. "But how very sad, Starling, that you never knew your parents."

"She might be lucky," Lavender said stiffly. "Not all parents are good. Mine were, of course, but I've heard of—"

"Were they kind to you in the home, Starling?" Mary asked, her forehead creased with concern.

"As kind as they could be. Money was short and..." Starling shrugged. "Charity begins at home, they told us quite often. We were expected to earn our livings as early as we could. I stayed on until I was eighteen, which was unusual. Most of the girls were put into service at fifteen years old."

"Why did—"

"This subject is *so* depressing." Lavender rearranged the placement of her spoon and fork. "Mrs. Seymour, do you mind if we talk about the treats we have planned for tomorrow instead?"

"Please call me Starling, Mrs. Frost. Everyone else does." Starling leaned back to allow Freda to take her last emptied plate.

"Want a game of billiards, Alasdair?" Paul said, tucking his thumbs into his waistcoat pockets.

"No. I've hardly seen Starling in the past two days."

"Lavender?"

She shook her head. "Ladies don't play billiards, I'm afraid."

"You should have asked me. I'm no lady," Mary said with a mischievous smile.

"I know that. You never let me win. I thought Lavender might." Paul rose to his feet and left with Mary for the billiard room.

"What shall we do?" Lavender asked Alasdair as he pulled her chair out. She took his arm before he realized he should have tended to Starling first, but as he tried to do so, Lavender gave him such a glance of reproach that he couldn't leave her.

"What do you want to do?" he asked gruffly.

"Nothing too strenuous." She touched the back of his hand. "Oh, you've scraped your knuckles. You haven't been fighting over me? Of course not. You're a married man."

He raised his eyebrows, trying to look bored. So far, his ignoring her had spurred her on very nicely.

"Anagrams, perhaps?" she asked in a low voice.

"Would *you* like to?" He glanced at Starling, who nodded.

Lavender plucked a few pink rose petals from a side vase while Alasdair set up the games' table in the sitting room. He placed a chair for each woman and each sat, Lavender offering him a complicit smile before she glanced at the first word whose letters she had to make into as many new words as she could.

He had to deliberately look away from her to set the timer.

Starling cleared her throat. "It's strange, isn't it? I have to try hard to guide this pencil properly without using my first two fingers. I watched Ellen today and she can maneuver the tiniest things without even thinking. I have eight buttons on this gown and she buttoned them all in half the time I can."

Lavender yawned delicately and put down her pencil. "I think I've made enough words."

Alasdair glanced at the timer. She still had another few seconds. Although he'd never played any game with her outside of a bedroom, he didn't doubt her intelligence for one moment. However, he nodded and answered his 'wife.' "It's wonderful what a person can do with a little motivation. I think Ellen's motivation was Freda. She didn't want to hold her sister back. Time's up. How many words do you have, Starling?"

"Four."

"I have twelve," Lavender said, modestly casting down her eyes.

"I win then. I have twenty." He grinned.

"Let me see," Lavender said, snatching the paper from beneath his elbow. "We can't have any cheating." As she leaned forward, she brushed his knee with her hand.

He involuntarily tensed.

Lavender teased her fingernail along his inner thigh under the cover of the table. "You wouldn't cheat, would you?"

"No."

With a slow smile, she put both hands on the table and took her gaze to her page.

"And my hair. I can't believe how clever she is with my hair," Starling continued. "I've never looked this good in my life."

"That *can't* be so." Lavender pushed a lock of hair behind her ear. "After all, Dare did marry you."

Starling gave a strange little laugh. "For my lack of looks."

He glanced at her. "Not so. Your other attributes were more important at the time."

Lavender's face froze, but he didn't regret his misleading comment. She had, after all, been ungracious to his wife.

Starling turned her attention back to her paper. "How do you spell 'rear'? Does it have two 'e's?"

"It doesn't matter. There's only one 'r' in the word 'engraving,'" he answered, puzzled.

"So there is." Starling concentrated on adding words to her list again. "You've done well by employing Ellen and Freda, Alasdair. Between them, there's nothing they can't do. They work in the kitchen, they wait on the tables, and they work as upstairs maids. I believe few servants are as flexible. The Burdons wish they had servants—"

"*Really*, Starling." Lavender frowned. "Are we to spend all night discussing servants? I'm sure the females about whom you are speaking would do very well for *some* households, but I wouldn't employ such creatures. I'd only have well-trained servants who don't speak unless asked and don't enter rooms until they've been invited."

"Was it you who told Ellen she couldn't enter a room until she was told?"

"I did," Alasdair said. "Drop the subject, please. Time's up. How many, Lavender?"

"Three. Starling was talking the whole time and I couldn't concentrate. How many do you have, Starling?"

"One."

"I have ten." He moved his chair back a little and picked up Starling's discarded paper, glancing over her list. "You have twelve words here, each with one alien letter." He examined her face, pursed his lips, and put the paper down. "The last word before I stretch my legs is 'distilled.'"

"No talking. I want to get at least ten this time." Lavender sounded pettish.

When he noticed the timer had run out, Lavender's total was nine. "Twenty-four altogether with my other words," she said with a satisfied little wriggle of her shoulders.

"I have ten. Twenty-eight altogether," he said, glancing at Starling.

"Twenty-nine," Starling said brightly.

"Is that what you came up with, after adding four and one?" Lavender's lips pursed with disapproval.

"When I added twenty-five and four. That's right, isn't it?" Starling asked him.

"If you just made twenty-five words, it's right."

"Let me see." Lavender snatched Starling's paper. "*Teller*? You can't have that. There's only one *e*. And what's *sild*? Do you mean sold? You can't have more than seven or eight right."

Alasdair scanned the paper. "No, she's spelt at least twenty right. I see what you've been doing, you wretch," he said to his wife. "You've substituted unlikely letters." He shook his head and laughed. "You deserve a good beating."

"What sort of beating is good?" Starling folded her paper.

"Perhaps the sort you do. The subtle kind." He stretched his arms behind his head, noticing that Lavender's gaze fixed on his chest. She pouted her lips, so he quickly turned his face to Starling.

"No one could possibly make twenty-five words out of the word 'distilled.' Lavender muttered. "She cheated."

"No," he said. "She doesn't."

Chapter 8

Alasdair sat in the bedroom chair and removed his shoes. "Why did you pretend to be hopeless at anagrams?" He watched while Starling took her nightgown from beneath her pillow.

She met his gaze. "I don't like competing. In anagrams, we only prove that one or the other of us is quicker at finding words." She disappeared behind the screen to undress. "Does someone always have to be the best? I think it's more interesting to find a word and substitute a letter, any letter," she said, her voice muffled for a moment. "Which changes it into another word. Then I don't have to compete with anyone but myself."

"You won easily. You didn't have to compete."

"Lavender wanted to. She thinks it's important to win. I would have made more words wrong the last time, but I started thinking of Ellen and Freda and forgot what I was doing." She lifted a pair of thin-soled, shiny boots from behind the screen. "But it doesn't matter. She thought most of my words were wrong anyway."

"Sild." Lavender did have a need to win but he wouldn't let her with him, not this time. "A young herring, if I'm not mistaken."

"I think so." One slender arm appeared above the screen.

"You know so, you wretch. Do you need any help?" When she didn't answer, he repeated, a little more loudly, "Do you want me to help with those eight buttons Ellen manages easily?" He saw no need for her to hide away to disrobe, not now that he appreciated her perception and enjoyed her candid observations. Taking no notice of her startled expression, he entered into her space behind the screen, turned her around, and began unbuttoning the back of her gown.

She stood motionless. "You do know how good Ellen and Freda are, don't you?"

"Of course." Curling spirals of hair escaped the netted mass and trickled gently around her delicate nape. Viewed like this, she seemed sweet and innocent despite her wealth of experience.

"But you were cross with Ellen this afternoon."

His sigh stirred the finer tendrils of her hair. "A guilty reaction. She caught me doing something I'm not too proud of."

"With Lavender."

Her statement needed no reply. Having unbuttoned her high bodice, he skimmed the fabric down her arms. Thus far, he'd seen little of her flesh. He liked her shoulders, straight and slender, and he watched them wriggle as she dropped her gown to a pooled heap on the floor. She stepped out and began to work at the hooks on her stays.

"Eat too much, did you?" he asked, amused by her efforts. Properly laced, stays were difficult to undo until the laces had been eased.

"I'm sure it wasn't this tight when I put it on."

"Which was before dinner and a good two pounds ago."

"Am I growing fat?" She sounded hopeful.

"It'll take more than a few meals before that happens."

"Do you think I'm too thin?"

"Not at the moment."

"What does that mean?"

"At this present moment I find parts of you very appealing. These in particular." He ran his thumbs across her shoulders, deliberately touching the smooth, creamy skin. Perhaps thoughts of Lavender had given him the slow heating in his groin, or perhaps the fact that he had been aroused and denied for two days had heightened his senses. He didn't know, and he didn't particularly care, because he had no intention of coupling with anyone. Not with Lavender and not with Starling. He began to unloosen her stays.

Her posture stiffened. Keeping her back to him, she unhooked the front and caught the whole thing at her bosom.

"Relax. I'm not going to make an advance." He scooped off her stays and, with determined hands, he covered the compressed creases of her chemise where the boning had pressed into her body. He massaged firmly. She stood as if poised for flight.

Pretending he didn't know, he worked his fingers around to the front of her rib cage, making sure he didn't let his hands touch her breasts. She stretched her neck to one side and the other and let her head droop. For the briefest moment, very fleeting, she leaned back against him. He flexed his hands, hoping he'd shown her that all men *weren't* the same. Most of them had the same physical reactions when they touched a woman's soft skin, but one of them didn't have to go further...unless a woman wanted him to, of course. Clearly she didn't which, being in love with another woman, he could accept.

Keeping his demeanor casual and hoping she didn't realize his body had grown more interested than he'd expected, he finished with a gentle tap of her bottom. "That's enough. Time we went to bed, I think." He cleared his throat.

"Thank you. That was very nice," she said in a husky voice.

He lay covered to the neck with the sheet by the time she had dressed in her nightgown. As she pattered over to the bed, he couldn't work out why he'd initially thought her plain. His first impression of her had been colored by the tight screw of hair on her head and her unflattering gray cotton uniform. He hadn't seen past her outward appearance.

Now that he did, he could see she had fine pearly skin, softly curling hair, arched eyebrows, and long eyelashes, fairer at the tips. Her big brown eyes lacked the hardness most ladies of easy virtue developed. "How long had you worked at the inn?" he asked, watching her slide into bed beside him.

"Six weeks."

Perhaps she wasn't as experienced as he'd assumed. Frowning, he turned down the oil lamp, leaving the room in total darkness. "These sheets are prickly."

"It's you. The sheets are made from the finest linen. If you wore a nightshirt, you wouldn't feel so irritable."

"I don't like being confined and strangled while I sleep," he said, hearing his own petulance. "Nor would you if you'd spent more than three months down..."

"You deserve to be uncomfortable when you won't be practical."

He muffled his request with the sheet. "Make me comfortable."

She heaved a noisy sigh. Nevertheless, she rolled him away from her and put her palms on his back the same way as she had the night before. He felt the same way he had about it the night before: hot and aching with guilty arousal.

* * * *

Starling awoke with her nose snuffled against hard warm flesh. She'd dribbled, too, she realized as she sleepily put her hand to her mouth. Alasdair's shoulder. Gracious!

"Do you know what time it is?" he said in an indignant voice. "Seven-thirty."

She stared at him. Lying on his back, with one arm beneath his head and the other around her shoulders, he was easily the nicest thing she'd seen in the morning—big, good-looking, and indulgent. "Seven-thirty?"

"The water hasn't been brought in."

She smiled at him, an action she realized had been entirely spontaneous and probably pathetic. She liked him, truly liked him, and not only because of the way his eyes crinkled when he was amused or the way he gave without expecting a thing back. She liked him because he liked her. He stimulated her, mentally and physically.

Last night, while they'd been playing anagrams, he'd instantly understood what she'd done. He'd laughed, not *at* her but *with* her. She'd not had that sort of silent communication with anyone before. And the massage. Somehow he'd guessed the stays were uncomfortable and without making a fuss, he'd helped. From the day she'd arrived, no matter what he thought of her, he'd treated her with respect.

He hadn't been born a gentleman any more than she'd been born a lady. He could only have made himself the way he was by sheer hard work. Again, she wondered how he'd really made his fifty thousand pounds. No idling onlooker, picking up random nuggets, would have broad muscled shoulders, a hard back, and that tight bottom she had seen on their first night. She swallowed. His skin was also smooth and touchable.

Waking up to herself, she lifted her hand and rolled out of bed, clutching her nightgown at the neck. "It's your own fault the water hasn't been brought in. You shouldn't have told Ellen she needed permission to enter rooms, and then she would have been here half an hour ago."

"Is she punishing me?"

"None of us likes to be reprimanded."

"If she'd come any farther into Lavender's room yesterday she wouldn't have liked what she saw."

"If you'd been rutting, she would have noticed that when she opened the door."

"We weren't rutting. Ellen wouldn't have seen anything more than a kiss, I expect."

"Do you usually kiss ladies with your trousers unbuttoned?"

He gave a dangerously long, slow smile. "Do you want to find out?"

"I don't expect I'll have a chance. Most of the time we spend alone together, you don't wear trousers at all." She bent to open her drawer, a little afraid that she'd sounded jealous and quite certain she'd sounded snippy.

"Come back to bed."

She stared at him, surprised. He closed his eyes briefly and said, as if he'd been forced into an explanation, "What do you expect when you wander around the room half-na...discussing...what happened between Lavender and me. Oh, for Hades' sake, cover yourself with my dressing robe."

"I don't see what you've got to be cross about." She marched to his wardrobe, opened the door, and pulled out a green silk robe.

"If you came back to bed, I'd show you."

She plunged her arms into the sleeves. "You'd show me why you are cross? Why would I want to know?"

"I don't care whether you want to know or not. I want—" A rapping at the door interrupted his rush of words.

"Come in," she called loudly. The door opened and Ellen stood outside, hot water jug in hand. "Oh, good. You're just in time." Starling flashed a quelling glance at Alasdair.

He shot her a smoldering glare.

"Ellen, Mr. Seymour wants everything back to normal tomorrow. Come at the usual time in the morning and do as you usually do. While there are guests in the house, it might be a good idea to knock at their doors and wait for their acknowledgment before you enter. Oh, and Mr. Seymour definitely doesn't want you and Freda to change jobs. Do you?" She fixed him straight in the eye.

For a moment, she thought he wouldn't answer.

He jutted his jaw. "If Mr. Seymour had the faintest idea what was going on around here, he might give his own orders."

Ellen glanced from one to the other. "Mrs. Frost said—"

"And while we're on the subject of Mrs. Frost," Starling said before Ellen had a chance to expose a not particularly admirable character trait of Lavender's. "She and Mr. Seymour are very old friends. I don't think any of us need to be too upset about a kiss between friends, do we? Mr. Seymour was very embarrassed. He thought you'd think the worst of him. He's sorry for shouting at you."

"Ha!" Ellen left the room.

"Thank you. Now I know she saw everything," Alasdair said tightly.

"Now she knows you told your wife and your wife forgives you."

Alasdair took a deep breath, brushing his fingers over his chin again and again. "You did well, Starling," he finally said. "I know I shouldn't have done what I did."

She turned around, unable to suppress her relief. "You're a man," she answered. "You behaved like a man."

"Touché," he muttered.

* * * *

In the afternoon, Alasdair took Starling and his visitors for a tour of the Emporium. The sun peered over the clouds. The warmth of the day caused shoppers to slow their stride to a saunter along the footpaths. Parasols were out in force, most wielded by experts. Carriages trundled by, the sound of the creaky wheels almost drowning out the flower seller extolling her wares.

Once inside the heavy main doors, Starling followed Alasdair through the vast homewares area, past the familiar leathery smell of the trunks and suitcases, and up the wide central staircase as he discussed the most recent additions and alterations with Paul. In this enormous store, the full staff numbered more than three hundred, including cleaners, packers, and loaders. Instantly recognized by the assistants, Alasdair was acknowledged with smiles, nods, and formal bows. Although properly reserved, he meticulously called, by name, each member of staff he passed. Impressed, Starling noted that success depended on more than money and looks.

Although he didn't introduce any of his employees to his party, Starling stood beside Mary, making certain her brown bonnet hid her face. In the five days she'd worked at Seymour's, she'd associated mainly with Mr. Porter during the day and the nine other girls in the boardinghouse at night. They knew her by sight but wouldn't expect to see her with Mr. Seymour's family or dressed in anything but anonymous gray. Her yellow and brown gown made her almost invisible, let alone the presence of lovely Lavender in a pinkish-purple gown and a smart scarlet pillbox hat that turned all heads.

Alasdair led the group to the back of the second floor where he sold fabric, gowns, hats, unmentionables, silk flowers, ribbons, and lace. "I took your advice," he said, smiling at Mary. "As you can see, I have a purely women's area. I have one in each of my emporiums."

"And I don't doubt you're making a fortune out of my idea."

"I'm doing well because you proved to me more than once that women are more enthusiastic shoppers than men." He grinned and chucked his sister under the chin. "Much more enthusiastic."

"And I may well prove the same thing again today." Mary gathered Starling's arm. "No doubt you know he employs women to sell the goods women purchase, like hats and gowns, as well as fabrics?"

Starling nodded. "I know he has nine women among his staff here. His ideas are considered progressive. That is why I wanted to work...um, for him."

"Perhaps you would like to inspect the fabric section here? I would be interested to know if it's as extensive as the one at Ballarat."

Starling glanced at Alasdair, who happened at that moment to be patting the hand Lavender had rested on his arm. "I don't think it would be fair to compare the two."

Alasdair focused on Mary, his eyes narrowed. "I didn't know Starling told you she worked for me."

"We interrogated her about everything the night you rescued Tammy. We know everything."

"Everything?" He raised his eyebrows at Starling.

"We still have a few little secrets," she said, but she couldn't tell by his expression whether he was relieved or disappointed. "I *would* like to inspect the ground floor, though."

"Pots and pans?" said Mary. "Why on earth?" Nevertheless, she traveled the length and the width of the lower floor with Starling, interested in the goods and furniture, discussing with her the merchandising ideas Alasdair had begun in his first business. "Like a trader born. Which, of course, he was."

Lavender stayed with the men, a good idea as speculation would center on the beautiful blonde and leave Starling a chance to learn about the various aspects of buying and selling from Mary.

"Breaking up the place into men's and women's areas is a moneymaker," Mary said happily. "He ought to pay me for that idea. No, no. He has, many times over. He never ceases to thank me and he has never discounted any idea of mine. His respect means more to me than any amount of money."

"Do you think he understands that?"

Mary shook her head. "He values money. He worked hard for it, though fortunately never as a manual laborer. I don't think Mama could have borne that. I doubt he has dwelt too long on thoughts of respect because as a man, he's never been denied it."

"Even when he had no money?"

"The more money, the more respect. That's how it is with men," Mary said regretfully. "Female employees are as responsible as males and work as hard, but men prefer not to buy from them, and many women won't because they accept men as cleverer. I see a time in the future when people are accepted for the job they do, not their gender."

"A time when women will be paid as much as men?"

"If they do the same job."

"It won't work. Men have to support their families."

"I know it won't work. It's a utopian ideal. We have it easy, letting men support us."

Starling didn't answer. She couldn't see a time in her life when a man had supported her or a time in her life when a man would. This day had shown her much about shops, and she could learn more. Alasdair's library held more than she could scan in a lifetime. These two weeks he had given her were proving a Godsend. When her time ended, better dressed and with the confidence she had begun to acquire by associating with people who accepted her as she was, she could certainly better herself. Fate had intervened to help her in her aim to buy and run a business.

"Time to leave, ladies." Alasdair, decorated with Lavender, stood behind them. Paul winked at Mary.

"I must say, you're a generous wife," Mary muttered. "I keep Paul close by when Lavender is around. She doesn't appear to understand the boundaries when left with other people's husbands."

"Seymour, what a timely meeting," a hearty male voice interrupted. "I want to talk to you about a piece of land I have in Port Adelaide. A perfect place to site a new business."

Without waiting to be introduced to a man who was obviously not an employee, Starling spun Mary around and headed for the front entrance of the shop. "Let's go to the carriage while they talk business. That ought to bore Lavender's boots off."

"I don't think she's worn boots in her life," Mary said, shaking her head. "Speaking of which, I think you ought to buy evening slippers. I don't see any need for you to wait for your things to arrive from Ballarat. Shoes never go astray, and if anyone can afford to buy shoes for his wife, it's Alasdair."

"More shopping?" Paul groaned as he maneuvered between them. "Come. If you're quick about it, I'll give you the benefit of my advice. Shoes, fortunately, are over here."

Starling took a steadying breath. Ellen had cleaned her boots to a high polished sheen and had replaced the laces. They'd pass without comment as old boots she'd traveled in. She would have preferred not to spend more of her promised forty pounds but Mary, she'd discovered, was as determined as Alasdair when challenged.

The shoes Mary finally convinced her she had to have cost two pounds. Because Mary assumed that Alasdair would pay, Starling couldn't see how she could insist on a cheaper pair, so she took them. Although one half of her was delighted to own a pair of black silk shoes with elevated heels, the other half mourned spending money on luxuries when she needed the essentials so much more.

Alasdair and Lavender finally caught up with them and, grouped, they found Alasdair's carriage, driven to the privileged position outside Seymour's.

"Ugh, that frog," Lavender said with distaste as Alasdair handed her into the carriage. "How could you talk to him for such a long time? He must be the ugliest man in the world. Hamilton Fredericks? Freddy Frog. That name suits him down to the ground, or perhaps I should say to the pond." She tittered.

"That frog, as you call him, is one of the most successful businessmen in Adelaide." Alasdair lifted Lavender's skirts out of the way so that he could sit between her and Starling. "He's also connected to the governor, a second cousin, I believe."

"Neither of which excuses the fact that he resembles a frog." Lavender shuddered. "Men with money and influence ought to be good-looking. Did you see how he looked at me? As if I were a morsel he wanted to shoot out with his tongue and grab."

Alasdair smiled. "Surely that only makes him human."

"I've often thought how well people suit their names. Dare Seymour. Courageous and all seeing. Lavender Frost. Well, it's for someone else to judge whether my name suits me," Lavender said, looking satisfied.

Mary leaned forward and, under the guise of pointing at something outside the window, whispered to Starling, "A beautiful perfume and color but cold and shallow. Yes, it suits her."

"Pale hair and violet eyes." Alasdair gazed too long into the latter. "But you were born Mayberry not Frost and you told me you weren't christened Lavender."

"My parents called me Lavender because I looked so well in the color."

"You would look pretty in orange," Starling said. "But it would be strange to call you Orange."

Paul laughed. "What about my name? Where do I fit into this hypothesis?"

"Some people don't fit. They just have names," Lavender said, shooting an annoyed glance at Starling.

Starling stared at her gloved hands. She didn't just have a name. She had an all-time description. Starling Smith, brown and anonymous, completely ordinary. "Starling Seymour. I don't think we can do much with that either."

"Oh, I don't know. We bought some rather beautiful shoes with that name." Mary smiled at Alasdair, who was frowning. "Only one pair, Alasdair. If I were your wife, I would have bought at least three. And an embroidered reticule."

"But I didn't make a bargain with you. I made one with Starling."

"True. And I remember every word of it," Starling said, like the meek and obedient wife she had promised to be. Recalling that he wanted her to give Lavender a reason to be jealous, she slipped her hand under his arm, leaned against him, and gave an *mm* of enjoyment exactly the way she had seen the blonde do.

A mistake because he relaxed and smiled, crinkling his eyes and widening his mouth, showing his good white teeth. Her insides dropped and swirled, taking away her breath.

She hoped he hadn't put her in the position of playing with fire.

* * * *

Starling again wore the gray refurbished gown to dinner, but she added her glamorous new shoes. Fortunately, anagrams weren't suggested as an after-dinner entertainment again, for Starling was so out of charity with Lavender that she might have forgotten her noncompetitive stance and won. Instead, Mary played the piano and everyone sang—except Lavender, who wandered around the sitting room, again upturning the ornaments and scanning their undersides.

"You don't like music?" Paul asked Lavender while Mary tried to find some newer music sheets.

"Orchestras. String quartets. Music that improves the mind, yes. Ladies—oh, what are you doing?" Lavender stood, her face aghast, glancing at the spilled coffee dripping from her décolletage to the waist of her lilac evening gown.

Ellen righted the cup she had been offering to Paul on a tray. "I'm sorry, ma'am. You moved suddenly. Let me wipe—"

"Don't bother." Lavender pulled a lace handkerchief from her sleeve and dabbed crossly at the coffee stain. "Really, Dare. This maid is incredibly clumsy. Why don't you keep her in the kitchen where she can't do so much damage?"

Alasdair's gaze sought and found Starling's. "It was an accident."

"If you'd had as much experience with servants as I have, you'd know you shouldn't let them get away with their mistakes." Lavender's eyes changed to slits and her mouth looked tight and mean.

"I think I can, Lavender. I think everyone deserves a chance in life." When Alasdair patted Lavender's hand, Starling's chest hurt.

Lavender made a face of glorious contrition. Her mouth drooped and her eyes filled with unshed tears. "Don't judge me harshly, Dare. I'm spoilt and I know it, but I've never had to practice tolerance. I want to be nice. I just don't know how to be."

Starling didn't know if Lavender was being clever or sincere, but as Alasdair devoted most of his attention to her after that, her intention didn't matter.

Because he also showed Starling that same understanding while she undressed for bed, she couldn't complain. As he had the night before, he eased the constrictions of her stays by massaging her rib cage. His wrists brushed her breasts once. Knowing his touch to be unintentional, she didn't react outwardly. But inside she relived the tingle of his touch until she shut her eyes for sleep.

Chapter 9

Starling poured a measure of hot water into the basin and unbuttoned the neck of her nightgown. Outside, she could hear the magpies begin their morning choir. She thought Alasdair still slept. She didn't expect him to come up behind her while she washed. When he lightly touched her back, she almost leaped out of her skin. Heart thudding, she dropped her flannel into the warm water and began to turn.

He stopped her with a kiss on the nape of her neck. His mouth tickled pleasurably. Without thinking, she smiled and rested her cheek back against his crisp, dark hair.

He moved her to face him, his expression indulgent. "This is more like it. If you can relax around me in private, you'll learn to do the same in public."

"I thought I did yesterday." Suddenly embarrassed, she focused on his dark stubbly chin, waiting to be shaved, then she moved her gaze to his sculpted torso. His palms flattened over her spine, not to keep her in place but simply to hold her. Lowering her head, she stared at the smooth skin of his chest and covered each of his nipples with a palm. His nipples hardened. Like hers.

As if she had always known what to do, she raised her lips. He slid his hand to her shoulders, lifted her, and bent his head. Her breath halted completely as his mouth took hers in a warm, soft kiss. Her heart began pounding in her chest.

His hand settled on the base of her spine, urging her closer to him. She liked his confidence. She liked the clean taste of his mouth and the warm linen scent of his skin. She trusted him. He would neither hurt her nor force her. During their last three nights in bed, he had proven he wouldn't break his unwritten rules. Although he apparently could kiss a woman into mindless idiocy, he would not take advantage of her.

His hands eased down farther until they cupped her buttocks, the warmth of his palms noticeable through the fabric of her nightgown. She found herself pressed against the entire masculine length of his body and she forgot to breathe.

His mouth angled and his kisses grew deeper and longer. Her own urges kept her clasped in his arms. Aching inside, she clung around his neck. Her breasts flattened against his wide chest, and she wanted to be even closer. Her body melted into his and she knew no one alive could resist this sort of giving and sharing. She arched desperately against him, experiencing an unknown need.

And then she understood why.

His hard pecker urged at the juncture between her legs and she had lifted to her toes, pressing against the exciting shape. Perhaps this sluttish behavior had been bred in the bone. Perhaps her mother had been the same, a loose female who had let a man land her with an unwanted baby. At the same moment as she realized she wouldn't follow in her mother's footsteps, he lifted his mouth from hers.

"Push me away," he murmured. "I'm acting like a man."

Flushed with shame at her behavior, she dropped her stranglehold on him and moved a step back. Nothing in the world could have prevented her from glancing below his waistband.

"You do kiss with your trousers unbuttoned," she said, cheeks tingling.

"I made a concession by putting them on. As you should know by now, I don't dress before I wash or shave. I'm covered. You have no reason to be offended."

Nor was she. No female in her right mind could be insulted by the flagrant bulge in his trousers. Such obvious proof of desire would flatter any sane woman.

She watched him button his flap. "I'm not offended," she said, finally. "You haven't tried to take advantage of me."

He gave a wry smile that hid his thoughts. "We shouldn't be sharing this bedroom, but if you move out, it'll cause more talk than I'm ready to handle. I'll kiss you with my trousers buttoned if that's what you want, but I can tell you now it won't make any difference. Naked or dressed, I won't be doing anything else."

"If you were in love with Lavender, you wouldn't want to kiss me."

He shrugged. "It would have been easy enough for you to discourage me, but you leaned against me and smiled. I happen to like half-dressed women with soft, cinnamon-colored curls who like me and kiss me back."

His hands reached out and bracketed her face. He stared directly into her eyes. "And you do like me, Starling."

She liked men in fully buttoned trousers with fresh-smelling dark hair. She liked men who rescued children, employed needy servants, and had a kind and clever sister. She appreciated men who held her without force, who showed her that she could be attracted and excited by them. No doubt about it, she never had met and never would meet a man like him again.

He had predicted she would know pleasure within the next two weeks and she had found excitement within two days.

However, a woman like her couldn't afford desires that would cause her nothing but grief. He liked her and she liked him, certainly, but neither had a commitment to the other. Squeezing her eyes shut she pushed on his shoulders, trying to deny the hot pulsing between her legs.

He dropped his hands from her face and said, with what she could only hear as disgruntlement, "And you kissed me, too."

She turned back to the bowl, fully conscious of the fact that he stood where he was for the whole thirty seconds she took to complete her wash. She could feel his gaze on her back. When she finished, she didn't look at him.

Shaking inside, she dressed while he washed.

"What do you want to do today?" he asked as she fought with her stays.

"What do you want me to do?"

The silence grew. Finally he said, "I thought I might take Paul to the club and leave you women to fend for yourselves. If you stick by Mary you can't get into too much trouble."

"Which makes me wonder just how much contact you've had with Mary. She talks to me and she asks me questions, almost none of which I can answer. I don't know anything about running a house, and I don't know anything about you. Our conversations are filled with me trying to avoid lying and her trying to encourage me to relax. I wish I didn't like her."

"I'm glad you do." He reached for his towel.

"Tell me when you've finished dressing and I'll call for Ellen. I can't do a thing with these blasted stays."

"I'm an expert. I'll help."

"An expert with stays? Are you bragging about your experience with women?"

"My common sense," he answered, coming out from behind the screen buttoning a white starched collar. "When we added merchandizing to importing, I had stays made in bulk. I saw plenty and I know how they work." He turned her around, put a knee into her back, and pulled at her laces. "Too tight? Tell me when they feel comfortable."

"They never feel comfortable."

"Then don't wear them. You certainly don't need to."

"You want me to look like your wife, don't you?"

He untied the laces, unthreaded them, and removed her stays. While she watched he threw the laced torture against the fireplace. "I'm paying you to pretend we are married and that's all I want from you."

"Then I don't understand what..." Her voice petered out as he slammed the bedroom door.

* * * *

Alasdair didn't understand *what*, either. He didn't know why he needed Starling's attention when he had the full attention of Lavender, the woman he had wanted for years. He didn't know why he thought he had a responsibility to be gentle with his hireling, to rehabilitate her so that she could experience the pleasure a man could give her. He didn't know what he wanted of her, what she could do during the day, or how she could be convincing in her masquerade.

He strode to the library and slammed the door behind him. After grabbing the daily newspaper, he dropped into a chair by the window and leaned back, closing his eyes. He'd gone from bad to worse in days.

He wanted to test her and he didn't know why he wanted to test her. Perhaps because he himself had failed—failed to think this situation through clearly. Failed to tell the truth when he'd had a chance. Not only that, he'd expected too much of her. Ladies filled the tedium of their days with luncheons, gossiping, and visiting, and he'd expected Starling to do the same. But not having a background as a lady, she had no acquaintances to visit and, other than Mary and Lavender, no friend with whom to gossip.

He opened the paper wondering if perhaps he wanted her to fail. If she couldn't keep up her façade, he could be done with the pretense and get rid of her. However, if she passed he would have to continue on with the farce. The paper dropped to his knees. He didn't know why he wanted to continue when, if he ended this fake marriage right now, he could have the woman of his dreams.

Then again, he didn't want the woman of his dreams to know she could so quickly call him to heel.

* * * *

"Now that you are here as the mistress of the house, I'm thinking we need more live-in maids," Mrs. Brighton said, smiling at Starling. "At this stage we make do, but a bachelor's establishment doesn't need as many staff as a married couple. We have plenty of room upstairs for more girls. And there's another room off the stables near Will's and Derry's if need be for male staff."

Starling adopted a thoughtful expression, assuming Mrs. Brighton was discussing this with her because as Mrs. Seymour she was expected to make a decision. She couldn't, of course, and she would again fob the woman off. "Once all the guests have left, we'll have a better idea of the staff we need," she said with what she hoped was an efficient and knowledgeable voice.

"The laundry's the main problem. I've been helping with some of the ironing in the past week but it's getting beyond me. I still have the running of the establishment...unless you take over as mistress."

Starling nodded. She knew how the ironing could get the better of a person. At the orphanage she had burned her hands on the irons so often that she had grown immune to the pain. Also, she didn't see how the regular staff of Alasdair's house coped with the laundry. At Saint Matthew's, every orphan had needed to work in the laundry. Each one, from the age of eight, needed to do the ironing and starching because all were taken into service by the age of fifteen.

Starling had expected to leave then, too. She knew her letters and numbers and she had basic reading skills. Had she not heard one of the home's sponsors say that if the girls had a better education they would be hired by superior establishments, she would have gone at that age, too. However, she knew if she had a better education, she wouldn't choose to be in service. Nor would most of the other girls.

Soon the orphanage buzzed with the idea that well-spoken girls could find higher paying jobs, which would attract higher placement fees for the orphanage. Laundry duties continued to be as much a part of an orphan's training as scrubbing, polishing, and mending, but within a year a nun had begun teaching grammar and pronunciation. Starling, showing a knack with the younger girls, was kept on to help teach the clear speech she had adopted herself so easily.

On her eighteenth year, Starling put her name down at Seymour's to be taken on as a shopgirl. When her nineteenth year loomed with no notification from the emporium, she assumed she would not be one of the chosen few. She left, determined to make her way alone. Teaching in the orphanage benefited a few, but running a business would benefit more.

With no money and no job, she contacted Meg, a former orphan who had been jobless herself until she had taken what she called "the easy way." Not recommending this for Starling, Meg got her a job in the laundry of the Star Inn. Six weeks later, Starling had her summons from Seymour's Emporium.

Five days after, she met Mr. Seymour and she was now here listening to the explanation of the running of the kitchen. Mrs. Brighton was telling her about not only the daily tasks, but also the weekly and monthly ones. The organization of a large household was not as new to her as Mrs. Brighton imagined.

She glanced over the four deep shelves holding sheets and pillowcases. Herbs sat between, adding fragrance. "For now, I think I've seen enough. I promised to go to the Burdons' to visit Tammy today."

"Mrs. Trelevan made ginger cake for her...if you don't mind."

"It's a lovely thought. I imagine the credit is due to you."

"I do what I'm paid to do." Mrs. Brighton inclined her head. "As Mr. Seymour's wife, you will naturally add your own touches."

Starling shook her head. "Mr. Seymour told me that his house runs perfectly without my input and I've seen how true that is. Everyone has his or her place and, fortunately, I know mine. Now, I must go."

She collected the cake from the kitchen. Seeing no need for a hat and gloves for the quick trip to the house next door, she put her shawl around her shoulders and hurried to the front door.

"Starling!" She turned.

Lavender appeared in the doorway of the sitting room dressed in her signature color. With her blond hair dressed in ringlets at the sides and her shawl beautifully draped to add elegance to her figure, she could have only appeared more lovely had she worn a color that added warmth to her skin. "Are you going for a walk? I'm so bored. Perhaps I'll come with you."

"I'm going next door to visit Tammy. If you'd like to come, too, I'm sure she'd be delighted to meet you."

Lavender stepped backward, wrinkling her pretty nose. "What on earth could you have to talk about with a child?"

"Come with me and find out. You might be as entertained as I am." Starling didn't want Lavender with her, and she was as surprised by her words as Lavender seemed to be.

The other woman dropped her ennui for a moment and looked relieved. "Any distraction is better than sitting here by myself. Mary's going over some accounts of Dare's in the library, though I can't imagine what use she thinks that might be. My father said women don't have heads for business and that they should be pure decoration."

Lavender's attitude annoyed Starling. Somehow, the lady had overstepped the patience limit of almost everyone. The servants worked around her in tight-lipped silence, and Paul and Mary, although scrupulously polite, found ways to avoid her. Alasdair was the only person who saw anything other than outward beauty in Lavender.

Forcing a smile, Starling held the door open for Lavender. Named Lavender, dressing in that color, and perfumed by the flower wasn't ingenious, but its very lack of subtlety suited Mrs. Frost.

Smothering her ungenerous thought, Starling walked in silence with the love of Alasdair's life down the slate path to the gateway. The gardener was cutting the spent blooms from the roses on either side.

"Afternoon." Derry pushed back his shabby cap. As tall as Alasdair— more than six feet—but younger, Derry had broad shoulders, a manly build, and a square jaw. His curly fair hair gave him the appearance of innocence, and his bright ingenuous eyes supported that impression.

"Good afternoon," Starling said. "What a lovely day." As if in confirmation, a host of chattering honey eaters swarmed through the scented air.

"They think so," he answered, grinning at the little birds. "They been waitin' to give their opinion." His admiring gaze settled on Lavender and stayed. He seemed not to breathe for a moment.

"I love your..." Lavender lowered her eyelashes, "...flowers. I wonder, would you mind picking a posy for me? These pink roses. I'd love some in my bedroom. Don't wait, Starling. I'll be along later."

"Are you sure?"

"I adore roses. If the young man doesn't mind, I'd appreciate a tour of the garden, too."

"The name's Derry, ma'am," he said as Starling turned back to the gateway. "Mr. Seymour's got some of them camellia trees out the back. Would you like to see them?"

Starling presumed the answer would be "yes." She hurried to the Burdons' house, glad Lavender had found something she preferred to do.

* * * *

Alasdair, with Paul behind, stepped into the front hall, shutting out the late afternoon sun. The three women chatted companionably in the sitting room. Alasdair greeted Mary and smiled indulgently at Lavender, who sat arranged in a carefully casual pose on the chaise longue under the window.

"Did you enjoy your day?" Starling moved toward him and held out her hands for his hat.

"I did. Did you manage to find something to do?"

"Been busy," she mumbled.

"*I've* been busy," he said with a frown.

When her warm brown eyes filled with pure satisfaction, he realized she'd been teasing him and for some days, too. He didn't need her to say, "Thought you might have been," to know that her grammar and speech needed no correction.

"Wretch! I'll pay you back for this, see if I don't."

"Can't." Her smile challenged.

"Can." Without thinking of anything other than the impudent curve of her lips, he swooped one arm around her waist and arched her against him. Bending his head, he kissed the mouth that had taunted him and fooled him into believing he'd hired a poorly educated, compliant female. She could only pretend to be meek. Forthrightness came more naturally. Her lips softened under his. Unable to stop himself he continued with a kiss that lingered until he heated. Only her hand pushing gently on his chest brought him to his senses. "Did," he murmured as he lifted his head.

A touch of embarrassment tightened his collar. Knowing he shouldn't have been inveigled into kissing this woman in front of others, he glanced toward Mary and Paul, who were giving each other told-you-so looks.

Lavender sat, arms crossed, an expression of chagrin on her lovely face. He couldn't remember a previous occasion when Lavender had demonstrated jealousy. "Perhaps I ought to warn you," he said to Starling. Unlike the other ladies, she still wore her day gown. "We have an important guest for dinner tonight."

"Who?" Mary asked.

"You'll find out."

"I should change." Starling's expression turned serious.

He smiled sardonically as he escorted her from the room. "You should, indeed." She could stop being so damned easy to be with, for a start.

He sighed deeply as he walked upstairs behind her.

Before searching out his evening suit, he rang for Ellen. While he waited, he idly fiddled with papers in his desk, trying not to watch Starling trying not to watch him. "Bring water for a bath," he said when the maid arrived.

"Yes, Mr. Seymour."

"And four towels."

Ellen shut the door behind her.

"If you are going to bathe, I'll change quickly and go back downstairs," Starling said, stepping toward the door.

"We're going to bathe together but not simultaneously. If you and I both get into the bath, there'll be no room for water, which would somewhat negate the reason for the bath. I'll use the screen if you still think we need it."

While he bathed, silence filled the room. "Are you there?"

"Yes."

He rose to his feet, dripping water, and reached for his towel. "You can come behind the screen. I'm respectable." He wrapped the towel around the lower half of his body.

She hadn't even begun undressing, annoying him with her false modesty. "Come here and I'll undo you."

She presented him with her back. In a few seconds, he had freed her from her gown and strolled to the window. He wanted to watch her, and he could have because the screen had been arranged to hide the view of the bath only from the bed. "Wash your hair," he said, irritated with himself for conceding to her every wish.

"I washed it three days ago. Why are you suddenly in a bad mood?"

"Get me out of it."

"Don't suppose I can."

"And I don't suppose *I* can," he said tersely. He relaxed a little when she laughed. "I'm somewhat tense. When you're out of the bath, I'll dry your hair. Perhaps that will give me a chance to unwind."

"Perhaps you ought to hire a cat."

The sound of surging water told him she had arisen. He wanted to see what she had to hide that made her presume she was so damned different. "I hired the next best thing. Are you covered?"

"Yes."

He turned around. She had tied her hair in one towel and had wound the other around her. Damn. She looked dewy soft. "Don't dress. Bring your comb to me."

"The towels are wet."

"They'll dry on you in this weather." He walked to the bed, sat, legs astraddle, and patted the area of coverlet between his legs. "Sit here."

After handing him the new comb from her dressing set, she settled with her back to him, dipping forward to remove the towel from her head. She flicked back wet curls of hair. "I hope you've done this before. I don't want my hair pulled out."

"As with everything else, I'm an expert. I had a mother and a sister, and they both liked having their wet hair untangled. Put your arms on my knees. It'll give you balance." And him an opportunity. Her skill at making herself into a separate unit was a skill he didn't appreciate. He wanted to get to know her, not intimately, of course, but to understand how a sweet young thing like her could have managed to sell her body to men without letting her experience color her language or show on her face. Other than her impression that all men were the same, she seemed to have skimmed through her six weeks of prostitution, and treating her roughly or implying her body might be for hire would only bolster her low opinion of men.

After untangling her curls, he combed the shoulder-length mass back from her face, resisting the urge to lift her hair and rest his lips on her white, unprotected neck. Wanting closer contact with her, he sucked in a breath, knowing he lied to himself—perhaps he loved Lavender, but lately he had centered all his erotic thoughts on Starling. He wanted a more intimate connection than her tentative hands on his shins and he imagined untying her towel and enjoying the weight of her breasts in his eager palms. "Turn around."

He slid one knee from beneath her arm and, given space, she swiveled to face him. She gave him a careful smile. "Who is the important guest?"

"Hamilton Fredericks," he said, his breath short and his blood pounding. "We saw him at the club today, and if I hadn't invited him to dinner I think he would have invited himself. Lavender has that effect on most of the male population." He had managed a casual voice, but he moved and her breast touched the inside of his bent knee.

She immediately moved back.

He breathed out. To support himself he rested a fist on the bed beside her opposite hip, leaving him chest to chest with her.

He stared at her mouth.

She stared at his shoulder.

"A kiss," he murmured softly. "You owe me for untangling your hair."

Her cheeks pinked. Her eyes focused on the arm that held him and then her attention slid to his hand on the bed. She cleared her throat, a noise that seemed to echo in the silent room, and concentrated on his chin.

He waited, leaving his mouth within reach. Her breath warmed his cheek. She raised her chin with acceptance.

With a careful expression on her face, she placed a hand on his shoulder and her soft lips on his.

Chapter 10

Within two seconds, Starling found herself stretched out on the bed. Alasdair's hot mouth played with hers. Tingling with pleasure, she combed her fingers through his damp hair.

He lifted his head, stared into her eyes, and slanted soft kisses over her mouth, exciting her so much that she dug her fingers into his back. When his hand curved around her bottom and lifted her into his hips, she relaxed. Nothing could be more enjoyable than his hard body rocking against hers.

Nothing could be tawdrier if the woman had been hired to fool the man's sister, especially if the man loved another woman. She stiffened.

His mouth wandered over her face, her throat, and the swells of her breasts. His lips lingered and lifted. "What is it?"

She turned her face to the wall. "You're the expert."

He took a deep breath, placing his hands on either cheek to turn her face to him. "You like kissing, I can tell, and you haven't minded when I've touched your body. You haven't minded, have you?" He flattened his palm on her rib cage and massaged as he had when easing her corset aches.

"I haven't minded."

"You can stop me any time. As soon as you don't like what I do, tell me and I won't do it."

"I think you shouldn't do anything."

"Don't you owe it to yourself to find out what you might enjoy? You'll never know if you don't give pleasure a chance." He dropped a kiss across her mouth and, lifting his head, he stared into the depths of her soul.

She wavered. He dipped his head again, covering her mouth.

The kiss asked questions and gave answers at the same time. He queried her appreciation of his lips, and she answered by placing her hands on his shoulders. He questioned her need to return his kiss, and she answered by doubling her elbows around his neck and increasing the soft pressure from his mouth.

Parting her lips, his tongue explored inside her mouth, behind her lips, over her teeth, even under her tongue. When he had learned every shape and texture inside her mouth, his tongue retreated to the tip of hers, where he teased until she responded by teasing back. His lips barely touched hers.

She sighed as his fingers tickled over the flesh of her breasts and tugged at her towel. He spread the fabric aside and brushed his open palm over one sensitive nipple. The towel dropped beneath her arm. When his chest pressed to her breasts, she experienced for the first time the naked pleasure of skin against skin.

Barely breathing, she closed her eyes and his warm, wicked, wonderful mouth took hers with possessive insistence. His tongue delved, hot and wet, filling her mouth with urgency. Mindlessly, she ran her hands over his back, caressing the silken firmness, smoothing over the muscle as he adjusted his body to fit with hers.

One of his knees parted her thighs and his male arousal pressed into the hollow of her hip. She suppressed an urge to reach down and touch him. Instead, despising herself for willing his hard pecker where her need ached, she tightened her bottom and curled her pelvis away from him.

He raised his mouth. Her arms dropped to her sides.

After a long stare into her eyes, he moved an elbow near her ear and supported his head on his closed fingers. Without speaking, and with his luminous eyes staring into hers, he moved a hand to her rib cage and caressed there, running his open palm over her quivering flesh. His thumb glided over the lower part of her breast. She wanted to guard herself, but she could only lie on her back, caught by his mesmerizing eyes and the slow seductive movement of his hand.

Her mouth dried. She swallowed and wet her lips with a nervous flick of her tongue.

"You look terrified," he said gruffly. "I can't believe anyone could use you roughly. You're so very sweet."

She couldn't answer. Her breath came in shaky, uncontrolled surges.

Circling his knuckles around the outer side of her breast, he connected with her arm, which he slid his hand down until he reached hers. He lifted her fingers to his chest, placing her palm right over one of his nipples. "I liked you touching me here earlier. Repeat the pleasure and you will see that I'm only flesh and blood like you. My nipples react exactly as yours do, and down there," he glanced at his arousal covered by the towel and flattened against his belly, "I have a similar reaction. I can't control the reaction, but I can control what I do about it."

Never once had she had cause to mistrust him. Never once had she cause to disbelieve him, and she did neither, hadn't even thought she might. Starling Smith was the only person she doubted, the orphan who had never known love and who wanted kindness so much that she hurt. Love had not been offered by this tall, strong man who made her feel more secure by the moment, but gentleness and consideration had.

She couldn't trust herself not to pretend that this was enough for her.

Pushing thoughts of Lavender to the further reaches of her mind, as he apparently had, she searched for insincerity in his face but found none. She couldn't deny this man a simple touch.

As she had this morning, she put one palm over each of his nipples. Of their own accord, her fingers caressed the surrounding flesh, noting how dissimilar he and she looked. Where she was soft, he was hard. Where she could be gathered and lifted, he could only be smoothed. His mouth curled with contentment. She appreciated him expressing pleasure. She appreciated even more the lowering of his lips to hers.

Undeniably, she enjoyed his mouth. His lips gave the love he didn't feel. His kiss could persuade her to pretend she needed nothing more. She enjoyed his warm hands closing gently over each of her breasts, softly squeezing and relaxing. When he took his mouth from hers and wet her nipples, she tightened her fingers in his hair, arching as his lips covered the peak of one breast.

Her emotions confused her. She knew she couldn't love a man she'd known barely a few days, but this sharing of sensations seemed closer to love than any feeling she'd yet experienced.

His lips returned to hers as if he needed to keep reminding her of his kisses. His hands, palms, and fingers caressed her nipples. She sighed, encouraging every move he made, and glided her hands down his back to the safety of the towel around his hips, stopping there.

He groaned, took her fingers in his, and delved them beneath the towel, loosening what she thought of as her protection. The towel slid off.

Her eyes opened as she touched the taut perfection of one rounded buttock. Not like hers, nothing like hers. His flesh was tight and hard and utterly masculine.

"Starling, Starling," he whispered and her name sounded like an endearment. His lips covered every inch of her face and her eyes closed to the glorious sensation of his mouth on her eyelids.

Touching him while he touched her was the most empowering experience of her life and, judging by the sounds he made, one of the most pleasurable of his. If only her days could be like this forever, clean, warm, safe, guarded by a man who had promised to stop whenever she said.

His hand edged between their bodies, placing her palm on his pecker. For one moment she let her fingers be swept along the length. Like him, his male appendage was solid and unyielding. For one moment she thought she loved him and he loved her. The vulnerability in his action lulled her. For one moment.

When he closed her fingers around his arousal and glided in her hand as she knew he wanted to glide inside her, she realized he didn't love her. He merely desired a woman. He hadn't even hinted he loved her. From the time he'd combed her hair, one action had led to another...as he had planned. She straightened her fingers and moved her hand to the coverlet behind her back.

His forehead dropped to her shoulder. "Flesh and blood, Starling, just like you," he said blurring his words against her upper breast.

The mist of his expiration cooled on her skin. She angled from beneath him, trying not to touch him, and sat up, dragging her knees to her chest and resting her cheek on one side.

For a minute or so, he lay beside her, flat out on his stomach with his face pressed into the bend of his elbow. Then he moved his jaw slowly over his arm as if he couldn't think unless he stroked his chin. Finally, he sat up, too.

He took one of her hands from her shin and held her fingers in his. His thumb rubbed over her palm and he turned her hand over. "Your hands are much softer," he said. "But your nails need reshaping. They're ragged." He brushed his lips across hers.

When she moved her hand back to her own leg, he sighed and tipped his head back until his gaze focused on the ceiling. "You don't need to say it. I know I was way out of line."

She shot a glance at him from around her arm. She would never have said that. The fault hadn't been his. She had encouraged him and hadn't given a thought to where her acquiescence might lead until she touched his pecker—flesh and blood perhaps, but no less beautiful for being real. Like him. Real: a man generous enough to take the blame that didn't belong to him. Real: a man wealthy and handsome enough to have any woman he chose. Real: the urges of the flesh that were difficult to repress.

Real: rough hands on a hired woman.

She eased out a breath. "I've never had nails long enough to cut because I've always bitten them. But perhaps I bit them because I never had anything suitable to cut them with."

"Never had scissors?"

"Only access to those big enough to cut off a finger instead."

Tightening his towel around his waist, he rose to his feet. "I don't think owning nail clippers has ever made me feel important before." When he smiled at her, warmth spread throughout her body, the warmth of the companionability she'd experienced with him for days.

Keeping her cheek on her knee, she watched him search through his top tallboy drawer, appreciating his back view perhaps more than she had before. She'd caressed that firm, rounded bottom and she'd enjoyed doing so.

He returned to the bed and sat beside her. "I'll cut your nails. I just happen to be an—"

"—expert at cutting nails," she finished.

"No need for insubordination. I wouldn't do this for just any female. In fact, I wouldn't do it for a woman unless I'd kissed her breasts first." He held out his hands for hers and didn't glance at her face, which had warmed.

"I don't want to know how many women's nails you've cut," she said tightly as he clasped her arm under his. The point of the scissors forced under her nail and snipped. "Ouch."

"Only yours. Other than that, I've cut mine, which gives me far more experience than you have. Keep your hand still. It isn't easy cutting a nail that's barely visible."

She rested her chin on his shoulder to watch what he was doing. "Have you kissed many women's breasts?"

"Changeable little thing, aren't you? Now, why would you want to know that?"

"I'm only checking to see if you're an expert there, too."

"Don't you have any basis for comparison?"

"No."

"I'm only an expert if you liked what I did, and I think I can safely say that you think I'm an expert. Leave your hand there. I haven't finished. Now, since you want to know how many women I've had, I can only tell you that I haven't counted. I've bedded a few women, but I've only made love to one."

"Lavender."

"Yes, the lady I plan to marry. Give me your other hand."

"Is there a difference between bedding and making love?"

"Not physically. Don't start worrying. You can certainly enjoy fucking without being in love. When you are, you want to hold that person in your arms longer and you want to look after them and save them from themselves. You feel protective. Lavender needs love. She's never been given it. Her parents were rather harsh and taught her values that...well, they're not my values."

Starling kept her face against his shoulder. Without knowing, he'd said he felt sympathy rather than love for Lavender, but, because Starling didn't know a thing about love, she didn't comment.

Although she wished she had an equal tolerance of Lavender, she didn't. Lavender had been given two parents. They couldn't have been harsher than the custodians at the home, who taught values and used severity to gain obedience. Lavender had been given everything that money could buy, plus the most beautiful face this side of heaven. Starling doubted that any woman could be sympathetic about the last. Envious, more like. Nevertheless, she resolved to be kinder in her mind to Lavender than previously.

She inspected her nails. "They certainly look better."

He smiled. "Never doubt an expert."

* * * *

Alasdair dressed and changed into a white cravat, gray-striped waistcoat, black tailcoat, and black trousers for dinner while Starling examined her renovated gray gown, doubting she would ever understand men. Alasdair wanted Lavender for his wife, yet he held out his promiscuity as a lure to Starling. And he had lured her with his kindness, his gentleness, and his ability to make her feel desired.

"Wear the blue gown tonight," he said, sounding abstracted. "We want to impress our guest."

She wavered, not sure she should try to impress anyone, though last night she'd been complimented on the new look Ellen had given her hair. Only a less pathetic creature than she would not court the same attention again. She put away the refurbished uniform. He finished and left. After pulling the bell cord, she slipped into her chemise. Without the stays, she could gown herself, but only Ellen could arrange her hair into a fine enough style to suit the blue gown.

Unbuttoned, she sat at the table. She heard Ellen's knock. "Come in. My, you were quick."

"I don't have to do Mrs. Frost's hair now. Freda's doing it."

"Won't that take her from her kitchen duties?"

"Yes, but I'll fill in where I can." The maid collected the hairpins from the tallboy. "And that will work out better," she said with a satisfied smile.

Sure she ought not comment on the situation she'd apparently not changed, Starling sat in silence. "Do you know the story of Adam and Eve?" she asked, lulled by the brushing of her hair.

"Silly story, that. I only know one snake what can talk."

"As a rule, most don't." Starling wished she hadn't given Ellen another opportunity to complain about Mrs. Frost. "But I wasn't thinking of that aspect of the story. I think the telling of it should have been the other way around with Adam tempting Eve. I don't see how a woman could tempt a man."

"You oughta watch Mrs. Frost then."

"I meant the average woman, not the ultimate. Mrs. Frost doesn't have to do anything to tempt a man other than exist."

Ellen snorted. "She spends more time tempting men than she does padding her hair and painting her face. Can I leave some of these back curls free tonight? It'd show how graceful your neck is."

Starling nodded. "Have you ever been in love, Ellen?"

"Yes, ma'am. I'm walking out with Derry. Was."

"The gardener? My, Ellen, what a catch. He's very handsome."

"Yes, ma'am." Ellen tightened her lips. "Very handsome and as thick as four planks."

"Should you describe him that way?"

Ellen swiped the cleaning brush over the hairbrush. She gave a harsh laugh. "I wouldn't have until today when he met Eve, the lady who offers her apples to every man what passes."

Starling frowned. "You mean Mrs. Frost? You can't blame Derry for being polite to her."

"Polite? If he wants that painted-up pretense of a person, I say let him have her and with my blessing, too." Ellen lifted the top section of Starling's hair.

Starling could hear the fury in Ellen's voice. "He picked her a flower because she asked for one."

"And he took her to the stables because she feels at home with horse manure?"

Starling glanced down, schooling her expression. "Your young man might admire her beauty, but if he loves you, you don't have a thing to worry about."

"I wish I could be like you." Ellen made a thin, rueful line of her mouth. "You trust your man, and he respects you enough to be honest with you. Derry's a womanizer. He takes what he's offered and he lies about it. He says that a man has to have...you know. I don't think a woman should give herself before marriage."

"That's what I was talking about before. Adam tempting Eve. I don't have the answer, but I wish that just once I had the apple."

"The master's a lucky man," Ellen said gruffly. "Let me finish your hair. I'm not cross anymore. What's done is done, and I can't change it." She put the pins and brush in the drawer, came back, and buttoned Starling's gown. "You could pull the shoulders down a little. The material doesn't need to be hiked up when it's cut on the slant."

Starling went to the mirror and shifted the material. Her hands no longer shamed her. The blue of the gown pinked her cheeks and whitened her skin. She turned her head this way and that. "The gown is beautiful, but don't you think I look a little bare with my shoulders showing?"

"Mr. Burdon sent over some orchids from his hothouse today. They're pure white and they'd set off your skin a treat. We could attach one to a ribbon and tie it around your throat. I'll get them."

Ellen was right. The tiny delicate flowers filled in her neckline, giving Starling an amazingly ladylike appearance. She slipped on her black satin shoes, certain she would never look as elegant as this again.

"Don't you look just lovely," Mrs. Trelevan said when Starling arrived taller than usual in the kitchen. "Them flowers was meant for you."

"The Burdons sent them over for me?"

"Course they did, but I didn't mean that. I meant that you look lovely wearing them."

"Thank you," Starling answered, blushing. "We have a guest for dinner. Mr. Seymour thought feeding another person wouldn't be a strain on the kitchen."

Mrs. Trelevan laughed. "He never does. Often tells me this sort of thing at the last minute. I can make do."

"If there's a problem, I don't mind if you give me—"

"Bless you. Don't you go thinking anyone will have to go short. Got plenty of food in this house, and we've certainly got enough for the mistress. It's the second remove I was thinking of. Might have to make an alternative. Freda! Drat that girl. Freda!"

"I imagine she's with Mrs. Frost. Can I help?"

"No, no, not in that gown, but I guess you could set another place."

Starling also arranged flowers on the dining table, taking longer than she expected. Dressed as a real lady, she felt strangely shy about presenting herself. When she arrived in the sitting room, she was introduced to the newly arrived guest, Mr. Hamilton Fredericks, whose eyes skimmed over her with masculine appreciation. Never before admired for her looks, she warmed inside and smiled with pleasure at the gentleman who, in truth, did resemble a frog with his bulky body and long, thin arms and legs.

"I'm privileged," he said with a courtly bow. He had flat curls around his face. "I hadn't heard about this marriage of Alasdair's. It gives me an opportunity to be the first with the latest gossip."

"I hope you won't gossip about this marriage," Starling said, catching Alasdair's glance. She surprised a half-smile out of him and a predatory gleam. "At this stage, it's a secret shared only by family."

"Then I'm even more privileged to be considered family," Mr. Fredericks said smoothly. "I won't say a word until given permission. May I ask why the secret?"

Starling glanced again at Alasdair.

"Why indeed?" His gaze left her face, reached the floral decoration at her throat, and flowed down her body to her black satin slippers. When he met her eyes again, she could see her hairstyle and the blue gown had changed her from a hireling to a desired woman.

She stood blushing with pleasure, recognizing the glow of confidence that came from within.

Then his attention shifted from her. A lovely vision dressed in mauve with violet stripes made her entrance through the double doors. Starling had the only view of Lavender's back. With a desperate lurch, she sprang at the lady.

Only the bottom button on Lavender's gown sat in the right hole. The other three had been misaligned. The lacing of her stays showed. If anyone saw Lavender from the back they would suspect she'd been dressed by a drunken lover. Starling knew she'd been dressed by Freda.

Starling reached over, put her arm around Lavender's waist, and turned into the lady, as if caught. "Oh, no, what have I done?" She pretended to tug away. "I can't think how, Lavender, but somehow I've trapped the edge of my sleeve in your buttoning. So clumsy. Would you mind coming into the hall with me? I can't get loose without undoing your gown."

"Really, Starling," Lavender's mouth said, while her eyes said "useless, stupid creature." "Hurry up about it then."

At that moment, Freda appeared with the dinner gong. "Not yet, Freda," Starling said. "I want you in the hall for a moment."

Freda put the gong on a side table, made an apprehensive face, and followed Lavender and Starling into the hall.

"See what you can do with this." Starling indicated the back of Lavender's gown.

When Lavender turned to Freda, Starling saw the back of the blonde's hair: a bird's nest of inexpertly pinned curls. A pit formed in her abdomen. Lavender's hair looked perfectly coiffed at the front. This disordered snarling where she couldn't see the style could be nothing other than deliberate.

Holding her arm over Lavender's back, she waited while Freda unbuttoned Lavender's gown, hid her stays, and neatly buttoned her up. Whether for the perceived transgression with Derry or the scathing contempt of her sister, Freda had purposely tried to make Lavender look ridiculous. Starling wished she didn't have to be in the middle of an obvious act of vengeance.

With a wide sweep of her arm, she wrecked the remainder of Lavender's hairdo. Wincing, she put her hand on Lavender's. "I'm so sorry. I can't apologize enough, Lavender. Perhaps I'm nervous or clumsy, I don't know, but now I've ruined your hair. Freda will have to take you back to the bedroom and begin again." She shot Freda a glance that said "or else."

"This isn't accidental." Lavender jerked her hand out of Starling's hold. She narrowed her eyes, shrinking her lips with anger. "Your jealousy is so petty. So unworthy. Come, Freda. Let's repair the damage."

"I'm wanted in the kitchen. Mrs. Trelevan's about to serve cheese soufflé with the first remove."

"I'll tell her to hold it back for half an hour," Starling said.

Lavender laughed. "Really, Starling. Soufflé can't be held back. It has to be served the moment it's ready. You tell the cook to make more," she told Freda, "and then come straight to my bedroom."

"Cook doesn't have time to make more soufflé. That's my job," Freda said. "I'll send Ellen to you instead. She's better with hair."

"If I have to listen to any more insubordination from you, I'll tell Mr. Seymour. Do as I tell you, now."

"But Ellen can't make—"

"I'm sure she can't. That incompetent creature can't do anything. Both of you deserve to be put off and only the fact that I'm dreadfully sorry for you has prevented me from speaking to Mr. Seymour." Lavender walked regally toward the bedroom wing. "Move along because I can't promise my good nature will last."

Freda glanced at Starling, as if waiting for instructions. Taking a deep breath, Starling nodded, indicating that Freda should obey Lavender.

With a dejected slump of her shoulders, Freda made her way to the kitchen. Starling wished that she had the right to countermand Lavender's orders. The sisters should have been left to do the tasks they did best.

* * * *

Starling had never eaten soufflé before and quite enjoyed the crisp chewiness. Everyone else left the dish. As Ellen came to collect the first set of plates, Alasdair stabbed his flat disk with his fork. "What's this?"

"Cheese soufflé," Ellen said brightly. "My first attempt."

He raised his eyebrows at Starling, not in a smiling way but as if he wanted a comment. She obliged him. "It's delicious, Ellen. Thank you."

He muttered something inaudible and toyed with his wine.

Despite the late beginning, dinner proceeded well. Starling had seated Hamilton Fredericks diagonally opposite Lavender, which probably suited Lavender because the placement put her closer to Alasdair. Staring at Lavender suited Mr. Fredericks because every time he spoke to anyone at the table except Starling he had Lavender in view. Each time the gentleman addressed the lady, he changed his voice from a decisive and rather charming one to a carefully bland tone, as if he didn't want to startle her.

Unfortunately, she made a joke of him, luring him into explaining a witticism to her and then, while he pondered an answer, turning her full attention to Alasdair. Neither man thought her behavior unbecoming. Perhaps Lavender saw her rudeness as a form of flirting.

After a stuffed mutton roast, a dish of buttered artichokes, and a clear soup had been served, Lavender emphasized a point to Alasdair by stroking the back of his hand. Ellen, delivering another dish, tripped.

A tray of cream-covered tartlets hit Lavender. One clung to the side of her face, one sat on her shoulder, and the others slid slowly from her skirts to the floor.

Lavender's face turned an angry red. "You're in this together, are you? First Starling, and now you." She gathered the tarts from her face and her shoulder and slammed them onto the table.

"No, Mrs. Frost. It was an accident," Ellen replied. She glanced at Starling.

Alasdair also glanced at Starling. His eyes stayed longer. "Clean it up, Ellen," he said.

Ellen grabbed Lavender's table napkin and wiped at the sticky meringue and cream on the side of her face. Lavender threw the maid's hand off her. "Don't touch me."

Ellen lifted the napkin up high, staring at two dangling ash blond curls in amazement. She swallowed. "I think these belong to you," she said with a strangled gasp. She dropped the false curls into Lavender's lap and giggled nervously. "I'm sorry, I'm sorry. I didn't mean to do that, truly."

"Get her out of here," Lavender said in a voice of repressed fury.

A muscle worked in Alasdair's jaw. "Out!" The motion of his head emphasized his order.

"I know whose idea this was," Lavender said with acid inflection as Ellen scurried from the room with as many tarts as she could gather in the napkin. Straightening her shoulders haughtily, Lavender stared directly at Starling. "I can only thank God that I was bought up as a lady. I wouldn't consider humiliating a guest this way. No lady would ever be so chummy with servants unless she wanted to use them in her vicious little plan." With a tilt of her lovely chin, she rose to her feet. Preparing to leave the room, she gave everyone a perfect view of her furious expression.

Starling gasped. One half of Lavender's face, the part that Ellen had wiped, had lost all color, causing her to resemble a half-painted plaster mold. One side was Lavender and the other, no one.

Experiencing a helpless ache of sympathy Starling rose to her feet. "Lavender, I'll help you clean up."

Lavender had been exposed as far more than a self-indulgent, spoiled brat. She'd also been exposed as a female who painted her character on her face. Possibly, in someone else a natural appearance wouldn't have been noticed, but Lavender's glamour relied on paint.

"No, thank you," Lavender said with an expression of disdain as she swept from the room. "I've had enough help from you for one day."

Starling glanced at the others, who stared back at her. Not knowing what else to do, she sat down again, wishing that the accident had occurred to her instead. She wouldn't have been half as offended and probably would have done no more than wipe her face and ask Ellen if she had hurt herself in her fall. However, she didn't think that the world revolved around her.

"There might not be any more tarts tonight," she said apologetically.

Mary smiled at her plate. "Not lemon tarts, at least. They did look lovely, too, especially the one on Lavender's shoulder. I think," she lifted her napkin over her face, "I'm going to cough." The noise she made didn't sound like a cough.

Starling didn't want to laugh. She could see Alasdair was definitely not amused.

Chapter 11

Starling undressed behind the screen. "I like Mr. Fredericks," she said, hoping a break in the silence of the room would ease the tension.

Alasdair hadn't said a word to her since Lavender had left the table. Mr. Fredericks had stayed another hour, offering intelligent and amusing observations. Not having been brought up as a lady, Starling's vision of right and wrong was how one person's conduct affected others. He pleased Starling by keeping the atmosphere light because the party was, collectively, more embarrassed by Lavender's non-reappearance than by her accusations. Starling didn't understand why Lavender hadn't returned. Perhaps continuing an absence was acceptable behavior and not vengeful sulking.

Venturing a tentative glance around the screen, Starling saw Alasdair propped against the headboard, exposing a muscle-hard and rigid upper body, arms crossed over his chest. His eyes shot silver daggers.

Apprehensive, she made her way to the bed.

"Why did you do it?" he asked in a dangerous voice.

With a shivery breath, she lifted the covers and slid beneath, sitting with the sheet drawn to her chin as protection.

"I've never seen such an exhibition of female spite in my life! Did you imagine that little bit of groping today gave you some rights over me?"

She slanted a glance at him. "I—"

"From the first you've been nothing but trouble," he said through barely moving lips. "I hired you to be my wife because I thought you could look like a woman a respectable man might marry. I expected you to choose clothes suited to your new position. What did you do? You found the ugliest, most ill-fitting gowns available."

"You told me to look plain."

"I told you nothing of the sort. My sister called me a miserly brute for not buying you finer gowns. She is under the impression I chose your clothes for you. When she chose one... You could see for yourself the effect her choice had on everyone tonight."

"It did?"

He narrowed his eyes at her. "As for your behavior toward Lavender, you have continually made a game of her, making sure she is not welcomed by my family and friends."

"If you mean the Burdons, she didn't want to meet them."

"And tonight, you insisted on treating her to an exhibition of spite worthy of an alewife. Fredericks, a cousin of the governor, sat at my table. Would he likely accept me as a gentleman now, eh, with a wife such as you?"

"He accepted Lavender as a lady."

His eyes flashed at her. "You have a harsh tongue, Miss. I offered you a great deal of money for this deception, but you have no more on your mind than making a fool of me."

"I had no more on my mind than making money for—"

"Money," he said with the disdain of one who has more than fifty thousand pounds. "Let alone you wormed yourself into the good graces of my servants. Why? Or are you planning to try blackmail? Is that it?"

"No. No."

"Of course not. You would only make a joke of yourself. You decided on a better plan this evening. You think I'm panting after you. Think again." His mouth narrowed. "I can buy women like you for four shillings."

Her heart dropped to the pit of her stomach. She slid down in the bed and pulled the covers over her ears.

He ripped the sheets down to her neck so that she could hear every horrible word he said. "You can't drag Lavender down to your level. She is a lady. How did you so easily manipulate my servants? By taking from them the tasks they prefer and promising them their jobs back when they've fulfilled your unworthy little schemes?"

She bumped out of the bed and stood, prepared to run if need be. "Learning from you, do you mean? You took my job from me. You promised me money when I had fulfilled your hopes and schemes. I didn't ask to be here. I know I don't belong. I don't know the first thing about servants or...or..."

"Civilized behavior? And you don't need to learn because I want you out of here tomorrow."

"Good," she said, wiping her nose with the back of her fist. "Because I can't stand living with a dog turd." She turned her back on him and marched over to the settee, where she sat clasping her knees to her chest.

He edged down in his bed and pulled the covers to his shoulders.

Her lips trembled and she sniffed, but she didn't move and she didn't cry. She clamped her jaw so tightly that her teeth hurt. He turned down the lamp and she sat in the same position in the dark, wishing she could open the curtains and at least gaze at the stars. When she finally heard him breathe slowly and rhythmically, she crept to his cupboard and wrapped herself in his dressing robe, amazed that for the first time in her life, she'd had the last word.

She wished she'd said "canine excrement" instead of "dog turd." He was right. She had no class. She would never pass as a lady.

* * * *

When Ellen came with the hot water in the morning, Starling pretended to be sitting on the settee, waiting. She put her finger to her lips and the maid left silently. With her back turned, Starling quickly lay down when she heard Alasdair stir.

She listened to him wash, tear open the wardrobe door, slam wood on wood, rip out a drawer, and slap it shut. *Canine excrement* hummed through her head. Finally, she heard the bedroom door crash. She arose from the horsehair-padded settee and rubbed her aching back.

Like the lady of leisure she would never be, she sauntered to the washbasin. He had left his used water. Soapy scum floated on top. Wrinkling her nose with distaste, she lifted the bowl and bent for the slop jar...which wasn't there. She only said dog turd once before she walked to the window, out of which a guttersnipe would hurl his used water. With the basin balanced on her hip, she lifted the window high.

Roses scented the fresh morning air and bees hummed with pleasure. The leaves on the trees glimmered in the early morning light. Lavender, who as far as Starling knew never arose until almost noon, walked through the vegetable garden. Wrapped in a shawl, she must have been taking a stroll before breakfast.

Starling had been unfairly blamed for the trouble Lavender had caused with the servants. Being drenched by the slops would be the perfect reward for the lady. Starling hefted her bowl, smiling tightly, expecting the blond beauty to come into range. More than likely she would enter the house by the French doors into the billiard room, right below. The moment she put her hand on the door, she would be drenched from her head to her toes. This retaliation would bolster Alasdair's belief that Starling had encouraged the servants to misbehave. Then, when she left, they would be out of his line of fire.

With her bottom teeth clamped over her top lip, she waited. As Lavender came closer, Starling chewed her lip. Her arms trembled. She would have loved to douse Lavender, but she just couldn't be so mean. Then the side door opened. Alasdair took two steps forward and grabbed Lavender into his arms.

Starling's chest expanded with righteous fury. As easily as Meg dashed water at rutting dogs, Starling threw the water at the entwined couple.

The lovers sprang apart. Lavender shrieked and Alasdair turned his dripping face up to Starling. He roared, "I'll kill you," as he leaped back through the door, leaving Lavender blotting at her gown and wailing.

Starling slammed the window hurriedly, put the empty basin on the tallboy, and jumped into Alasdair's bed, pulling his blankets over her trembling limbs. With hot eyes and a swollen throat, she tried to regulate her breathing into something that might resemble the deep pattern of sleep. The door crashed open. She snored.

The blankets were ripped from her and she was gripped under the arms, lifted to her feet, and shaken by a dripping man with an expression as threatening as the low growl in his throat. "What is this need to make me look ridiculous?"

"You left your scummy water here. What was I supposed to do? Drink it? Put me down. I can't pack while I'm hanging in the air."

He lowered her feet to the floor. "Do it," he said tersely. "Right now." He grabbed at a towel and rubbed his hair.

With an insolent sway of her hips, she walked to the cupboard. No one had to tell Starling Smith to leave more than twice. She found the brown paper wrapping where she had put it in the bottom and some string. Taking her time, she folded her new gowns and the one that Mary had brought her, placing all the underwear except the petticoat and chemise she intended to wear on the top. With eyebrow-raised insolence, she took out the brown-striped gown, her new shoes, and the new hat she had bought—a plain straw pillbox decorated with a smart brown, spiky feather. He watched every move with a satisfied smile on his face.

"Do you intend to watch me dress?" she asked with hauteur.

He sat on the bed, patting a yawn from his mouth. "Who knows what you might steal if you were left alone."

"I've always liked that dressing robe of yours."

"It's worth about two pounds."

She ignored the bait and moved behind the dressing screen. When she had dressed in the gown, she saw he had changed into a dry shirt, which he had tucked neatly into his waistband. Despite him being the sort of man who jumped to erroneous and unfair conclusions, her belly performed an unnecessary clenching that almost made her groan aloud. She wanted him. She should have given in to him when she'd had the chance.

Experiencing almost physical pain, she wrapped her old boots into the parcel and tied the string. "You owe me money," she said, dragging on the knot.

"You owe *me* money."

Her gaze flew to his. "You would pay me forty pounds, you said."

"Forty pounds for fourteen days." His eyes flared. After staring at her for a full minute, he firmed his mouth, scowled, and opened a side compartment in his desk with a key. He took out a bag of money and a sheaf of loose papers, which he skimmed through. "You worked five days. I owe you fourteen pounds, or thereabouts, but it seems you owe me seventeen pounds and some shillings."

"Five pounds."

He passed the papers to her. "Total those bills. I think you'll find I'm right."

"I'm not paying for the underwear," she said when she saw he had added his purchases to hers. "I didn't buy it. You did and you threw away the stays."

He took the receipts from her and folded them. "You misled me. I thought you were staying for fourteen days. Our deal was for forty pounds. I threw in the extra because I had a verbal contract with you. I'll break it when you give me the money you owe me."

"Well, I don't want your underwear."

"You're wearing it."

"My old underwear was thrown away. I've nothing else to wear."

He waited.

"I don't have any money, you know that. Here, take this hat. I've never worn it. You can get your money back."

"Two pounds. If I take off five for the underwear, nightgown, stockings, and the holdall, you still owe me ten."

"This isn't fair. I shouldn't have to leave in debt. You promised me money."

"Which you spent faster than you earned."

"I couldn't wander around wearing worn-out boots and borrowing gloves from your sister."

He shrugged. Now that he appeared to have calmed down, she tried for reason. "Take back all the gowns. Have them. Have the evening shoes. I've only worn them on carpet. You can resell them for full price.

That will leave me owing you about two pounds. Let me borrow that until I get a job."

He shook his head.

"Why not? What's two pounds to you?"

"At the regular rate of four shillings, ten times with you."

"Ten times?"

"That is, if you want to work off what you owe me. I'll tell you what, if you make it enjoyable, I'll pay you six shillings a time."

"Is that what this is about? You want me to be your whore?"

His thumb tapped on his chin. "It's either the full two weeks, as per our contract, or you can pay me in kind what you owe before you leave. It's your decision."

"It wasn't my decision last night. You told me to leave."

"You went to great pains to force that situation, didn't you? You thought I'd send you off with forty pounds. I won't, Starling. We agreed on two weeks and if you don't intend to stay, all you have to do is strip off your clothes and lie on this bed."

He pulled his shirt out of his trousers and began undoing the flap. Now absolutely certain he didn't want her to leave, she smiled. Alasdair needed her to stay to give Lavender a reason to be jealous. "Six shillings for three minutes? I'd be mad to pass that up."

"It won't take three minutes," he said, crossing his arms.

She evaded him. "No, it'll take nine days, because I'm staying."

With that, she untied the string on her parcel and lifted out her clothes.

Chapter 12

"Ellen, I'd like to see you and Freda in the library immediately."

Starling hastened to the book-lined room and waited, scanning the bookshelves and wishing she had time to read a novel. Alasdair kept books on every subject a person might want to learn about, from the manufacture of cotton in America to weaving with pure gold to politics and law. A person could spend a lifetime in this room without finding the motivation to leave.

Above the fireplace hung a large oil painting of apples in a ceramic bowl, beneath which a porcelain figure of William Shakespeare sat surveying a manuscript. She recognized his form from the inside cover of a play, one of his she had read and hadn't liked. A woman didn't kill herself when she lost the man she loved. She found a job and worked even harder to support herself.

After stroking the leather binding on an illustrated book titled *Birds in the Southern Climes*, she settled herself into a linen-covered chair by the central table.

"Ma'am?" Ellen and Freda stood in the doorway.

She motioned them to enter, leaving them gazing at the exotically patterned carpet. Many a time she'd been in their position, awkward and embarrassed, chastened by being left to stand beside the desk of the head nun of Saint Matthew's, Mother Sarah. At those times she would have confessed to murder in order to be allowed to leave. However, she'd never committed murder, or theft, or even deceit. Her worst deed had been pride.

She knew that people would work hard, given just rewards. Having a proper teacher in the home had been her lucky start, but some of the girls didn't want education. They left the home with red, raw hands and went straight into service. Starling, justly rewarded, had a chance of a better life. So, too, did Ellen and Freda and would when Starling ceased her indulgence of their shenanigans.

If they continued to focus on personal grudges, they would become unemployable. Such good workers could rise high if they had a mistress capable of undertaking their training. Starling couldn't continue to hope that Lavender would become the true mistress of the house before another undisciplined incident occurred. "Did you deliberately send Mrs. Frost off improperly dressed last night?" she asked Freda.

"Yes, ma'am."

She turned to Ellen. "Did you deliberately drop food on her and wipe off her face paint?"

"Yes, ma'am."

Both maids stared at their feet.

"I don't want to hear justification. There is none for jealousy or spite." Yet she herself had tipped a basinful of water over Lavender not two hours ago. She winced. "I won't have a repeat. If anything else happens to Mrs. Frost, I'll be very disappointed in both of you. You," she said to Freda, "will resume your kitchen duties, and you," she said to Ellen, "will continue as a ladies' maid. Should Mrs. Frost not want your services, I'll tell her that she is at liberty to hire a maid for herself."

"We won't shame you again, Mrs. Seymour," Ellen answered. "We know Mr. Seymour blamed you. Freda heard him yell at you this morning and we want to tell him it was us, not you."

"What happened this morning was my fault. I want you both to swear to me you won't do anything other than your jobs, and then all can be forgotten."

"What about Derry? I can't let her walk in and snatch him from under my nose."

"You don't know that she has. If he strays, it's as much his fault as it is Mrs. Frost's."

"A man can't be blamed for—"

"Should we expect men to be weaker than we are? Of course not. If we don't give in to our baser urges, nor should a man."

"You're right." Ellen straightened her posture. "Derry has to work out for himself what's important to him. If my feelings aren't, I s'pose I'm not either. I swear I won't take out my jealousy on Mrs. Frost again."

"I swear, too," Freda said. "Mine was spite, and I don't want to be a spiteful person."

"You're both good girls." Starling cleared the lump in her throat. "Now off you go."

She sat for a good half hour. Alasdair loved Lavender. He had shown how much by insisting Starling stay to give Lavender a reason to think he could get by without her. Of course, Starling wanted to stay, but as much for being with him as for the money. She liked sleeping beside him at night and waking beside him in the morning. She liked being secure in his family. She liked picking flowers and arranging them and idling around and eating cake. She liked being respected. She liked being liked, and she knew that despite Alasdair being in love with another woman, he was attracted to his fake wife.

She also knew that he would never act on his attraction even though he'd had ample opportunity. Although she couldn't quite understand how he could love one woman and desire another, she appreciated that guilt made the man a mess of contradictions. Despite this, he was strong and thoughtful, kind and clever, quick-witted and generous—that was, when he wasn't telling her she was a slut and he wished she would leave.

If he distrusted her, as he had pretended, he would have hidden his money. No doubt of it, his agonizing over Lavender had addled his brain.

She covered her mouth with her knuckles. A person couldn't choose whom to love.

* * * *

"Listen to this." Paul lowered a copy of *The Morning Chronicle*.

Starling sipped her tea while Paul spent some moments, head down, gathering himself for his announcement. Finally, he read out, "'The performance is clever considering his unfortunate defect... With two legs he would no doubt be an excellent dancer...' Signor Donato." His eyes gleamed. "A one-legged dancer, currently enjoying a season at the Theatre Royal."

"Let me see. I don't believe it."

Paul handed the paper to Mary.

Alasdair gave a loud whoop, and the tickle in Starling's belly grew to a fit of laughter she couldn't stop.

Then Lavender, dressed like a bunch of violets, entered the sitting room. "I hope I'm not interrupting."

Everyone stopped laughing and turned to her.

"Oh, the playbills. Are we going to the theatre at last?" She leaned over Paul's shoulder and scanned the paper. "They're putting on the oldest plays imaginable. I saw *Much Ado about Nothing* when it premiered."

Paul stared at her. "Well, you certainly don't look your age."

Starling, Alasdair, and Mary glanced at him. He shrugged, and Starling again experienced the hot tickle that forewarned a giggling fit. Laughing now would belittle Lavender, and she had no intention of being unkind to a woman who took herself so seriously.

"I'll check the dinner menu." With laughter burning inside her, she sped from the drawing room to the kitchen, where she gave way to uncontrolled gasps.

Mrs. Trelevan said, "Bless you," three times before she'd stopped.

When she re-entered the drawing room, she discovered that the others had decided to go to Her Majesty's Theatre on Friday night. "Have you seen *School for Scandal,* Starling?" Mary asked.

"Oh, I can't go. Really, I can't."

"If you're sure..." Lavender said, primping her sleeves. She shot Alasdair a quick glance.

"Of course you have to come. And to balance the numbers, why don't we ask Hamilton Fredericks to come, too?" Mary said.

Lavender gave a pretty, dimpled smile. "Such an opportunity for him. If only some lady would kiss him, the frog might turn into Prince Charming."

"I think he is Prince Charming." Starling lowered her gaze meekly. "He's one of the most considerate people I've met."

"There, it's settled then. We'll dash off a note to him." Mary rubbed her palms together. "I hope he'll come, but with Starling as the lure, I'm sure he will. Don't frown so, Alasdair. Mr. Fredericks knows Starling is married, and he's an absolute gentleman. He wouldn't say a word out of line."

Lavender's face set. "I didn't notice him paying Starling any special attention."

"You left early last night." Mary gave an agreeable nod. "From all I've heard, Mr. Fredericks is one of the most important men in the city. Even the governor goes to him for advice, and I believe that more than one very well-connected lady has set her cap at him. He's never taken the lure, of course, because he's far too intelligent, but he—"

"Who told you this?" Alasdair frowned.

"You did. But I noticed how taken he is with Starling, myself." Out of Alasdair's sight, she smiled at Starling.

Apparently, Mary had noticed the strained relations between Starling and Alasdair. Perhaps she thought she could spark a reaction from her brother, using the means Alasdair hoped would work with Lavender. Starling glanced down at her softened hands, the nails he had manicured. "Mr. Fredericks doesn't know I exist. It's Lavender he's taken with, not me."

Lavender smiled. "As for that, I couldn't say, but I did notice last night how often he looked at me. He's friendly with Sir Dominic, is he?" she asked Alasdair.

"I told you before that he's a cousin."

"Would he have a private box at the theatre?"

"I imagine so, Lavender. Most of those who can afford one, have one."

"*You* have one as well." Lavender's eyes widened. "How your circumstances have changed. I remember when you thought taking me for a stroll in Melbourne was a high treat."

Before Alasdair and Lavender could begin a "do-you-remember?" conversation, Starling interrupted. "I can't go to the theatre. I can't go out anywhere in public with Alasdair." Her voice quavered. Mary and Paul might despise her when they knew the truth, but they would hate her if she continued betraying them by living this lie.

"Why not?" Paul glanced at Alasdair, who stood utterly rigid. "He's not too bad looking. He'd be better looking if he could smile occasionally."

"I can't go on with this any longer, Alasdair." Starling rose from her chair, fully prepared to leave this group of people who were not her relatives and who owed her no kindness or friendship. "Shall I tell them, or do you want to?"

"I'll tell them." He stood beside her and tightened his arm around her waist. Bemused by his support, she leaned into him. "The truth of the matter is..." He took a breath. "We wanted to keep this marriage a secret a little longer. We thought that once the word went around, there'd be an endless stream of invitations and interruptions. We wanted to be with family for the first few weeks until we all got to know each other. And then we planned to take an extended holiday, just the two of us together."

When he smiled down at Starling, she couldn't breathe. Every word he had said had been a lie, yet she couldn't contradict him, literally, because he stole her words with an absolutely word-shattering kiss.

* * * *

Alasdair presented himself at the dinner table a confused man. He didn't know why he hadn't ended the charade when Starling had given him a reasonable way out. He didn't know why he continued complicating his life.

"I've been wondering, Alasdair," Mary said, breaking into his thoughts. "And I'd like to know why you chose Kapunda to build one of your emporiums."

"The place is growing rapidly."

"Is that because of the copper mine?" Starling asked, scanning the vegetable dishes. Alasdair had noticed her enjoyment of every morsel of food she ate, unusual in a female because most watched their waists. However, she didn't appear to possess an ounce of vanity, and she certainly didn't know how naturally lovely she was.

Mary nodded. "Many more workers are needed in boom times. This attracts women as well as men."

Starling passed the condiments to Paul. "Families."

Alasdair glanced at Starling. "And new establishments."

"And you stock the goods people need for their move," Mary said, smiling.

"In Kapunda, everything."

Starling helped herself to a spoonful of creamed corn. "And does this new money provide other job opportunities, too?"

Alasdair's eyebrows lifted. "Where were you ladies when I was investigating this? You both ought to work for me."

Starling gave him an indignant glance, which he ignored.

"Why do you think the store is taking so long to turn a profit?" Mary asked.

"So, you saw that?" he said, pleased.

"It was hard to miss when I compared that store's books with the others, as you asked me to."

"The last manager lined his own pockets and skedaddled. The new man seems to think we should continue as we'd intended, and at this stage I'm inclined to agree. He knows his area best."

"My father said that the person who knows best is the person who controls the money." Lavender leaned back, apparently satisfied she'd imparted words of wisdom.

"Oh?" Annoyed yet again by her parent's opinion, Alasdair glanced at her. "And did you believe your father?"

Lavender's shoulders stiffened. "I never really thought about it. Doesn't one always believe a parent?"

"Until one starts to think for oneself." Alasdair added an extra dab of mustard to his plate. "I never met your father, but I know he owned a bank. The money he controlled had been earned by others."

"He managed his own income well." Lavender gave a satisfied smile.

Alasdair nodded. "I don't imagine too many people doubted your father was clever."

"And that's why I give you the benefit of his advice occasionally."

"I don't want it, Lavender. I don't think the way your father did."

"Perhaps if you did, you'd—"

"Have some more roast beef," Starling said smoothly. "No? You can take the plates then, Freda. I agree with you, Lavender. I think Alasdair has taken some poor advice lately, and I think most of it's his own."

Alasdair leaned back in his chair and eased his thumbs into his fob pockets. "Do tell," he drawled.

"Your waistcoats." Starling's quick bite to her bottom lip told him she'd decided not to go on with the thought. "You only wear gray or black. Don't you ever long for bright colors?"

"Do you?"

"Of course."

Mary shook her head. "So Alasdair did choose those day gowns."

"He prefers to see me in dull colors."

"And what colors would you choose for yourself?" Alasdair lifted his eyebrows.

"Burgundy, puce, mauve, pale bluish-green, blue, of course, anything cool. Even lavender."

Lavender giggled. "You'd look like a peacock in my colors. I think you're safer sticking to brown."

"She looked gorgeous in that soft blue the other night," Mary said. "Didn't she, Paul?"

Paul nodded. "And lovely tonight in that mauve and lilac floral."

Alasdair gave a tight smile. "Lavender's being a little too tactful, my love. I think you'd look like a whore in showy purples, don't you?"

Starling considered his statement. "I don't know," she said finally. "What's a whore?"

"A rather gaudy bird found in taverns or on street corners."

"Wild or domesticated?"

"Able to be tamed, but rarely kept caged."

"You seem to know a lot about them."

Alasdair opened his mouth to answer, but Mary said quickly, "That's enough, Dare. Paul, tell her what a whore is."

"Me? Why me? Dare can tell her later." Paul folded his arms. "All right. I can see he'll carry this on all night. A whore is a woman of the night, not the sort of person we'd discuss over dinner. What am I thinking of? Not the sort of person we'd ever discuss, ever."

"A woman of the night? What does that mean?"

"You can drop the subject, now, Starling," Alasdair said, placing his napkin on the table. "I think you've made your point."

"Is she a bad woman, Paul?" Starling raised her chin. "Is that why we can't discuss this?"

"Whores are immoral women," Paul answered with clear reluctance. "They earn their living by charging men for the use of their bodies."

"What are the men who buy their services called?"

"Desperate." Paul laughed. "They'd have to be, to pay a woman."

"I see. The immorality is in accepting payment. Men can use whores, but they don't really need to. If they're motivated, they can find women who don't charge. I imagine these unpaid women aren't called nasty names, either, and they and the men who buy whores' services can be discussed over dinner because they're not immoral."

"They are," Mary said, glancing at Paul. "The church teaches that there should be no congress between males and females without the sanctity of marriage. It's as immoral to make any sacred act into a transaction for money as it is to have marital relations without the commitment of marriage."

"That's what I was taught." Starling kept her gaze on Mary's face. "But while men want women..." She raised her palms as if helpless. "The rule of supply and demand is not only true in retail, but it's also true in life. I don't believe we should condemn women for making choices we might not, of necessity, make."

"And a more unsavory subject couldn't be found to discuss over dinner," Lavender said with disdain. "I'm sure the gentlemen are not interested in hearing about women who only want their money."

"They're not if they know that's their only attraction. But I suspect men have the same ability to fool themselves as women do." Paul gave Alasdair a significant glance as he pulled out Mary's chair for her. "Can I interest anyone in a game of billiards?"

"Does a person need to be experienced to play?" Starling asked, replacing her napkin on the table.

"Nothing more than willing."

"I'm willing. If you can teach me the game, I'd love to join you."

"I'd like to learn, too." Lavender aimed an apologetic glance at Alasdair from under her long eyelashes. A conversation about whores and women wanting men for their money would be lost on a woman who'd never known poverty. "My father might have been wrong when he said ladies can't play billiards."

Surprised by Lavender's acknowledgment, Alasdair reached out one finger and touched the pad to her cheek. "Fortunately, I happen to be an expert teacher."

Starling's lips clamped. With a tilt of her chin, she led Paul to the billiard room.

Alasdair entered the room with Lavender and Mary. The latter took a seat in a single chair beside the fireplace and stared expectantly at the billiard table. Lavender clung to Alasdair's arm, also watching while Paul found a suitable cue for Starling and showed her the best hold. He then set up the balls for her on the lamp-lit table. Glancing at Alasdair, he said, "Your turn."

"Generous of you. Lavender, are you ready?"

The beautiful blonde gave him a soft smile and moved to the table.

Alasdair put a cue into her hands and curled her white fingers under his. She stayed close enough to let her breasts touch his arm.

Starling ignored Lavender's byplay and went on with the business at hand, learning a new game. Clearly, she didn't mind what he did.

Alasdair wanted her to mind. He wanted to show her that Lavender was more than interested in him. A real new bride would be shocked to see another woman trying to fascinate her husband, and to be credible, Starling ought to be fighting for his attention.

He frowned, shocked by the thought that he was acting like a disgruntled husband.

Chapter 13

For the first time, Alasdair noticed how hard Lavender worked to keep his attention. She brushed against him at every given opportunity. As a host, he had been lax. Without realizing, he'd turned his interest to Starling, continually mulling about the experience she must have to make him want her so badly. A wise man would let her leave. A wise man wouldn't twist his tales until he sounded addled in the hope of forcing her to stay with him.

"Is *that* what this is about?" she'd asked. "You want me to be your whore?"

A foolish man would have answered yes and taken her and sated his damned hunger.

Trying to respond to Lavender, he let her hand linger on his as he showed her how to strike the ball. Starling didn't once glance their way. A little possessiveness from his wife wouldn't be out of order. He wouldn't mind in the least if she grabbed him and slapped him. If she fought for him, verbally or physically, he could have an excuse to snatch her away, race her to the bedroom, hurl her on the bed, and get between those long legs of hers. Once he'd had her, he could forget about his ridiculous yearning and concentrate on Lavender.

The game began with Mary being the first one out, and Paul the next. When Alasdair's time out arrived, he went through the French doors onto the balcony, determined not to stand around admiring Starling's derriere as she bent over the table chasing the ball. He clenched his fingers into fists and rested them on the stone balustrade, wishing he hadn't lost control of the entire situation.

A female who was less than respectable had no right to amuse him with her remarks, make him laugh out loud at her blatant provocation, or inflame him to the point where he had practically begged her to stay in his house and keep teasing him until he couldn't string two sensible words together.

He smacked his fist against the railing, wishing he'd never thought of teaching Mary a lesson. The only person who had learned a lesson here seemed to be him. He was an expert all right: an expert in entangling himself with completely inappropriate women. Why couldn't he simply say to Starling, *This is ridiculous. I'm as randy as all hell and I can't take the woman I love because if she knows, she'll use me the way she used me before. So, since you've had men before, and I'd hardly be despoiling a virgin, could you please, please share your lovely body with me just once?*

He groaned, rested his elbows on the hewn stone balustrade, and put his head in his hands He couldn't beg. That was the root of her attraction, of course. He'd never had to beg a woman in his life...not even Lavender.

Clenching his jaw, he tried to count the stars in the black sky, lost his way, and attempted to identify birdcalls. His diligence was rewarded by the soft tap of a female step and the gentle curl of arms around his waist. She snuggled into his back the way she did in bed. He breathed out and straightened. Clasping his hands over hers, he said, "I don't know if I can take much more. I'm abiding by the rules but fast getting to the stage where I'll accept even this as an invitation."

A little noise of contentment warmed his back. She disentangled her hands from his and flattened them on his abdomen. Fighting the compulsion to move her fingers for her, he rested his palms on the stone again, leaving her to explore if she wished.

Her hands moved closer to his groin. His breath began to rasp. Finally, she walked her fingers near his aching cock.

"Please," came from his lips as a groan.

She laughed.

Then he glanced down and almost reeled with shock. Over his trouser flap rested one pampered white hand. Instantly subsiding, he turned to face Lavender. If he had made an ass of himself by letting Lavender know that Starling didn't want him... He smiled as if he'd known her touch her all along.

Lavender eased into his reluctant embrace. "Can't we get away from the others? I'm sure they won't notice. They're too interested in the game."

He shut his eyes as he rested his face against her perfumed hair. If he took Lavender, he wouldn't want Starling. His eyes widened with remorse. He'd reversed the two women in his mind. "Now isn't the time," he said, guilt making his voice sound thin. He put her away from him.

"You said you want me." Her lovely eyes, dark in the night, glistened. Her mouth flattened at the corners like a child about to have a tantrum.

"We *are* away from the others, sweetheart. Let's enjoy each other's company."

She gave him a long, assessing smile; lifted her face; and pressed her moist lips against his. Her seeking tongue repelled him. He would have pulled back, but her hands took each side of his jaw. Her body pressed avidly against his. More numbed than excited, he straightened his back, slanting a placating mouth near her lips.

"Lavender," said a soft, impartial voice. "It's your turn."

Alasdair lifted his head and saw Starling. "She's wanted here," he said in a shaky voice.

"Please yourself." Starling turned away.

He gritted his teeth and dropped his hold on Lavender, who appeared utterly astonished.

"Doesn't she mind?"

"She'll punish me later."

Lavender gave a wide, triumphant smile. "You really do want me. You've been putting me off for days, and I thought I ought to leave, but if you can face your wife's fury, you certainly still have feelings for me. As I do for you." She squeezed his hand and left, following Starling into the billiard room.

He trailed, watching while she took up her cue.

"We're winning," Paul said to Lavender. "One good shot from you and we'll have these two crying into their pillows all night."

"We don't mind if you win," Mary said. "You haven't cheated or jostled the table or done anything underhanded. He usually does," she said, nodding at Starling. "This is your warning for the next time you play with him because by then he'll be desperate. He's only nice the first time so that he can fool you the second time."

"That seems to be a masculine trait." Starling glanced at Alasdair.

Lavender sighted her white ball with the cue and let fly. She missed. "Do better if you can," she said in a light voice to Starling.

Starling leaned forward, concentrating; then she shot her ball forward. The red slammed into two whites, sending one into the center pocket and the other, rather more slowly, to the back pocket, where it hesitated, teetered, and dropped in.

"Amazing," Paul said with a gloomy expression on his face.

"It just goes to show what a person can do when she tries." Starling pretended to manicure her nails with the end of her cue.

A chuckle issued from Paul. "See that, Alasdair?" He replaced Lavender's cue in the rack. "Your wife's not just a pretty face."

Alasdair inclined his head. "Far from it."

Lavender folded her arms across her chest. "Games," she said with a tilt of her eyebrows. "They're so boring. I didn't want to play in the first place."

Starling placed her cue in the rack. "It was beginner's luck."

"It was determination." Alasdair swiveled around and leaned one hip against the table. "You don't need to be so modest when Lavender says she doesn't care."

"I didn't say I don't care. I said that the game is boring. I doubt that a lady would ever have a natural aptitude for it. Starling," Lavender said, smiling prettily, "that maid, Ellen. You were right. She *is* better with my hair."

"You look lovely tonight," Starling replied, and Lavender's eyes widened.

Lavender had done well...for a spoiled brat. Alasdair didn't doubt she'd make a good wife. She had, after all, been brought up as a lady with all the attendant virtues, goodness, kindness, and consideration for others.

Unlike Starling, who clawed her way using instinct and guile. And her soft, lush, clever mouth.

* * * *

Alasdair read in bed for half an hour, turned down the lamp, and drifted into a restless sleep. Snippets of dreams, meaningless and disturbing, wafted through his mind. He kept waking to shake them off. The last, an erotic fantasy in which he performed endless and impossible feats of sexual stamina, found him tangled with Starling and strangled by a sheet.

He untangled the linen from around his neck but stayed in sweaty silence against her back. Investigating her hip, he found only the fabric of her nightgown. He moved his nose to the nape of her neck, breathing in the hot smell of sleeping woman. His breath stirred her hair, tickling him around his face, and he nuzzled closer. He could make her want him. He'd tasted desire on her and only her inhibitions held her back.

He proceeded cautiously, first rubbing his knees into the backs of hers, then rocking her hip against his arousal. She wriggled away from him and made a sound of protest. Resigned, he rolled onto his opposite side.

He slept eventually but not until he had thought over and discarded his every plan of action. None would work, not on a perceptive female like Starling and not when he could manage another week before asking Lavender to be his wife.

* * * *

Starling opened her eyes and saw the flesh of Alasdair's chest, so she closed her eyes again. She could hear the loud steady beat of his heart. Fortunately, in his sleep, he wouldn't know that she had draped herself over him again. One arm stretched over his chest and one knee rested on his thighs. Her other arm curled under her body with her hand opened against his rib cage. He drew her like a magnet.

She took a deep breath into his shoulder. Asleep he was gorgeous, big, warm, and snug. His chest was smooth and hard. A girl would be mad not to want to run her hand over his skin, and being completely sane, she did. His steady breathing ceased. He drew in a deeper breath. He had been awake, not asleep. His fingers tightened around her shoulder.

She made a sleepy sound, pretending her touch of him had been unconscious.

"I give in," he said. "If you want me, I'm yours."

She ached. She wished he meant he cared for her, but she knew exactly what he was saying. With a half smile he lifted her knee higher, brushing her inner thigh over those parts of him that proved him a desirous man— very desirous, hard and waiting.

Her flesh quivered. His body excited her and her heart thudded as he took her thigh across his male appendage, back and forth gently. He left her leg high above his hip and slid a warm and sure hand up the back of her knee under her nightgown. Her breathing sped up and she heated. She couldn't deny for one moment that she liked his touch. Without doubt, he would not breach her virginity...unless she wanted him to.

Despite knowing him for a promiscuous man, careful with his money and willing to lie, she also knew him for a compassionate and thoughtful man, slow to anger, quick to smile, and ready to help anyone in need. Then, too, he was fine looking. Many of Meg's customers had been dirty, unshaven, and crude, but Meg said their appearance didn't matter. In the end, all men were alike.

Starling frowned. Alasdair was no money-waving customer, and she was no whore. They were simply two people who had been left together in a bed night after night. Anyone, given those circumstances, would experience the same companionship she did. Tears prickled behind her eyes. She lied to herself.

She craved his touch, his kisses, his smiles, and his big, careful hand stroking her hair. She wanted him to see her the way he saw Lavender, as a beautiful desirable woman, worthy of more than forty pounds. She wanted him to respect her opinions and take note of her wishes, and she wanted him to trust her.

As soon as his hand reached her bottom, he spanned one soft portion and turned himself into her. With her nightgown now to her waist, she was at a disadvantage. She pushed at his shoulders. "No, don't."

"Shush." He rolled on top of her.

Beneath him, legs sprawled apart, she had no leverage. She squirmed. His weight doubled hers. A quick movement of his hips took his hardened arousal from her belly to the juncture between her legs. Left with only the power of her words, she knew true intimidation when he captured her mouth. She couldn't concentrate on his kiss. If she couldn't stop him, she would be lost. He would thrust inside her and spill his seed. She felt him slide his heavy pecker against her and she panicked. Tearing her mouth from his, she said, "No. You can't. I've no douche."

He lifted his head. "What?"

"I can't have a baby. You can't give me a baby. Please, stop."

"I haven't started."

"Let me go, Alasdair." She wriggled ineffectually and stilled when she realized that her movements shifted him closer.

He lifted himself to the full extent of his arms and closed his eyes. Swallowing, she flattened her hands beneath his shoulders. Although still in the same position, at least he'd hefted his weight from her. Somehow that consideration gave her more confidence. She lifted her knees, hoping she could buck him off, now partially free.

"If you want me to stop, don't encourage me," he said huskily. His arousal sought and pressed.

"I'm not encouraging you. I'm lying here waiting for you to leave."

"You're lying beneath me as wet as a September day. You want me, Starling. Admit it."

Her every thought seemed to be centered between her legs. The slick sensation of him sliding against her provoked a swollen, throbbing need. She tightened her face, her breathing, and every emotion she had. "No. You did this, not me." She pushed his shoulders, hard. "You can't do this. It wasn't in our agreement."

"Don't be a half-wit. If you want to fuck and I want to, what can an agreement made almost a week ago matter?"

"It mattered yesterday."

"I didn't want you to go."

"And we both know why, don't we? You can't change everything to suit yourself. You know I only agreed to pretend to be your wife because you promised this wouldn't happen."

He pushed with his arms, moving his body farther down hers. The top of his head rested on her collarbone and a far safer part of him nestled between her legs.

"I don't think I'll give you a baby," he said. "But if I do, I won't desert you. I'll support you and the child."

"In luxury, I suppose?" Perhaps her father had said these same words to her mother. Perhaps every man said this to every woman.

"In comfort. But it won't happen. Between what you know and what I'm prepared to do, we won't conceive a child."

"I don't know what you're prepared to do, but I do know that you won't be given an opportunity to conceive a child with me."

"You're a hard woman." His thumb caressed her hip bone. "But I'm a determined man."

"I won't change my mind. I'm illegitimate. I'd be the last person to wish that state on another." She dragged against him and he lifted to let her leave. "Besides that, you don't interest me," she added shakily, watching as he made himself comfortable on his own side of the bed.

He put both arms beneath his head on the pillow. With the sheet covering him only to the waist, she saw how his movement changed his body shape. His abdomen tightened and his chest expanded as if he had transposed most of his muscles to that area. She averted her eyes when he smiled.

"All right. Luxury. It's hypothetical, after all, and if you want luxury for yourself and my child, you can have luxury. Now, we'll have to define luxury."

At that moment, Ellen knocked at the door. Neither spoke until she entered, then only Starling spoke. "Good morning."

Ellen glanced at Alasdair, but he had pulled the sheet to his chin and appeared to be asleep. "Good morning," she whispered.

"No need to whisper. He's faking."

"I'm not. I'm fast asleep," he answered, sounding disgruntled. "I never speak to Ellen in the morning. She'd die of shock."

"I would," Ellen said. "It's too early to talk."

"That's a shame. I want to discuss luxury." Starling sat up. "I wonder if it's anything like this, lying in bed while someone cooks breakfast."

"That would be my idea of luxury," Ellen answered. "That or staying in bed all day. You've run out of soap. I won't be long." She left the hot water on the tallboy and closed the door.

"I like Ellen's second idea. How about it, Starling?" Alasdair reached over toward Starling with a hopelessly lewd expression on his face. He tugged her ankles, one in each hand, and insinuated his upper body between her legs. "Luxury indeed," he murmured, tightening her heels around his back.

Still upright, she angled her knees together, letting them press against his chest. "Stop it. She'll be back."

"Not for a few minutes." Dropping his hold on her feet, he ran his hands up her legs to her knees, which he pushed apart easily. Without any warning, he dipped his head between her legs. She gasped. His tongue stroked where his male part had been. The delicious rasp transfixed her. She experienced the glory of the wetness and the excitement of knowing he wanted to taste her. Oh, luxury indeed, but one she couldn't allow. Flushed and throbbing, she jerked backward and fell out of bed.

She picked herself up, shot him an accusing stare, and marched over to the hook behind the door. Totally defiant, she lifted off his green silk robe and covered herself. In that time, he did nothing but lie on his stomach in the bed.

He turned and sat up. "You're right," he said. "You do look good in cool colors."

"You always change the subject when you've done something wrong."

His mouth twisted wryly. "You know me rather better than I'd hoped, but is it so bad to want to give you pleasure? I think you've had little enough of it. If you don't want me inside you, I can bring you to climax with my mouth. That won't give you a child. If you'd relax for a moment, I'd—" He stopped speaking when he heard the door handle turn.

Starling quickly moved to the doorway and took the soap Ellen held. "Thank you," she said, hearing her voice as a throaty whisper.

The maid closed the door again.

Climax? What did he mean? Climax meant turning point, but Starling hadn't heard that word before in relation to intimate congress. Perhaps the turning point came when men spilled their seed, but she didn't spill seed, or if she did Meg had never told her that part. But Meg had told her everything. She knew men. And they were all the same.

"I am relaxed. It's just you. I don't like you touching me." She straightened her back, tensed her jaw, and went behind the screen to wash.

"You can lie to yourself, but you can't lie to me." The bed squeaked and the wardrobe door opened. As she poured the water, he asked, "Can you ride?"

"Horses?"

"Yes, Starling. Horses." He loomed behind her. "It would be nice to get away from the others today."

"I was brought up in an orphanage. When I left there, I worked at the inn. I've seen horses—in fact, I've even patted one—but I've never had a need to ride. Anyhow, I will be getting away from the others today. I promised to go over and see Tammy."

"You're not being indiscreet while you're at the Burdons', I hope. Children seem to pick up on the strangest things, and Tammy's a talker."

"I know that." She turned around to look at him. He'd partially dressed. Just when she'd steeled herself to cope with his naked pecker, he'd hidden that interesting part from her. "We don't discuss much more than men, politics, and religion."

"Men? The child's six. You can't talk to her about men."

"She brought up the subject. She needs someone to help her decide between her two swains and she asked her dolls' opinions, but I believe neither of them helped much. So, she consulted me. I agreed that you're brave, but I could see her dilemma. Derry is extremely handsome and he does have fair hair."

"You think Derry's handsome, do you?"

She smiled. "And he has the added appeal of great strength. I have it on the highest authority that he can carry a girl around on his shoulders for hours. It would be hard to beat that. A man like him would be easy to fall in love with."

"He's courting Ellen," Alasdair said tersely. His face tensed and his eyes glittered.

"I believe you're jealous."

"You're mine until the end of next week. Don't go looking at Derry, and don't go trying to steal him from Ellen. He fell in love with her the moment he saw her, and he'd only want you for the same reason I do."

Her face drained. "Thank you."

"Don't fool yourself, Starling. He loves her. When she first arrived at this house, he spent every spare moment with her, and he's the one who helped her to cope with her disability. If you come between them I'll—" He didn't finish. Instead, he grabbed her by the upper arms and lifted her toward him. Because his eyes stared at her mouth, she thought he might kiss her, which hardly seemed a punishment, but he didn't. He breathed deeply and let her go. "If I find out you've been carrying on with anyone else, I won't pay you. You were hired to be a faithful wife to me."

"I don't remember that being in our original terms."

"I'd hardly want a wife who rutted with the gardener. If I find out you're playing around with Derry, I'll make life very difficult for you, make no mistake."

Chapter 14

The sun glittered on the gum trees' new orange leaf tips. In the shade, a few black lilies bloomed. A tiny flowering creeper, splashed with slender mauve flowers, had twined around the shrubs growing on the banks of the trickling River Torrens.

Tammy, dressed in a blue dress and a darker blue bonnet, clung to Starling's hand. "Where did the well go?"

"It's there, but Mr. Seymour had a cover nailed on top. He doesn't want any other little girl to fall in." Starling toed the fractured brick edging, which, along with the few nailed planks, was the only indication that a well lurked beneath. The tunnel had been filled but a pile of muddy soil still sat between the digging and the well. "He was very upset when he heard his favorite girl had hurt herself."

"Am I really his favorite girl?" Tammy hopped from foot to foot.

"I would think so. He doesn't buy sweets for me."

"'S'pect I'll have to marry him when I grow up."

"Would that be fair on Derry? Aren't you afraid you'll break his heart?"

Tammy scooped up a handful of soil. The dry dirt drifted away. Wrinkling her nose, she pulled off the sling supporting her left arm. "Between you and me, Miss Starling," she said wiping her hands against each other, "I think he's forgotten me. He likes your princess more."

Starling put Tammy's arm back into the sling. "You need to let your bone heal, dear heart. Let it rest."

Tammy gave a grown-up sigh of resignation. "You women. Always nagging. S'pect the princess never nags. That's why Derry likes her. Do you like her?" She raised her large blue eyes to Starling's.

"Just between you and me, Tammy," Starling answered, wavering between truth and tact. "I try. She can be very nice, but princesses don't think the way we do. Remember the princess who couldn't sleep with the pea under her mattress? She was very rude to her hosts. And the princess who wanted the frog to give back her ball wasn't very kind. Both those princesses had to change their behavior before the handsome prince fell in love with them."

"Derry kisses her on her neck."

"I beg your pardon?"

"He kisses her on her neck. I saw him. But I s'pect he was only thanking her because she helped him with his trousers. There's Mr. Seymour." Tammy took her arm out of the sling again and waved. "If he comes over, would you ask him?"

Starling sucked in a breath. Had the child confirmed that Lavender was dallying with Ellen's swain? "Ask him? Oh, no. I really don't think we should speak about Derry kissing princesses."

"Ask him if he'll take me for a ride on his horse," Tammy answered loftily. "My arm's better, truly."

Her chest still fluttering, Starling nodded. "Oh, of course."

Alasdair pulled up his horse a few feet away. "Now, Miss Burdon, you keep away from that well. I don't want you frightening me half to death again."

"I frightened me a little bit, too." Tammy tugged on Starling's bile yellow and brown gown. "Ask him."

Starling brushed at the smudge Tammy had left on her skirt, though she knew no one would notice dirt on the brown material. She cleared her throat. "Miss Burdon would like to grant you one favor, to repay you for saving her life. She would, she says, ride with you."

Alasdair grinned and nodded. "Miss Burdon, please step up here."

Starling lifted Tammy to Alasdair. He took the child from her. "What's his name?" Tammy asked as she tangled her fingers in the horses' mane.

"Comet." Alasdair put one arm either side of the child and crossed the reins in front. "Hold here, Princess."

"I'm not a princess anymore," she said as the horse ambled in the direction of the Burdons' house. "Miss Starling says some princesses are rude and some aren't very kind. I think I'll be a fairy instead. I'm about the right size, aren't I?" Her voice trailed into the distance.

Breath bated, Starling stood while Alasdair reached the perimeter of the Burdons' property. She began to breathe again when he handed Tammy over to the waiting housemaid. Because he smiled courteously, Starling had to believe that Tammy hadn't told about Derry and Lavender. After Tammy had skipped beside the maid through the gate in the fence, Alasdair turned his horse and urged the gelding into a controlled canter back to Starling.

As he drew closer, he called, "The Jackworthys are visiting. I'm afraid you can't compete with an eight year old. Tammy wants to see Helen, a person she truly admires." His horse loomed beside Starling and circled.

"I suppose I'll go home then." Starling indicated the wooden cover of the well. "In a few years this will rot. Until it's filled in, the well will always be a danger."

"I'll get Derry onto the job."

Starling began to walk back to the house, a little overpowered by the tall horse ranging beside her.

"Why don't you come for a ride with me?"

"I told you I can't ride."

"I can teach you."

"I don't need to be taught. I don't need to ride."

"I'm bored. I don't usually take so much time off work, and I wouldn't have unless I had recently married a pretty young bride who needs my attention. Therefore, it's your responsibility to indulge me, Starling."

She frowned. "How long will it take?"

"About half an hour. There's not much to riding other than practice."

"Half an hour? I suppose I can spare half an hour to alleviate your boredom."

He reined his horse to a halt. "We'll go upriver. It's more private past that area of scrubland."

"Now, why would we want privacy?" She placed her fists on her hips.

"Put your foot here." He held out a stirrup with his foot. "I'll help you up."

"This is a trick. I'm not going anywhere private with you."

"It's not a trick. Put your foot here and grab my arm."

"I'm sure I shouldn't trust you." With a resigned sigh, she put her foot on his, grabbed his arm, and almost had hers jerked out of its socket when he pulled her up behind him. "Well, I don't know how I did that," she said, amazed when she found herself settled over the horse's rump, one leg either side. She eased forward, trying to tug her skirts down, but they covered her knees and wouldn't stretch any further.

"See?" He sounded smug. "That's why we need privacy. I don't want the locals looking at my wife's legs."

"I'm not your wife."

The horse took a step. Starling lurched and grabbed Alasdair's jacket.

"You are for the next week. Put your arms around me. You'll crease my jacket with that death grip."

She gripped him around his waist. With every step the horse took she grew more insecure because the stride had a toppling sway. As soon as she became accustomed to the motion, Alasdair made the animal change pace. She bounced against him and back. "I'm going to fall," she squeaked in his ear.

"Not without me," he said over his shoulder. "Hang on tight and we'll both stay put."

He soon reached his destination upriver and reined the horse to a walk. He stopped when he found a clearing surrounded by gums. With his right leg over the head of the horse, he slid off, leaving her sitting behind the saddle. "Don't leave me," she said, her heart thumping, clutching the leather seat.

"Scoot forward into the saddle." He picked up the reins, doubled them across the horse's withers, and held them bunched. After she'd settled herself into a more comfortable position, she dragged her skirts beneath her bottom but still couldn't manage to cover more than her knees. He put the reins into her hands.

From there everything went from bad to worse. He shortened the stirrups, forced her feet into them, "Heels down, back straight," and made her ride by herself. She knew she shouldn't have trusted him. By the time her spine knew every bone and her body had forgotten everything but the motion of a horse, she had horse hairs growing from her sweaty hands and she'd rubbed blisters into her inner thighs. Not only that, but she could make the horse stop and start, turn in circles, and go faster when she had the presence of mind to cling tightly. And instead of walking beside her and telling her exactly what to do, Alasdair now leaned under a tree and watched, arms crossed over his chest.

"Is half an hour up yet? If I'm tired, I don't know how this horse feels."

Alasdair glanced at the sun. "It must be almost midday."

"Midday? If it is, I've been doing this for two hours."

"Thereabouts."

"You said it only took half an hour to learn to ride."

"You learnt how to ride in the first half hour. You've just been practicing."

She lifted her chin and encouraged the horse to walk toward him. However, the horse would neither stand on Alasdair's feet, although he made no attempt to move them, nor knock him over. Instead, the silly creature gave him a whuffly kiss.

"I fail to understand why children and animals like you. Those of us with a little more sense can see you as you are." With that, she swung her right leg over the back of the horse and tried to drop down.

That action made Alasdair grab the horse quickly. "Don't ever get off a horse like that," he said, tersely. "Take both feet out of the stirrups first."

"Everyone gets off that way." She balanced on her right foot because the horse had moved from where she landed and her left foot had somehow snagged in the stirrup leather.

"Should the horse not stand completely still, you'll be dragged by the leg, as you can see at the moment. Occasionally, even the best-trained mount will move off when the weight on their back shifts. If anything happens to startle it at that moment, you're in trouble."

He helped with a little twisting, and she freed her foot, but putting both feet on the ground didn't help. "I can't stand," she muttered. "My legs won't work. I don't think I'll ever be able to put my knees together again."

"Now, wouldn't that be a shame?" When she glanced at him, he grinned. "It'd be an advantage for a girl like you."

"It'd be an advantage for a man like you."

"Perhaps I should take advantage of it while I can."

"My arms still work."

"Hit me and I won't help you into the shade."

"You deserve to be hit."

"I'm all talk, Starling. You know I won't touch you. You do know that, don't you?"

"Yes, I know." She heaved a sigh as she clung to his offered arm. "It's just that you never give up on trying to convince me I want to be touched."

"It's my job. I'm a man. Come on. A few more steps and you can sit down. Play your cards right and I'll give you a leg massage."

She groaned as she sank to the ground beneath a shady gum. "Would it help?"

"What? Playing your cards right or a leg massage? Both would help."

"How do I play my cards right?"

"Smile and relax. I said relax," he said, kneeling between her legs, which he moved apart. Using both hands, he kneaded her calf. "I can't do this under your skirt. Lift it a little, will you?"

She lifted the fabric and pulled the bulk between her knees, challenging him with her gaze. He took no notice and, chastened, she dropped her hands to her sides. Her head lolled back as he continued to work at her lower leg until he'd eased the stiffness. Then his hands moved to her knee, and he pushed her skirt to her thigh. She re-covered her knee. He leaned back on his heels. "I've seen your underclothes before. I bought your drawers and your stockings, remember? If you want me to help, you can't afford to be coy."

"I don't feel very comfortable when you're between my legs."

"That's not something I hear very often," he said, his expression a little too smug.

He put one hand on her inner thigh where the skin burned and the other on the opposing side. She couldn't concentrate on either her tender skin or her aching muscles because his touch not only warmed through the fabric of her undergarments but also tingled the juncture between her legs. Trying to breathe evenly, she closed her eyes.

He began to work on her other leg, lower and then upper. The tingle happened again when he massaged her thigh, so she breathed through her mouth. He worked with one hand on each leg, starting firmly and growing more careful as he reached her upper thighs. Each circling made her more conscious of being a woman than someone with aching muscles.

"How does that feel?"

She needed to swallow before answering. "Much better."

His thumbs moved and her already heightened awareness turned to an excited throb.

Pulse thudding, her belly contracted.

"How does that feel?"

"Alasdair," she whispered. "You know what you're doing, don't you?"

"I'm far more conscious of what I'm not doing." His eyes looked shivery and the dark edge emphasized his pale irises.

He rose onto his knees, letting his arms drop by his sides. She couldn't fail to see the rodlike shape beneath his buckskins. She gave a shaky laugh because she couldn't speak; she shut her eyes briefly to the knowledge that she liked seeing him this way, liked seeing his desire for her. The man had looks, money, and—if she didn't keep her head—her. "You ought to stop doing this."

"You like it as much as I do." He lifted a hand to her hair.

Very slowly she relaxed her jaw. His thumb caressed her cheek.

"I told you...." she began shakily, and although he didn't interrupt, she didn't continue. However, she lifted one hand to his front, tracing lightly over the fly of his trousers.

His hand tugged at her hair. "This is unseemly, Mrs. Seymour."

She rested her hot cheek on his hip.

"Not here. Not like this."

"But you're the one—"

"I can't. I couldn't."

"Not by the look of you."

"I'm in two minds." His expression tight, he pulled back from her. "My thinking mind says that I shouldn't accept favors from a girl like you."

"And what is a girl like me?"

"One who perhaps needs a little more than a quick fuck behind a tree?"

She blushed. Whether her embarrassment was caused by the fact that she certainly wanted more than the word he said or by the fact that he'd been the one to stop the whole thing, she couldn't say. She didn't know what type of girl she was, but she suspected that she differed very little from others. Once aroused, she couldn't be sensible. Too many times she'd forgotten his plan to send her off after this next week. Too many times she'd forgotten her plan to help her fellow orphans.

He rose to his feet, extending a hand. "Do you think you can bear to get back on the horse?"

"Perhaps walking will ease this stiffness."

"Yours, maybe, but not mine."

She didn't waste time blushing again. She simply let the first blush grow hotter as she tested her legs. "I suspect a hot bath will help."

"You don't feel much better, do you?"

"The massage helped. I might walk like a broken peg, but at least I can walk."

He gathered the grazing horse, swung into the saddle, and rode to a fallen tree stump. New leaves sprouted from the base. "If you sit sidesaddle in front of me, I can take you back in relative comfort. For your next riding lesson, we'll use a ladies' saddle."

Because the prospect of walking the distance daunted her, she did as he asked. The horse walked back in the hot bright sun, but Starling felt no discomfort. The side of her body brushed against Alasdair's front. Once or twice his hands covered hers, but she heard nothing but the clop of hooves, a pair of scything wings in the air above, and the beating of his heart.

Along the river, beside the back gate to his house, he pulled up the horse. "I suspect this will be the longest day of my life," he said.

She glanced at him and his mouth dropped over hers. Because she couldn't bear to do otherwise, she responded. During a gloriously long, deep kiss, his hand covered her rib cage, perilously close to her breast.

The kitchen door banged in the distance. His arm dropped and her hand moved to her lap.

Starling cleared her throat. "I'll go inside," she said, sliding off the horse.

"I'll stable the horse." Alasdair reined in a half circle and waited while Starling opened the back gate.

Starling saw Ellen swish rapidly through the vegetable garden with the kitchen knife in her hand. "Oh, there you are, Mrs. Seymour. Mrs.

Brighton was wantin' you. Soon as I pick the spinach for Cook, I'll tell her you're back."

With an embarrassed nod, Starling headed toward the side terrace entrance, noticing her boots had picked up clumps of dirt and grass. She stopped before the first step, using the tread as a boot scraper.

"Why aren't you talkin' to me?" she heard a male voice say. She turned and saw the gardener speaking to Ellen.

"Get out of my way," Ellen said.

"No. I want to know what I done."

Starling subsided on the top step so that she could wipe her boots against the grass. She ought to have taken the kitchen route instead.

"S'pose you know that better than I do."

"I ain't done nothin', Ellen."

"It might be nothing to you, but it's not to me. Let me go!"

Starling had never been placed in such an awkward position. An embarrassed eavesdropper, she decided to remove her boots instead of trying for a quick clean, but the laces held tight. If she couldn't leave the area within a few seconds, she would keep hearing a conversation not meant for her ears. She could only imagine the couple was not aware of her presence.

"You don't want to listen to a pack of lies."

"But I do every time you open your mouth, Derry. This time I saw you. I saw you take Mrs. Frost to the potting shed."

"I showed her the camellia cuttins. There's nothin' wrong with that."

"Oh, I think you showed her far more than the camellia cuttings. I take care of her clothes, you see. She had your potting mix under her petticoats. I know what you did. You can't keep your tool out of—"

With one boot off, Starling hopped to the doors and wrenched at the door handles. She stepped into the house and sat on the carpet in the billiard room, tugging at her other boot. When she had removed both, she glanced at the couple through the glass panes, assuming she hadn't been noticed. With her boots in one hand, she passed the kitchen.

The back door slammed. "What's the matter?" she heard Mrs. Trelevan say.

"Here's your blinkin' spinach. I'm done with the garden, and I'm done with Derry," Ellen answered in a high-pitched tone. "I've had enough of his whoring and his lies. If he wants that painted doll, he can have her with my good wishes."

"Now, now," Mrs. Trelevan said.

Starling crept to the main hallway hoping now that the staff knew of Lavender's escapades, they would be kind enough to keep their information from the master of the house. She wished she didn't care, but strangely, she did.

Although Alasdair knew Lavender's moral code, he would still be shocked and hurt that the woman he loved would betray him with another man.

Chapter 15

Starling ate luncheon with the others, all of whom had decided to shop in Rundle Street in the afternoon. Not again prepared to risk her position by leaving the house, she mentioned important tasks she needed to do and took her time refreshing the flowers. Then she inspected the rooms, wishing she were the mistress. She saw that Alasdair used the library rather than his study for most of his work at home and realized the light in the room was possibly the draw. The morning sun made the space very appealing. A good housewife would combine the two rooms and leave the study at the back of the house for a nice quiet conservatory because of the view over the garden and the afternoon sun.

She sighed, knowing she could not change a thing, not about the house nor about her relationship with Alasdair, as demonstrated by her uncharacteristic behavior with him this morning. Despite the fact that he would offer her no more than the odd caress, she kept testing, craving his attention, and needing his smile. Even when she didn't see him for an hour she thought of him.

Finally, more to occupy her mind than her hands, she went to the kitchen. "It's hot outside," she said to Mrs. Trelevan, who was kneading pastry on the table. "Though not as hot as last year."

The cook smiled. "Hot in Ballarat, last year, was it?"

Starling looked elsewhere and nodded.

"Did you get much rain in winter?"

Starling smiled and shrugged.

Mrs. Trelevan pursed her lips. "At least it doesn't get too cold in Ballarat."

"It's inland. No sea breezes."

Mrs. Trelevan laughed. "I come from Ballarat, meself. The frosts are real bad and the winters are almost like back home in England."

Starling sighed with regret and stared at the floor. "It was a silly story anyway. I don't know why he couldn't admit he met me here."

"He wanted to give you a reason not to have all your luggage with you. Stands to reason that if you married him on the day he brung you here, you would have packed your things beforehand. I surmise he married you a week or two before when he disappeared for a few days. I don't know why he had to keep you a secret from us. We woulda been thrilled. I don't understand why he wouldn't let you bring your things, though. Even if he wanted to buy you everything new, he might have known you would need some of your old gowns."

"He wasn't thinking clearly."

Mrs. Trelevan shook her head. "Good to see, when he's normally so smart. The right woman will turn any man's head."

"Did you meet him when he was setting up his emporium in Ballarat?" Starling asked, desperate to change the subject.

The cook's eyes met hers. "I first met Mr. Seymour in Ballarat, yes." She rolled her pastry into an oblong shape almost thin enough to see through.

Starling pulled a chair from under the pine table where Mrs. Trelevan worked. She began to grease the dish the cook had placed by her right elbow. "He went there trying to forget Mrs. Frost, I believe."

Mrs. Trelevan shook her head. "He didn't appear to have a problem forgetting her. Course, he was busy workin', but when he took time off, he took it with a certain female what kept him occupied. I always used to think how clever he was about everything but women. That one, she were too hard for him, and I reckon Mrs. Frost is, too. But men can't be blind all their lives, and by marryin' you, he made a very smart choice."

"How well did you know him in Ballarat?"

"At first just to look at. He's a fine-looking man. Even someone my age notices fine-looking men. Then he started to get a reputation. There was lots of hard workers in Ballarat, but he was lucky, too." Mrs. Trelevan dropped the pastry into the greased dish.

"Well, it was a smart move to set up a shop in the gold fields."

The cook cut her pastry to fit the pie dish without speaking.

"He was fortunate not to have to mine gold like the other men."

The cook eyed her, as if mulling her answer. "My husband was a ratter."

"A ratter?"

"When he heard tell of a strike, he used to bide his time, and when he thought the coast was clear, he'd crawl in and nick what he could, just enough to keep me and Bobby, that's our son, in food. After some while a certain lucky miner started putting on a guard at night.... Well, what happened to Joe weren't Mr. Seymour's fault."

"What happened to Joe?"

"He and Bobby got caught. The miner said he wouldn't press charges, but no one cared about that. Caught is guilty and justice is quick. The other miners strung Joe up and they was going to string up Bobby, too. Mr. Seymour said the boy didn't know nothin' about the stealing and he'd only been in the mine because he was helping out there." The cook cleared her throat. "Mr. Seymour had an interest in the mine. I don't know if anyone believed him, but they let Bobby off. To make the story true, Mr. Seymour gave Bobby a job. Now there's not a story of Mr. Seymour's I wouldn't go along with, not a one. Love me boy, I do."

"I'm sorry about your husband," Starling said softly, mulling over the word *interest*. Alasdair's tale of making his fortune without dirtying his hands was most likely another Ballarat story concocted for his own convenience to hide from the respectable the fact that he had made his fortune working as a miner.

"Me, too. Loved him as well. He weren't a bad man, only weak. Without him, Bobby had a chance to grow up respectable, but we both miss him."

"Where is Bobby now?"

"Turned sixteen last year. Worked here in the stables until then. Mr. Seymour found him a 'prenticeship as a carpenter, and he works and lives over Norwood way. See him every Sunday." Mrs. Trelevan began chopping chunks of meat into neat squares. "All of us here have reason to be grateful to Mr. Seymour. He bought Mrs. Brighton from her husband."

Starling blinked. "He bought her?"

Mrs. Trelevan shrugged. "She thought she ought to work off the price, but Mr. Seymour said it weren't her debt."

"I didn't know that we were allowed to buy and sell people."

"Men do what they like. Mr. Brighton sold her at public auction. Said she were a good worker but too old for him. She wasn't sorry to leave that man, no, not at all. 'Bout the most humiliating thing a man can do, what her husband done to her. Mr. Seymour didn't expect nothin' for his money, and he pays Mrs. Brighton a regular wage, but between you and me, I reckon she'd rather work in one of his shops. She can as soon as you're settled in."

Starling glanced away, knowing she wouldn't be settled in, ever. That would be Lavender's place. "Freda told me what he did for her and Ellen," she said, her voice slightly gruff.

"He collects strays." Mrs. Trelevan lumped the meat into a pile and began to chop two large onions. "Reckon he found you somewhere that does him no credit and that's why he's giving us the story about Ballarat.

Not one of us would judge a thing he does, not one. He don't seem to realize that, but for him we'd be on the scrapheap. That's where me and Freda put the underwear you came here in, and that's where we'd put anyone who said a word against you or him. Tell a lot about a person by their underwear, you can."

Starling pressed her hands to her cheeks. "I wish I hadn't begun this lie."

"Owning cheap and darned underclothing's not shaming. It's shaming when it's dirty or not darned, and your underwear had more darning than calico in some places. Now, Mrs. Frost! Real expensive her stuff is, but treated as she treats people. Throws it away as soon as it don't flatter her."

"Would you like me to scrape these carrots?"

"No. You're the mistress, and you shouldn't be helping the cook. I'd like you to grease up your hands. Almost right now, your skin is, and you shouldn't let any opportunity slip. Was you a kitchen worker?"

"Laundering made this mess of my hands."

"Well, now. Where would Mr. Seymour find a laundress, I'd like to know?"

"Right under his nose in his Adelaide store. Can I do the table setting?"

"Bless you. You don't need to ask what you can do in your own home."

Starling took her time arranging the table. When she finished, she decorated an ornate epergne with piled-high fruit and trailing ivy leaves. After that, she collected a stack of mending from the laundry and worked in the sitting room. When the light began to fade, she left to bathe and change for dinner.

In the middle of a particularly hearty splash of water onto her shoulders, she heard the door click. "Ellen?"

"No. It's me." Paper rustled, a floorboard creaked, and Alasdair walked past the screen. "It's still hot outside," he said, pulling out his tallboy drawer.

Starling draped the wet flannel over her breasts and bent her knees to hide under the water.

Alasdair lifted one eyebrow. "The only thing this modesty does is make me more curious. Do you have some deformity you don't want me to see?"

"I think I'm normal."

"Let me judge." Even from six feet away, she could see the gleam in his unusual eyes. Amused or interested, she couldn't tell. After swallowing a strange constriction in her throat, she floated the washcloth to the edge of the bath and watched the drips trail over the edge. "Your body is beautiful, Starling," he said huskily. "I have thought of little else all day. I didn't get a lot of work done in the office. That's why I came back early."

"I don't suppose that pleased Lavender."

"I compensated her." He smiled. With his gaze drifting from Starling's breasts to her face, he walked over to the screen, where he took off his jacket. He removed his fob and disappeared from view. When he came back, he wore nothing but his trousers. With that same unreadable expression on his face, he picked up a towel and held out the length. "My turn in the bath."

Eyes averted, Starling stood. As she stepped over the edge of the bath, he wrapped her in the towel—arms, too. With very little skill, he began to dry her, and she imagined she would be red-streaked wherever he rubbed.

"You're not very good at this," she said in a voice vibrating with his energetic movements.

"But I'm good at this." He tightened the towel and his arms around her. His mouth dropped to hers.

Imprisoned, she could do no more than accept, but she neither wanted, nor needed, an excuse. She couldn't imagine anything more wonderful than a kiss from Alasdair. He ended that kiss with small, gentle ones.

"I would stop," he said ruefully. "But I've been under a lot of pressure." His arousal pressed near the juncture of her thighs.

Her heart pounded. "My legs are getting cold."

"And so is the bath water."

One quick kiss, and he ended his grip on her and the towel, which slipped. She grabbed the covering, foolishly embarrassed. He slipped off his clothing and lowered himself into the bath, but she didn't look. Grasping the towel, she moved out from the screen.

"The parcels on the bed are for you," he said.

She glanced at the brown-paper-wrapped pile. "No, keep them. I can't afford anything else."

"They're gifts, Starling. You are staying the allotted time."

"Gifts?" Her throat closed over. Holding the towel, she prodded one parcel. "Can I open them now?"

"Of course."

She opened the topmost, the biggest, and tucking her towel tightly, she held up a morning gown of pale green, the short sleeves cuffed with white lace. Beneath lay a beautifully cut brown jacket, piped in emerald and lined with the same color in silk. "Brown," she said, probably too loudly, because Alasdair answered.

"I could only choose between black and brown. I thought brown suited you best."

"It seems to be a consensus. They're lovely, Alasdair, but perhaps too smart for me."

When he didn't speak, her chest sank. She'd questioned his gift. Wincing over her ingratitude, she opened a smaller parcel. An ornately carved tortoiseshell comb studded with beaded designs sat on the paper. "The comb is lovely," she called, her fingers stroking the smooth finish.

His only answer was a splash. She opened the next, a red glass bottle with a spraying device at the top connected by a tube. Saying nothing, she clasped the perfume to her and smiled. The last parcel awaited. As she unfolded the paper, the material spilled out, tangling with her fingers. "Burgundy," she said, delighted. "It's very stylish."

"Do you like it?"

"I love the color. My, it's a dressing robe. And slippers just like yours. They're beautiful, beautiful."

"Try them on and let me see."

Although his voice sounded casual, she could hear the underlying forced casualness. He wanted to see the fragile fabric wantonly clinging to her skin. Her heart thudded and her flesh tingled.

Dropping the towel, she slipped into the robe; tightened the long, soft sash; and lifted the lace edging the neck. The silk masterpiece flowed in layers. She loved this robe, her own, which he had given to her as a gift. He'd remembered how much she liked his, and he'd remembered she had said she would look nice in cool colors. She'd made each of those statements to irritate him, yet he'd made this effort for her.

She scooped her hair into a loose knot at the back, which she fastened with the exotic Spanish comb. Her fingers trembled on the perfume bottle as she misted over her throat.

Moving to the cheval mirror, she examined her reflection and could not see Starling Smith, brown and ordinary. She saw Starling Seymour, desired wife of wealthy Alasdair, with soft curls hanging in front of her ears and her face made delicate by the width of the comb. She saw Starling Seymour, a woman with ivory skin and brown eyes set aglow by the color of her dressing robe.

Perhaps she saw selectively, but she could see more than she'd seen before, a seductive, throbbing, and willing woman, one who had somehow managed to attract a stunningly handsome and very generous man. After a last adjustment to the robe, she stepped behind the screen and waited for his comment.

Alasdair stared. "I was wrong," he said in a soft voice. "You don't look like a whore in gaudy colors. You look like a very sophisticated and very lovely lady."

"I'll never be a lady." Her voice came out husky. "And I've never worn a color like this. I feel different, not so ordinary anymore."

His mouth curved. "The name Starling suits you. You remind me of a Starling, all the beauty hidden until the light catches the shimmer on the wings."

"You've found something beautiful about a Starling?" Her eyes misted.

He shrugged. "It's an elegant bird, discreet. Haven't you heard of a murmuration of starlings?" His hand reached out to her. He didn't need to speak. His eyes said, "come to me," and she did.

She walked to the bath and kneeled down. His hand curled around the back of her neck and his lips found hers. The kiss pressed long, deep, soft. Her fingers touched his wet shoulder, slid and drew patterns that didn't cool with the water. Her mouth opened and played with his, brushing gently. His hand urged and his head moved, circling so that he could take more than her lips. He took the edges, the surrounds, her chin, and her cheeks. She loved him and she loved what he was doing.

Her hand moved to his chest, male and hard. His breath whispered, sped, and his heart pounded under her palm. His mouth lifted from hers. "If I don't do something about my aching cock soon, I won't be much good for anything."

She drew back.

He stood, reached for the towel, and quickly dried himself.

She swallowed past the heavy lump in her throat. He hadn't asked her to relieve him. Meg knew nothing about men, nothing, and Starling wished that she'd never listened to a whore. Not all men were urgent, not all men were rough, and some—this one—seemed so tender that he made desire into far more than a physical experience. She trembled with an emotional need she thought she would never know.

She offered him her lips again.

This kiss was demanding, passionate, hard. His insistent tongue made her breathing speed out of control. Somehow, as he kissed her, he murmured words that excited her, descriptions of his size and his arousal. She wanted desperately to touch him. His fulfillment should be hers.

Her fingers entwined with his. He groaned deep into her mouth and used her hand with his, pressing her palm down hard, sliding the skin of his oiled perfection over the thickness beneath. Logically, she shouldn't enjoy this decadence, but logic had little to do with lust.

His words became urgent, his kisses frantic. He would be like this making babies. With him, she would always feel desired and special. Then, he quickly removed her hold. For some seconds his breath came in panting gasps. Although he said nothing, she knew he'd completed his needs.

Her head dropped to his shoulder and his face rubbed over her hair. His lips pressed against her forehead. "Thank you."

"No," she answered, lifting her head. "Thank you. Thank you for the gifts. Thank you for everything."

He straightened. His forehead creased. His hand slid from her neck and his chin lifted from her hair. "You're honest," he said with a cynical edge to his mouth. "You pay your debts. Whereas I..." He made a resigned face and shook his head. "I'm damned, I suppose. I could say I don't know what I'm thinking, but I do know. I'm thinking about fucking and I can't stop. That's what comes of having a woman in my bed, be she mine or not."

He stood until she felt compelled to let him go. She tried to look into his eyes, but he gazed at his clothes on the bed.

You don't exist when they've finished, Meg had told her, and Starling could now see the truth of that statement.

He'd eased the ache and he didn't need her any longer.

Her lips curved into a wry smile. When he didn't desire her, she turned back into a brown, ordinary, menial worker—no longer Starling Seymour, but only Starling Smith. When she glanced into the mirror, she could see herself as she really was, nothing much, simply a woman in a burgundy dressing robe.

During dinner that night, she was a woman in a gray, refurbished gown. No matter how beautifully Ellen had decorated her hair with the new comb, she looked nothing compared to Lavender, who shone like a lilac in moonlight, who had added to her confidence and superiority.

"I probably shouldn't accept gifts from married men." Lavender gazed right into Starling's eyes as she spoke. Her smile looked triumphant. She took a tiny sip of carrot soup. "But Dare and I have been friends for so long that I can't see the harm in it."

"Gifts?" Starling asked carefully.

"Only one. A white fur cape. It seemed meant for me somehow. The lining was the most glorious shade of lavender. I had to have it, and Alasdair insisted on buying it for me. I would have been ungracious to refuse, but it was so expensive. I think possibly the most expensive thing in the shop. It's bad of Dare not to tell his wife. You're bad, Dare, truly."

She gave him a roguish tap on the arm with her fan. "I'm sure you bought something for Starling as well."

"I bought her cooperation," he answered coolly. "Do you want port, Paul?"

Cooperation. Lavender's fur had been a gift. Starling didn't look at Alasdair again, but because he'd not once glanced at her, she doubted he would notice.

One week more and she could leave this man before he managed to rip her heart in two with his emphasis of her unimportance in his life.

Chapter 16

"I don't understand my brother anymore," Mary whispered to Starling as she walked up the stairs to their respective bedrooms. "Have you two had a fight?"

"I suspect so. I'm just not sure why."

"I've never known him to be so moody. If Paul ignored me and showed favor to a scented doll with the morals of a horse fly, I'd break his fingers."

"Wouldn't you wonder why he showed the preference?"

"I'd infer he'd lost interest in me."

"Alasdair can't ignore Lavender forever," Starling said with a weary rub of her forehead. "She's his guest and he's loved her for years."

"It's not love. It's blindness."

"All cats are gray in the dark. It's the light that spoils the vision. That's when Alasdair can see what he really wants."

"That's when he's the blindest. Don't let him get away with it. You're smarter than Lavender. Show him."

"Compete? That's not my style."

"You're right." Mary reached for Starling's hand. "If he was smart enough to marry you, he's smart enough to work out why. Good night, Starling. I'll see you at breakfast."

Starling continued on to Alasdair's room, certain only of the futility of her feelings. After she'd undressed, alone, she climbed into bed, alone. Sometime during the night, she reached out and found him beside her.

* * * *

The morning tap at the door woke Alasdair. As Ellen brought in the water, he pulled the sheet to his neck. When she left, he stretched his arms above his head. Starling hadn't moved, hadn't flickered an eyelash. He'd known yesterday that his presence no longer threatened her.

He smiled at the irony. Yesterday he thought she wanted him, felt a desire equal to his, and yesterday he'd made a dunderhead of himself buying gifts to please her. Beneath his head, his hand knotted into a fist.

He wanted her, but he couldn't have her. He'd gone farther with her than any reasonable man would, given a solid determination to marry another. Unfortunately, he could taste her desire, but *fortunately* she was able to repress her passion, leaving him with nothing to do but frustrate her, deny her everything she denied him.

She stirred. Her hand flattened over his rib cage. Her elbow bumped his cock. He waited and watched her through narrowed eyes. She rubbed her cheek across his chest in a languorous waking movement. He let his breath out slowly. His heart began to thump. He tensed every muscle in his body. Very slowly her elbow brushed back and forth across the tip of his erection, an action that tightened him between the legs like a pause before a throw.

"Are you awake?" She glided her palm to his navel.

"Guess."

"Is this a sign?" Four fingers touched his arousal.

He had to swallow before he could answer. "Not necessarily. If you'd test more often, you'd find out."

"Alasdair," she said with a sigh. "You know what would happen if I tested more often. You'd fail, you know you would."

"You would, too. When you touch me, you get aroused. You want me, but somehow you've learnt to close off your mind." He grabbed her hand and lifted her arm above her head. At the same time, he turned into her, pinning her knees with his. She looked alarmed now and wide awake.

"I'm holding you to our agreement."

"I'm letting you set the limits. I always have. You know what you did yesterday. If you'd wanted to go further, you could have, and if I'd wanted to force you, I could have. But I didn't then, and I won't now. But I will do to you everything you've done to me."

"You have." She tried to throw him off.

"I haven't brought you to climax, and I owe you that."

"I'd hate to be the one to tell you about the differences between a man and a woman. Women don't—"

His lips took hers while still moving. Just because she hadn't experienced the ultimate pleasure didn't mean she couldn't. Perhaps when she did she would crave his touch: want more, beg and scream for him. He parted her legs with his, sliding his arousal against her hot flesh. Her freed hand pushed at his hip. He lifted her wrist to the other above her head, holding them together in one hand, never once easing the pressure of his mouth on hers.

Imitating with his tongue inside her lips how he would love to plunge between her legs, he lifted his thighs to ease his hand between their bodies. His fingers parted and explored her. Tightening his buttocks, he angled his arousal to rest at her entrance. She made a sound, an unwilling, breathless moan. Despite the urge, he didn't move. His fingers found moisture but as yet no evidence that he could take her over the edge.

Knowing her to be a novice in touching, he used his tongue in her mouth with persuasive skill. His fingers used the same rhythm as he stroked upward until he finally felt a response, first just the slightest hardening and then a full pulsating arousal. That response did far too much to him.

"Let me fuck you."

"You promised."

"I'll make it good, Starling. I'll make it good."

"No." She dropped her knees and tried to push them between his. Her hands fought his grip.

She dried with her fear and lost her arousal. He could only blame his desperate words. "I understand 'no.'"

"You shouldn't hold my arms, Alasdair. It's not fair."

"Use them, but on me, not against me."

When, with absolute reluctance, he stopped gripping her wrists, she lowered her hands but only to his face, which she cupped either side. "I trust you. I don't know why I panicked."

"Trust puts an awful lot of pressure on a man. Hell, Starling. Call me a bastard and let me act like a bastard."

Her thumb traced a path across his cheekbone. "You don't need my permission to act the way you do. You *are* being bad. I don't understand men, and I don't understand how you can contemplate being unfaithful to the woman you love. When you tell Lavender the truth, you'll hurt her. Or don't you plan to tell her the truth?"

"I'll tell her I hired you and I'll tell her why. Other than that, there's nothing to tell. Is there? You feel nothing, don't you?" He gazed straight into her eyes and circled his thumb around her center of pleasure. Her lips parted and her eyes widened, changing into hazy pools of desire.

"I feel nothing," she agreed in a forced voice.

He smiled at her lie, feeling her swelling response to his caress. "Well, then. There's no harm in it."

When he touched her lips with his, brushing them the way his fingers brushed her womanly places, her knees lifted again around his hips, giving him access, making herself available. She rocked, arched against him, and her hands clutched at his shoulders. His mouth filled with the taste of her desire, and he knew the harm. A primal life force thudded through him, a compulsion to thrust inside her, and instead of giving in to his desire, he breathed hard and expressed his lust with his tongue.

Her hands spread across the skin of his back. She made her kiss into one of the most exciting experiences of his life, and he didn't know how. One part of his mind stayed cool, noting the practiced teasing of advance and retreat, and the other lost itself in the hot, wet sensation of her lips and the insides of her mouth taking his tongue in a tantalizingly deliberate firm draw. Too easily could he imagine that same surrounding of his cock, the slow dragging, the soft wetness, the glide, the desperate pressure. Too easily could he imagine the invitation of her hands sliding to his buttocks, caressing, rounding, and urging.

Unable to help himself, he probed. She tightened, and when just the tip of his cock entered her, she arched. Her knees began to shake with the same rhythm as his flicking thumb. He could feel every nuance of her buildup, the tension before the explosion, and he wanted to feel her gush of excitement while inside her.

The frustration of not having her permission made him sweat. He'd asked and been refused. Should he bleed from every pore, should his every nerve ending beg, he wouldn't allow himself a sensuality she denied. Soon, she would see what she'd missed. Twice she almost reached climax and twice she fought herself, pulling back, tightening and moaning. Never before had a woman done this to him, even Lavender ,who had been a virgin and had more reason to be confused about her body's reactions. To say Starling puzzled him would be an understatement. She would deny herself that which she didn't deny him.

"Take the pleasure, sweetling," he murmured. "I give it willingly."

Her hands fell back on the sheet, her head twisted away from him, and in a series of convulsions she climaxed. He found himself breathing as erratically as she. He found his head on her shoulder.

She edged her hips a little to the side, effectively nudging his arousal aside and moving out of the vicinity of his hand. He'd never felt so superfluous. She'd used him and lost interest. He pounded with frustration, experiencing a despair he didn't understand.

He rolled off her onto his back and flattened his palms beneath his head. The morning sun glinted on the window, casting patterns of lace on the wall. In an attempt to disguise his arousal, he lifted one knee, masculine vanity and wasted. She didn't care and never had. "There." He forced out an even tone. "Now we're square. I don't owe you a thing."

"By the end of this week you'll owe me forty pounds," she said in a shaking voice.

His lips curved over his teeth. He rolled over to face her. Lifting himself on one elbow above her, he said, "And not four shillings more."

"No." She turned her face to the window. "Not four shillings more. I don't need to earn my money that way."

"And I don't need to pay for a woman's services. I never have, and I won't start with a female I hired. Forget what happened between us yesterday because it's been negated by what happened then. Nothing. Payment for payment."

Clothed only in frustration, he sprang out of bed, grabbed his drawers, and forced his feet into the legs. Unbelievable as it seemed after the words between them, he hadn't lost one inch of his aching arousal. With no intention of letting her see his agony, he sat on the side of the bed.

"Doctored," she muttered.

He spun around furiously. "Doctored? Hardly, my little bird. What do you think this is? A hairbrush?" His hand grasped his erection. Such was his arousal that he almost responded to himself, and such was his anger that he wanted to, right in front of her. Fortunately, he still had some pride. "It's only proof that any female with opened legs tempts me. And yours, my dear, opened and begged. You came so fast that I'd say you found the one profession for which you have a natural bent."

She blushed, a full, awkward reddening. This proved one thing beyond the shadow of a doubt. She didn't know he lied. She had no idea of the effort he'd expended in giving her an orgasm. After taking this revenge, he had no qualms about the bulge in his trousers.

She didn't look at him and she said not a word. He washed and dressed in a fraught silence.

He didn't speak to her during the day or at dinner. When Paul, Mary, and Lavender left the house for the theatre with Hamilton Fredericks, he went into the library and shut the door. There he finally gave vent to his feelings.

Papers he had stockpiled for months flew out of his hands, floated over the room, and settled on the floor in untidy piles. Quelling the urge to grind them with his heel, he gazed at the pages, clenching and unclenching his fists. Finally, he collected each and sorted them again.

As he noted dates and the corresponding profits in the margins, he thought of frightened, widened brown eyes; laughing, sparkling, teasing brown eyes; glowing, desirous, wanton brown eyes; and puzzled, hurt, angry brown eyes. His elbows lifted to the table and he dropped his head into his palms.

He had to admit it. He wanted, yet couldn't take, an ex-whore who had likely been tupped by far worse men.

* * * *

Starling sat alone in the sitting room. Embroidery skills like Lavender's had not been needed in the orphanage, but every "bird" had been taught darning and mending. Some pricked their fingers more often than they pricked the material, but Starling had always managed quick, neat stitches. She liked sewing and enjoyed finishing hems, which she had been adding to the new sheets for the past three hours.

Although she'd watched Lavender monogramming her handkerchiefs and thought she could imitate the intricate patterns, she resisted the urge to leave a splashy *S* for Starling, not Seymour, on the dog turd's sheets. If she did so, only she would understand the joke, and an unshared joke was like an unshared smile, wasted for the lack of being offered to another.

With that, she wasted a sigh. From now, she could count the days until she left. Alasdair would count them, too. He would be only too glad to get rid of her now that she had proved immovable. She wanted Alasdair to make love to her, but he couldn't when he didn't understand the term "make love." He used the same word she'd heard in the inn and invested it with the same meaning: nothing.

Intimacy with Alasdair could never be nothing to Starling. Every motion of his head, every shrug of his shoulders, every smile, bright or bland, had significance for her. She loved him but she hated him, too, hated him for not caring, for not knowing how much he hurt her. He could think she would only pleasure him for money until the end of his days, and she would never put him straight.

She wouldn't give her body because she'd given far too much already, her heart, a stupid—she wiped her eyes—piece of flesh situated about one foot above the piece of flesh he wanted.

She hated him, his humiliating words, his smug smile, his snapping gray eyes, those stubby black lashes that could hide his expression so easily. No longer could he impress her with his wide shoulders, his beautiful taut body, or his gentle hands that could make her body feel like a length of precious silk. All those had been given to him or taught to him. He couldn't impress her unless... Oh, Lord. He could, with every one of his generosities. He could, but she would never let him know. Dog turd. Seducer. Altruist.

With the first two in mind, she folded the sheet. After her industry, she deserved a book to read, a calming story that would take her out of her meaningless life and into that of someone less ordinary. The fact that he'd shut the door to her book supply should mean nothing to a woman who meant to march through life, toss decisions over her shoulder, and turn into a true independent heroine. Squaring her shoulders, she knocked on the library door.

"Yes!"

She opened the door. "May I borrow a book?" She shook, knowing herself to be anything but dashing, fearless, and original.

Alasdair moved his head in an upwardly inclined nod, indicating more impatience than acquiescence. Miss Eliza Bennett, individual and strong-minded, walked over to the bookshelves and pulled another book by her creator, *Mansfield Park,* into her undaunted hand.

"What did you take?"

Starling Smith, who'd rarely been given the courtesy title of *Miss*, turned around and hid the book behind her back. "You have thousands. Hundreds."

He rose to his feet. "Why hide your choice from me? You couldn't have taken *How to Turn a Man into a Eunuch in One Easy Lesson.* I suspect you read it years ago."

"You have no right to talk to me that way."

"That's what I am, a eunuch. In working order, ready whenever called but never given the pleasure of satisfaction. Is that what you want, my dear? To lead me around by the cock until I promise you anything your heart desires? The day will never come, of that I give you fair warning. I'll never pay for your favors."

"In that case, we don't need to discuss the subject."

She edged toward the door. He moved like a cat about to pounce on a sparrow, shoved the door closed, and leaned his elbow on the wood beside her head. "Show me the book," he said in a threatening voice.

"I said borrow, not steal."

"Does your type know the difference?"

She smashed the cover into his shoulder and winced when she saw his expression. The black edging around his irises expanded until it almost touched his pupils, giving the impression of a bottomless pit. Dry-mouthed with contrition, she kept her expression hard and cold. "Did you have time to read the title?"

"If you are using a whore's trick to excite me, you don't need to," he said with soft menace. "I'll offer you the same price as before—nothing."

Without knowing where she found the front, she relaxed. She tilted her head up the way Lavender did. She let her eyes melt as Lavender's did. She smiled with yielding innocence, put one finger on the top button of his shirt, and traced a slow path to the next, the next, and the next until she reached the waistband of his trousers. She wouldn't go farther. She couldn't because she wanted to and he wanted her to. A pulse throbbed in his neck. He moistened his lips. "That's what you get for nothing," she said sweetly. "Nothing."

"I'll take it," he answered, not moving. "Give me nothing a little lower, and I'll give you the reaction you're asking for."

"You've already given me the reaction I expected."

"You little liar. You want me so much, you've done everything but ask. You'll have to ask because you'll get nothing until you do."

"Really," she said sweetly. Her finger progressed to his trouser button. She could see the shape beneath, she could see he was, as usual, aroused, but testing him seemed to be important. Suddenly, touching him with her palm felt imperative, but until she glanced at his face she didn't realize how easily he'd tricked her. He'd challenged her to touch him and his face relaxed now that she had. She dropped her hand quickly.

With a gleeful laugh, he grabbed her, sliding his hands from her back to her breasts. "I'll have to buy you a front buttoning gown."

She raised her arms to push him away, but her wrists glided around his neck. In truth, she *had* practically asked. She'd come to him and she'd insisted on his attention. His mouth gave her as much as it took. She almost sobbed as his touch on her nipples made the whole of her breasts swell and ache. He could do anything with her, anything, and the dog turd not only knew it, but he reveled in the power.

Almost desperate with a need to please him, she let him lift her skirts. When he separated the seam in her underdrawers, with shaming compliance she spread her legs. He drew in a long breath and touched the dampened area between her legs. Despite her trembling compliance, she knew the harm. Every time he touched her, she wanted a little more. She wanted to know how his simulated love would feel inside her, and she knew that she would this time. He'd stopped stroking her to undo his trousers.

Still kissing her, he lifted her higher against the door, pulled one of her knees around his hip, and let his erection seek. She loved the feeling and knew that from time immemorial women had enjoyed the very same thing. As she angled her hips to take him, she heard the front door slam.

She froze. Alasdair arched his head back. "Damn," he mouthed. "Damn, damn, damn. Don't make a sound. No one knows we're in here."

In the oil-lit room, Starling saw reality for the first time that night. She saw a born whore shoved against a door, skirts up. Instead of a couple in love, she saw a man with his trousers opened, urging against the whore and swearing. She saw two rutting pigs, herself and Alasdair, joined in sweaty lust. Her fist thumped his shoulder and she tightened her face. He leaned forward and tried to take her mouth, but she turned her head away. "Stop. Let me go.'

The uncaring beast angled his hips and teased partway into the woman he didn't give a shake of his head for, while outside in the hall, separated from him only by a door, his family and his beloved Lavender made their way to their respective bedrooms.

Starling gasped. Using a whisper of repressed rage, she said, "Any further and I'll charge you five sh...pounds."

His eyes flitted over her face. She could see him consider.

Efficiently, as though he'd judged the price too high, he buttoned his trousers. With an expression of implacable coolness, he moved her from the door and leaned his back against the wood. Prevented from opening the door, she stood in silence, listening to the retreating murmur of voices.

"They've gone," Alasdair said, moving to his desk chair. "You have my permission to leave, too."

Flushed, after shaking out her skirts, she ran her hand over her hair and opened the door. Lavender had trooped halfway up the stairs, but when she heard Starling, she stopped, fanning herself with the theatre program.

"Did you enjoy the play?" Starling asked, unable to hold the gaze of the angelic-looking beauty.

"It was passably entertaining. Dare won't mind, will he, if I spend some of the next week with Hamilton? He wants to show me the sights."

With a light shake of her head, Starling said, "You must do as you wish, Lavender. I'm sure he does."

Lavender smiled and caught Starling by the arm. As they walked together, Lavender said, "He always has." She poked a blond curl behind her shell-like ear.

Starling couldn't bear looking at the other woman's satisfied expression.

Lavender giggled. "Hamilton thought it would be nice to get together as a group sometime next week. A picnic, he said, if the weather's fine."

"I'm sure Alasdair would adore seeing you charm Mr. Fredericks."

"Surely you don't imagine he can see past you?"

"Surely you don't imagine *I* can't see through you?"

Starling shut the bedroom door, leaving Lavender in the hallway with an expression of outrage on her face. No longer did Starling care about upsetting Alasdair's guests or upsetting him.

If she never spoke to him again, it would be too soon.

As it happened, she didn't have to worry. For the next four days, he volunteered not a word to her unless others were present.

Chapter 17

During the past four days, Alasdair had noted one thing. He had Starling's complete attention. He knew for a fact that she wanted him as much as he wanted her. He stared out of the carriage window, barely noticing the passing scenery. Lavender had asked him to take her to Hamilton Fredericks's house, where she had been invited for a luncheon with some of the local dignitaries. He had invited Alasdair and his wife, too, but Alasdair had pleaded a previous engagement.

"I don't have to go. I'd rather be with you." Lavender leaned into Alasdair, taking his hand in a clasp she lifted to her bosom.

"Fredericks is expecting you. I promised I'd have you on his doorstep by noon, and I promised I'd be in the store by twelve-thirty. I don't break promises, Lavender." He'd promised to love Lavender forever and in certain ways he did. He could still read her like a book, and her smiles still lightened his mood. Strangely, those smiles no longer had the same physical effect on his body. His blood didn't pound when she touched him, and he didn't long to pull her into his arms and kiss the petulance from her face. He'd lost his youthful passion for her and was now more in control of his feelings,

For sheer physical appeal, he couldn't think past Starling, but this would wear off if he spent less time in his bedroom with her. For the past four nights he'd gone up to bed long after she did, woken before Ellen's rounds, and leaped out of bed first.

Lavender pressed her lips on his fingers. "The first time we lay together, I remember you telling me you would always love me."

"I was eighteen and still a romantic."

"That's not what I mean. I gave you my virginity. I made a dreadful mistake when I let my parents marry me to Richard. I couldn't ever love anyone but you. He knew that." She glanced at his face. "He knew when I crept out to meet you."

"You should have left him when I asked you to."

She lowered her eyes. "I can't live without money. I told you so at the time."

"And I couldn't wait around forever."

"Only men are granted divorces, and he wouldn't divorce me. "

"I didn't see those practicalities when I was twenty. I thought you could leave and live with me."

Her pretty lips moved into a pout. "The scandal would have ruined my parents. I thought of you as my refuge, my love, but not my lover. You were more a husband to me than Richard."

"But I wasn't your husband, Lavender. I couldn't afford you, as you said."

Her eyes glossed with tears. "I should never have married him, but I did, and now I am free...and I don't think I should be punished for my mistakes for the rest of my life." She slid her arms around his neck. "Please don't send me back to Melbourne. I want to stay with you."

He touched his mouth to hers, then he leaned back. "But I'm married now."

"And I'm poor now, just like you were. I'm at your mercy."

"As I was at yours."

"You surely don't intend to pay me back for my thoughtless, stupid words all those years ago?" Her eyes widened.

He shook his head. "How could I suddenly lose a wife?"

"You've only been married for a week or two. Surely you could get an annulment."

"Are you waiting for marriage?"

She shook her head. "I'm in no position to do that. I wouldn't have objected if Richard had taken a mistress."

He examined her gloved palm. "And you see yourself as being mine?"

"Why not? As I said, I'm poor now. I don't have a single penny."

"I was hoping for a rich widow," he said with an evil grin, curling one of her ringlets around his finger. "I thought you would have inherited your father's fortune."

"Not even the family home. Richard shot himself." She took his fingers into her lap. "My father scotched the scandal. He made sure the coroner found that Richard had been killed by an unknown intruder. He didn't know about the money, then."

Alasdair glanced into her glistening eyes. "What money? His or Richard's?"

"My inheritance. After Papa lost the bank, he gave it to Richard to invest. The wrong ship sank, and with that Papa's money. Mama inherited his house as his widow when he died, and she let me live with her. When Mary asked me to come to Adelaide... Oh, Dare. Tell me you love me. I need love so badly."

He spanned the back of her neck with his hand. "If only you'd married me six years ago. I would have adored you and protected you for the rest of my life. As it is...I do love you, Lavender. Of course I love you."

"How rich is Hamilton?"

"You'll see as soon as you step inside his house. He can afford to indulge his every whim."

"What if I'm his whim?" she said pettishly. "What if he wants to marry me?"

"You don't have to make any decisions today. We're here. I'll walk you to the door."

The carriage halted on Robe Terrace. Alasdair stepped out, rolled the steps down, and extended his hand to Lavender. She climbed out slowly, staring at Fredericks's house. Two storied, the magnificent edifice faced the city parklands, a very prestigious position. A turret had been built on either side of the slate roof. She laughed aloud. "The frog prince resides in his version of a castle. What a shame one kiss won't turn him into Prince Handsome."

"He doesn't need looks to be accepted into society. He had the right parents."

Fredericks's housemaid opened the front door. Lavender left Alasdair without even a wave.

Alasdair didn't think of her again until Travers, his clerk, opened his office door. "Four-thirty, Mr. Seymour."

"What? Oh." He rose to his feet, remembering he had to collect Lavender. He should have been more sympathetic this morning after she'd bared her soul.

Shrugging into his jacket, he firmed his jaw. He'd committed himself to marriage with Lavender, but he couldn't yet reconcile Starling's position in his house.

He only had three more days with the wary little bird. In that time, he would have her and get her right out of his system.

* * * *

Hamilton Fredericks's face almost split in two with the width of his smile at Alasdair. "Lavender has promised a perfect day for tomorrow. We thought...a picnic, perhaps?" Fredericks turned his gaze to the blond-haired beauty by his side.

"All of us, Dare. You and Starling, and Paul and Mary, too." Lavender clung to Alasdair's arm and turned her glowing eyes to his. "Hamilton's cook has begun the preparations already. He'll pick us up in his carriage at midday. Say yes, Dare, please say yes."

"Yes." Alasdair shook Fredericks's hand. As a wife of an ambitious man, Lavender would be perfect. The lady could twist men of Fredericks's ilk around her little finger. When Alasdair married her, he need no longer worry that Starling's appalling treatment of her had lost him a valuable social contact. "Thanks, Fredericks. We'll enjoy it. I'll take this pest off your hands now. I'm sure she persuaded you into this."

"I consider it an honor to be persuaded by a lady of such beauty. She tells me she won't be returning to Melbourne."

"No." Alasdair's eyes searched Lavender's suddenly innocent expression. "I'll find accommodation for her when Paul and Mary leave."

"A hotel?"

"I can't impose on Starling and Dare for the rest of my life." Lavender heaved a sigh. "I'll look around for a nice little house of my own during the next few weeks."

"Nonsense," Fredericks said. "I have a vacant house in... If it comes to that, Seymour has a..." Clearing his throat, he glanced at Alasdair, who quickly evaded the other man's eyes. "My house in North Adelaide is ready for occupancy right now. It's furnished, Lavender, and I insist that you use it."

Lavender, lips pressed together, stared at Alasdair, too.

"We'll discuss this at a more appropriate time, Fredericks." He nodded formally at the other man, then he indicated the awaiting carriage to Lavender. Silence lingered on the way home.

He should have offered one of his city houses to Lavender. She had told him she had no money. But he didn't want her in the only one presently vacant. He'd earmarked that for Starling the moment Lavender had said she didn't mind her husband having a mistress. Starling couldn't live on his forty pounds forever. Surely being a rich man's mistress would be an acceptable position for a woman with few prospects.

He closed his eyes. He could only hope.

* * * *

The picnic day dawned bright and clear. The perfume of a thousand flowers scented the air, which throbbed with the humming of bees.

Alasdair toyed with the idea of staying in bed long enough to drape Starling across his body as he had with such success before. He'd never been so horny for so long in his life, but instead he stretched, rolled out

of bed, pulled on his trousers, collected a clean shirt, and went down to
the laundry to wash and shave.

"No. I won't, Freda," he heard Ellen say. "Every time she can, she
sneaks out of the house to meet him in the stables."

"Maybe she really is interested in plants."

"She's interested in what he's planting under her skirts. You and me
know that. We both know what they've been doing."

"He says she's a whore. Does it count if she's a whore?"

Ellen laughed bitterly. "I've a mind to ask Mr. Seymour. Then we'd see
who'd be smiling at who."

Anger welled inside Alasdair. With no names mentioned, he had a
very clear idea who "he" and "she" were. His damned whore imitation
wife and the randy young gardener.

Mentally his fingers tightened around the soft, white, defenseless
neck that too many times he'd wanted to touch with his tongue and
warm with his lips. He clenched his hands on the laundry trough until
the sinews ached.

Leave her to stew? He ground out a harsh, cynical laugh. No longer.
The next time she flashed her four-shilling glance at him, he would
give her satisfaction. A man as good-natured as Derry couldn't provide
what she needed.

* * * *

Starling dressed carefully, hoping she, like Lavender, could look
gently born and cared for now that she had better clothes.

The green gown, made from a light, soft fabric, fitted as well as a
bespoke outfit. The skirts looped at the back. Combined with her straw
hat, the outfit suited well enough for a picnic.

She misted her new perfume over her throat. Regretting her hopeful
smile, she shook her head. She shouldn't have wasted a precious drop
on trying to appeal, not when she would soon leave, luckily with
nothing to regret.

After one last adjustment to a curl behind her ear, she greased her
hands. She couldn't regret almost two weeks of pampering. With her
smooth hands and nails almost to the ends of her fingers, she could be
taken for a lady. Or, at least, not be taken for a menial worker. This was
another gift from Alasdair, and one she could use.

Now with promised money, confidence, and new clothes she
would manage taking on a business without needing to depend on
anyone for support.

Alasdair's smile surprised her when she arrived in the sitting room. Not for days had he relaxed his aloof attitude.

"You look nice today, Starling." Lavender shot a glowing smile at Alasdair.

"She does." He cast a possessive glance at the blonde's lovely face.

Starling began to shake. These two made her feel like a slug on a lettuce. "There's no sign of rain, I hope?" She walked to the window and moved the lacy covering aside. "Mr. Fredericks is turning into the carriageway now."

In the brougham, Lavender seated herself between Mary and Starling. The men sat in the forward seat with Mr. Fredericks, who tried to hide the fact that Lavender's concentration on Alasdair disappointed him. Starling wished she could give him what he wanted. She wished everyone in the world could have what he wanted because then she would, too.

For the picnic site, Mr. Fredericks had chosen Morialta Falls, sited at the end of a well-worn track into the bushland. The faint gushing sound of the creek over the rocky outcrop had the effect of building anticipation, and Starling enjoyed stepping through eucalypts so tall that she had to narrow her eyes and crick her neck to see the shady canopy at the top. The place looked like a green tent with shedding bark poles. Masses of delicate shrubs and flowers grew beneath the trees.

"South Australians are probably the only people in the world who can find entertainment in a filling creek bed," she said to Mary, who laughed.

Two black cockatoos flew screeching overhead as Princess Lavender directed the gentlemen to set up the blankets under a single spreading eucalypt some distance away from the water. Lavender waited for her minions to serve her, and they did. The men helped her get settled in the most comfortable spot. They carried baskets to where she pointed. They arranged their bodies to shield her from the threatening sun and the wispy breeze. Even Paul joined in the competition, albeit with a silly smile on his face. When Mary frowned at him, he widened his eyes with innocence.

As the minutes ticked into a half hour and then an hour, Starling's eyebrows began to lower. She'd been ordered to pass a glass to Lavender, fill the glass, hold the glass, shake the blanket while Lavender rearranged herself more prettily, stand, sit, move aside, and finally serve Lavender's food. Not only did Alasdair treat her this way, but Paul did, too.

Mr. Fredericks tried tempting Starling with delicacies, but before she tasted a single tiny cucumber sandwich, either Alasdair or Paul interrupted with another order. Mary seemed to be deaf, dumb, and blind. Not a word did she say while her husband made as great an ass of himself as did Alasdair. Mary seemed to be engulfed in indolence as she trailed a leaf in the grass and relaxed in the sunshine.

"Let me serve you some of this sliced meat," Mr. Fredericks said to Starling during a moment's respite.

She smiled at him and lifted a glass of cider to her lips.

"Have you tried the strawberry sponge, Lavender?" Alasdair asked. Lavender shook her head. "Starling, would you mind? The knife is by your right elbow. Could you cut a slice for Lavender?"

Starling set down her glass, cut of a wedge of cake, and passed the delicacy on a plate to Lavender, who by now sat so close to Alasdair that with the slightest relaxation, her cheek would rest on his shoulder. Alasdair sat legs straight out in front, the weight of his body taken back on his elbows. A heel kicked into the center of his chest would topple him onto his back.

Starling resumed her former position and took the plate Mr. Fredericks offered.

"Are there almonds in that cake?" Alasdair asked Lavender. Instead of answering, she broke off a scrap and put the cake into his mouth. Although Starling had picked up a fork, she couldn't swallow. Nothing would pass the lump of anger in her throat.

"This looks nice," she said to Mr. Fredericks. Determined, she collected a wafer-thin slice of corned beef on her fork. "I'm so hungry I could—"

"Could you cut me a piece of cake, too?" Alasdair glanced at her, then he glanced back at Lavender's cream-encrusted fingers, which she slowly surrounded with her mouth.

Starling placed her fork back on her plate. Carefully, she put her plate on the rug. Straight-shouldered, she leaned forward, cut a precise wedge, slid the cake onto a fresh plate, found a cake fork, and rose to her feet.

Three deliberately placed steps took her to Alasdair's side. Only her eyes moved as she stared down at him. He held out an imperious hand. She considered him, the perfection of his sculptured face, the smooth-shaven chiseled jaw, the wide chest covered with a gray waistcoat. Her eyes drifted from the waistband of his buckskins to his firmly muscled thighs, his crossed legs, and focused on his highly polished shoes. She stared at his aloof face again.

He raised one eyebrow. "Do I have to starve while you admire me?"

"You're a very handsome man." She bent down, upturned the plate, and slammed the cream-filled cake against the juncture between his legs.

He spun out an oath in a voice of repressed fury. The impropriety of her action and the sudden thinning of his mouth gave her no choice other than to run.

Unable to pick up her skirts and uncaring of her hat, she dashed toward the safety of the trees at the bottom of the rise.

Chapter 18

Alasdair raced through the trees, crunching over dry leaves and small twigs littered across the undergrowth. Despite having to duck the lower branches, he gained ground on Starling. He took his pace down to a lope when he spotted her panting behind a red gum with bole wide enough to make into a dining table for twelve. The scene about to be played had an inevitability that took his steps to a stroll and his breathing to deliberate. As he drew nearer, he could hear Starling's short, quick gasps. She had run quite a distance.

"I'm sorry," she said between breaths. "It was an accident. My hand slipped."

"It does that quite often. In bed at night...in the morning before I can escape you. You want me so badly that you can't think of anything else."

"I agree that you are an attractive man. Most of your employees think so, and I'm just as human as the rest. But I'm not available. Since you've never needed to pay for the services of a prostitute, why chase me?"

"Because I want you," he said through his teeth. "You have to give your trust and when you do, you'll be repaid tenfold. That's the only way you'll find the ultimate fulfillment. You won't while you look at fucking as a transaction. Then being laid is just a job, not an emotional experience."

"I don't want an emotional experience. I can't afford an emotional experience."

"You can't afford not to have one. When a woman slams a plate where you did, a man can be nothing but flattered. You could have rubbed the cake in my face, but you didn't. You went for my groin, which showed me where your every thought leads."

"You take the strangest actions as compliments." She tilted her chin.

"You've given me every reason for confidence. You don't resist when I kiss you. When I touch you, you melt. You like my hands on you. Just a nudge and you open your legs. Just a caress and you come. You're wild for me, and yet every time I try to take the final step, you empty your mind of everything but money."

She pushed from the tree. "Money's important. Without it, people sleep in the gutter, wash in puddles, and wear rags. You live in luxury. You have a hot bath whenever you like, and you wear a clean shirt every day. You couldn't possibly understand what it's like to be cold and dirty."

"Couldn't I?" His mouth twisted. "I'm sure you weren't cold and dirty in the home."

"Sometimes at night I was cold, but I managed to avoid being dirty. I didn't really know about dirt until I left. In the outside world, dirt is a way of life."

"You have to choose the life you want." He took two steps closer.

"I know. And I have."

"I don't like you going to Derry. You told me that you didn't want to earn your money like that," he said, taking one last step right into her.

"I've never taken money from Derry."

Her simple statement dropped him into a hole as deep as forever. For a moment, his jealousy stunned him. Then hurt took over and wound him into anger. "Swear to me you're lying," he said, his lips barely moving

Eyes averted, she shook her head. "I don't want Derry's money. You've promised me forty pounds, and that's all I'll need." She put a hand on his chest to push him away.

"So I've been paying for Derry's pleasure while foregoing my own." He focused on her hand, no longer dry and chapped, no longer red or with chewed nails. Her hand looked white and delicate, yet she held him so easily. "You've played me for a fool for the last time. I won't wait for your permission. I'll have you now." He put one hand on either side of her head on the tree trunk and pushed his body against hers, forcing her against the tree.

She jerked her head away but his mouth came down and kissed the side of her neck.

"Derry's had no pleasure from me." She angled her head away. Her shoulder bumped his chin. She stilled. "Alasdair, please believe me."

"You've been seen. The servants know, probably everyone's known from the start. Oh, no. They didn't tell me. They're too loyal. I overheard a conversation between Ellen and Freda. You're breaking Ellen's heart, but you don't care, do you? But why should you? None of us means a thing to you."

Frowning, lips pressed together, Starling stared at him. The fight went out of her and she sagged. "You're wrong. You're so wrong. I do care. I don't want anyone to be hurt, least of all you. What do you want me to say? What do you want me to admit to?"

He squeezed his eyes shut and his voice came out as a whispery plea. "You made Derry pay. You didn't give him freely anything you won't give me."

"I didn't. He paid, and he'll keep on paying. He surely will."

"I don't want you to go near him again. I want you for me and only me. Tell me! Tell me I'm different. Tell me that's why you keep me away. Because you're afraid that if we make love, you'll want to stay with me."

She lowered her head and his cheek brushed against her hair. "I don't want to care about you. I don't." She lifted her face, and he examined her expression. Her mouth twisted into a pleading smile. "I want to leave in two days with no regrets."

He let his hands drop from the tree trunk. For a moment she remained unmoving, then she slowly relaxed until her arms hung by her sides.

Although she seemed defeated, Alasdair had been. He couldn't imagine anything he wouldn't forgive her. His mouth sought hers. His arms went about her supple waist and gathered her to him. Somehow, with her lips, she could give what no other woman could—a feeling of oneness. He didn't care how many men she'd had in the past. Only her future mattered, her future with him. How lowering that as a prospective mistress, she would mean more to him than his wife.

His mouth touched hers. His body clamored and hers did nothing to ease the ache. She molded against him, lighting a desire that made him groan, while her arms circled around his neck. To be different from the other men she'd known in the past, he couldn't take her in quick lust. A momentary satiation wouldn't be worth the disillusion he would see in her eyes.

"I have to have you, Starling, I have to," he whispered, spreading his fingers across her back.

"You'll be married soon. You'll forget me soon enough. Oh, Alasdair, you don't understand 'no.' You never have. To you the word means 'later.'"

He laughed softly. "It does, with you. I have an agenda now, and I won't rest until I fill it." His lips brushed across hers again and again and finally settled with passion.

At no stage did she try to push him away or stop him. However, he didn't attempt further liberties, knowing that anything he started with her this time he would finish. He didn't have the insensitivity to make love to Starling and return to the woman he intended to marry as if nothing had happened. He doubted he could. Contentment would show

on his face, and Lavender would guess in an instant what he had done.
He would have liked his nether regions to display as much sense, but he
imagined he would subside during the walk back.

Not a man to frustrate himself any longer than he had to, eventually he
stopped kissing the lovely lips beneath his. Then he started again when
she seemed bereft, when her mouth looked lonely and unloved.

"We'll have to return to the others." He took a deep breath, setting her
away from him with reluctance. His eyes swept the full length of her,
appreciating her slim curves and the elegant way she wore her clothes.
"You're a mess." He smoothed his thumb across her lips, smiling when
he couldn't wipe away her recently kissed appearance. "Let me help
tidy you up." He picked a broken twig out of her hair and turned her
around to brush leaf litter from the hem of her skirt. "That's better. Now,
where's your hat?"

"I lost it somewhere. I'll have to find it."

"I'll buy you a hat for every day of the week."

She noticed a sticky glob of cream on the front of her skirt. "Do you
have a handkerchief? I'll have to get this off."

He had the same mark on his trousers from the cake with which she
had anointed him. Delving his hand deep into his pocket, he drew out a
clean white handkerchief as requested. "A bird in the bush deserves two
hands." He laughed softly as he rounded her bottom with one hand while
he scrubbed at her skirts with the other. He lifted his head and saw the
expression of yearning on her face. His mouth dried. "Don't look at me
like that," he said huskily. "You're making me shake."

She swallowed and shut her eyes. "I'm not immune," she murmured.

"I know you're not, love. You feel the way I do, but we'll do something
about it—later."

"No. We'll never do anything about it. I'd rather remember you
as...different."

"I will be. I'll give you pleasure."

"You won't be. You'll be taking the same thing every man wants."

"You can't expect a platonic friendship."

"I don't expect any friendship. I expect the money I earned by
pretending to be your wife *in name only*. It doesn't matter how I feel
about you, and it doesn't matter how you feel about me. There's nothing
between us, and I won't let there be anything between us. I have a choice,
and I'm choosing a new start in a new life. You don't enter into my plans.
Only your money does. It's final, Alasdair. A few moments ago we
kissed goodbye."

"Don't be ridiculous. We'll be sleeping together for another two days."

"Not if you plan to seduce me. I'll move into another bedroom if you don't give me your word right now that you won't touch me again."

"I won't give you my word."

Her hips twisted and somehow she moved out of his grip, which had grown tighter with every passing second. "Let me have that." She held out her hand for his handkerchief, which he passed to her. With quick and efficient strokes, she brushed the front of her skirt, cleaning off the traces of cream and cake. "I won't offer to do you," she said, returning the white linen square.

"You never have" he said, defeated. "That episode down by the river. It was a tease, wasn't it? A way to make me turn a blind eye to whatever you wanted to do?"

"No. For a while, I thought I'd do whatever you wanted, but I know now that I don't want any other woman's man. That's for the exotic birds of the world, not the starlings. I respect you for not making a promise you don't intend to keep, enough not to make any of this difficult for you. I'll move into another bedroom for the next two days." She walked away.

With her firm words, he lost his chance of making love to her and his hopes of keeping her. His brain deadened. He watched her, his shoulders stiff and his chest constricted. He pressed his palms together and brought the tips of his fingers to his lips. Every breath ached. Even the sky turned black.

He would never have her.

* * * *

Starling returned to the picnic party with her retrieved bonnet placed carefully and a neat bow tied under her chin. Paul and Mary smiled expectantly, Mr. Fredericks moved as if about to rise to his feet, and Lavender sniffed disdainfully, reaching out to stay him. For a moment, he stared at Lavender; then he, too, smiled at Starling.

Assuming she needed to apologize for her behavior, Starling hauled in a breath, not knowing where to begin. At that moment, Alasdair hove into view, striding toward the picnic party as if he'd been for a Sunday stroll. Lavender gleamed a glowing, knowing smile at Mr. Fredericks, although she couldn't know anything. She couldn't be sure that Alasdair had caught up with Starling.

"So there you are," Alasdair said to Starling.

Mr. Fredericks said, "Seymour, you're a lucky man." He refilled a glass passed to him by Lavender. Thunder rolled in the distance.

Alasdair raised his eyebrows politely.

"To have a wife like Starling. She's an intelligent woman, quiet and in control of herself."

Lavender laughed. "Though, if I might mention the cake..."

"She went to the source. Any other woman would have attacked you, my dear. You were fortunate she has a sense of fair play."

"You must think we're all mad," Mary said to Mr. Fredericks. "This argument has been brewing for days. Newlyweds tend to skirt the issue but we thought...well, none of us likes to see silent arguments that could be settled with a few words. Lavender, you've been such a sport. The way you tried to make Starling jealous was wonderful. I don't think Paul and I could have done half as well without you."

Lavender inclined her head.

"You're a good actress." Mr. Fredericks stared at Lavender. "You took me in for a while. I honestly thought you were trying to steal Mrs. Seymour's husband."

Starling blushed. "Rather than have you praise me for my appalling behavior, I must apologize."

"Accepted," Alasdair said. "My behavior was appalling, too."

Lavender brushed imaginary crumbs from her gown, glancing at Mr. Fredericks. "If you think she's so perfect, I can't imagine why you bother with plain old me."

"You're hardly plain or old. You're a very beautiful woman, my dear." Mr. Fredericks recorked a wine bottle and glanced at the sky. "It's getting late. I think we ought to leave before the weather breaks." The sheltering tree gave a shiver of restlessness. Fat raindrops began to fall.

Lavender wailed. "Oh, no. My gown. I left my shawl in the carriage."

"I think we will have to run," Mary said, standing and beginning to drop food into the baskets.

Aided by her prettiest pout, Lavender kneeled, wrapping the remains of the cold meat in greased paper. "I don't suppose anyone noticed the meats were drying out." She heaved an audible sigh as she placed the packaged meats into a basket. "Look at the mess in here. I suppose I'll have to tidy up or Hamilton's cook will have a word or two to say."

Starling widened her eyes, impressed by how swiftly Lavender could change from the spoiled princess to the martyred slave. She helped pack, and the picnic was ended in a flurry. Black clouds crashed together, and almost as soon as they had entered the brougham, heavy rain began to fall. She was glad of her new pelisse—a gift she could take when she left.

Lavender, wrapped into her shawl and with a carriage rug over her knees, extolled her own virtues to Alasdair during the trip home, numbering among them the effort she had expended on the picnic, which the others had neither noted nor appreciated.

"Not so," Paul said. "It was the most entertaining picnic I have ever attended."

Lavender used her blackened eyelashes to great effect. Immediately after dinner that night, she made her excuses and went up to her bedroom for what she described as "an early night." Alasdair retired to his study, and Starling beat Paul at a long and wearing game of billiards while Mary immersed herself in her embroidery.

Some two hours later, Starling left for the bedroom wing with Paul and Mary trailing behind. Alasdair joined them, his distant manner preventing light conversation. At his door, he gripped Starling about the waist and bade Paul and Mary a firm "'good night." He swirled Starling into the bedroom and closed the door.

"You don't need to manhandle me. I wouldn't have shamed you. I would have waited for them to retire before going to my own room."

"You don't need to go to your own room."

"Do I have your promise you won't touch me?"

When he deliberately turned his face away, she gathered up her nightgown, her burgundy dressing robe, and left.

She had chosen a small bedroom on the other side of the landing. Decorated predominantly in white, with a muslin curtain covering the window, the room had possibly been meant for a child, with a single bed, a set of drawers, and a small painted cupboard. The area filled her needs. Because she couldn't ask a servant to prepare the bed for her, she had smuggled up clean sheets from the hemming pile.

Once this sparse room would have been the culmination of her dreams. Now, the lack of luxury emphasized her fast rise in the world and her compulsory descent. A good preparation, in fact, for the life she would live after the next day, a life without Alasdair, paid for by the lies she had told these past two weeks. She sat on her bed, huddled over, hurting so badly that she could barely breathe.

Her lie today about Derry could be no worse than her evasions to Paul, Mary, and the servants. She didn't want Alasdair to learn the truth about Lavender. Once the careless beauty married the best and most honorable of men, she would never again want, need, or crave another man.

Starling was not meant for Alasdair—never could be, never would be. The dream had died, had never been real in the first place. Lying on her back, arms by her sides, she told herself she had lost nothing. Instead, she had earned enough money to start her own business. Any more would have been greedy. The brief moment in time she'd felt desired and beautiful would last her until the end of her days.

She curled herself into a tiny ball.

Chapter 19

Some time past dawn, Alasdair heard his bedroom door close. He opened his eyes.

"I don't want to give you any excuse not to pay me," Starling said in a cool voice. "Ellen will think I've been here all night."

He pulled his sheet to his nose, not deigning to answer. Not for the world would he tell her he'd missed her warmth, the tickle of her hair on his face, and her shy sweetness in the morning. In one more day he would have Lavender.

* * * *

"Starling!" Lavender held out a dish of melted cheese to Starling. "I asked for a Welsh rarebit for breakfast and the kitchen sent me this peppery concoction."

"Welsh rarebit?" Starling didn't know the dish. "I'll see if Mrs. Trelevan has something else."

"I asked for Welsh rarebit," Lavender said, tapping her foot. "Is it too much to expect?"

Starling didn't know, but bearing the plate she went into the kitchen, where Mrs. Trelevan was making stuffing for a haunch of beef. "Mrs. Frost would like Welsh rarebit. She says this one is too peppery," Starling said, putting the plate on the table.

Mrs. Trelevan looked vague. "Too peppery?"

"It's the dish I made for Madam," Freda said with a shrug. "I asked her if she wanted mustard, but she said she don't discuss cooking with servants. So, I made her a Welsh rarebit the way Mr. Seymour likes it."

Ellen, standing in the doorway and adjusting the frill on her cap, said in a despondent voice, "I've finished the bedrooms. Need any help in here?"

Freda smiled at her sister. "Madam just sent back the delicious breakfast I made for her."

"You shouldn'ta done nothing mean, Freda. We promised Mrs. Seymour we wouldn't." Ellen glanced at Starling.

"I obeyed orders. That's all I done." Freda frowned and crossed her arms.

"Make her a plain rarebit without mustard," Starling said. "I'll explain to her that you used your regular recipe."

Mrs. Trelevan said, "Begging your pardon, ma'am, but that woman is nothin' but trouble."

Mrs. Brighton came in from the garden with a basket of herbs. "I've just heard she's not going back to Melbourne with Mr. and Mrs. Elliot."

Ellen paled and put her face in her hands. Freda moved around the table and took her sister into her arms. "You said you didn't care what Derry done."

"I do." Ellen sniffled. "I love him. I'll never get him back if she doesn't go."

"You never tried to get him back," Mrs. Trelevan stated bluntly. "Don't reckon he would have looked at her if he'd had a promise from you. Seems to me you asked everythin' from him without ever giving nothin' of yourself."

"You're not suggesting that I should have bedded him without marriage?" Ellen asked in a stifled voice.

"No. I'm saying you never even got betrothed, though he asked you times without number. You kept testing him and testing him, but he passed the test the moment he met you, seems to me."

"He treated you like a queen before your hand healed," Mrs. Brighton added, with a wary glance at Starling. "He made you up posies of flowers despite the ragging from the stable boy. He told everyone he loved you. He waited for a year, Ellen, and not once did you ever consent to do more than walk out with him. I don't blame him for thinking he's free to do anything he likes."

Mrs. Trelevan nodded. "Until a man's betrothed, he's free. You have to face it, Ellen. You don't have no right to complain about anythin' he does."

"I thought you all supported me," Ellen said, mouth rebellious and eyes glistening.

Four pairs of eyes met.

"If you want him, you'll have to do something about it." Starling watched Freda pour a melted cheese concoction onto a freshly cooked slice of toast.

"I can't," Ellen mumbled. "He doesn't love me anymore."

Starling tapped her fingers on the table. "I think that you ought to hear that from his own lips."

Ellen stared at Starling; then, eyes downcast, she walked out into the garden.

Mrs. Brighton put a sprig of parsley on the cheese. "That needed to be said."

"I think she was always afraid he didn't really love her." Freda handed the plate to Starling. "She really thought losing her fingers made her deformed. I don't know how many times I told her that it never made no difference to him. When you love someone, you don't notice their faults."

With a smile of resignation, Starling took the dish and left. "You certainly don't notice," she muttered to herself, "if someone is beautiful."

* * * *

Alasdair saw Starling in the passage. "That's for Lavender, I presume. She told me the kitchen staff gave her bad food."

"Not on purpose," she said. "And not bad. Just a trifle heavy with the mustard. There's no need to reprimand them."

He turned to watch her enter the dining room where Lavender, not very patiently, awaited her breakfast.

Determined to take back control of his staff, he strode toward the kitchen, "I hope we've done the right thing," he heard Mrs. Brighton say. He grasped the handle of the door. "Madam went over to him again last night. I saw her hurrying across the lawn to the shed. There's no doubt she's—Mr. Seymour! Well. You did give me a fright. I didn't see you there."

* * * *

His mind repeating again and again the conversation he'd overheard, Alasdair retreated to the library and stayed there all day, messing with his papers until he'd confused his accounts too much to bother trying to make sense of them. Thereafter, he sat in his chair and stared out the window.

He'd made a basic mistake about Starling. No matter that he wanted her more than he'd wanted any other woman, she'd deceived him. For a while, he'd wavered between picking her up by the scruff of her neck and throwing her naked into the street or ripping off her clothes and ravishing her until she begged for mercy. Both gained him sexual satisfaction, and each would avenge the loss of his pride. He gave a sour laugh. Even now he could think of little more than having her, a gutter-bred woman who had laughed in his face—not openly, but by sneaking out to pleasure his gardener.

His head throbbed, fit to burst. The only way to gain the upper hand was to withhold her money. Because the servants knew about her behavior, that should be reason enough to refuse to pay her. Unfortunately, what the servants knew had no bearing on the case. He'd hired Starling to fool his sister, and she'd done the job so easily that Alasdair should have suspected from the start that he was dealing with a very clever woman.

All was not lost, however. He had achieved his aim with Lavender and could have a well-born wife with the right connections as soon as he wished. With this in mind, he remained scrupulously polite to Starling during dinner and after, when he accepted Lavender's challenge for a game of billiards.

The single game they played seemed to take longer than the creation of the world. By the time he finally escaped to the sitting room, the others had gone up to bed. He wished he'd been with them because he knew Paul and Mary wanted to leave early in the morning. Although he meant to tell Starling he knew the truth about her sluttish behavior, he didn't find her in her room. Noting the folded nightgown on the pillow and the lamp she had lit, he punched the doorframe with frustration. What a great nodcock he'd been and how blind. She'd only wanted this single bedroom so that she could be free to visit Derry whenever she chose.

With his jaw clenched hard enough to make his teeth ache, he walked over to the window, not expecting to see anything but the night shadows. A figure outside moved across the lawn in the direction of the stables. His chest tight, he strode into the hallway.

"Oh, there you are, Alasdair," Mary said, sounding relieved. "I've been knocking on your door for ages. I couldn't believe you'd be asleep yet. I wanted to speak to Starling. Do you know where she is?"

"I do," he replied grimly. He tried to push past Mary.

She smiled. "Relax, my dear. I don't want her for the whole night, but I have to say more than a quick goodbye to her. It might be six months before I see her again. I want to thank her for her hospitality and for being married to my favorite brother."

"No need."

"You men." She patted him on the cheek. "You don't have the slightest idea of the work that goes into running a house or entertaining guests as demanding as some of us have been. She's such a lovely woman, and I'm so proud of you for choosing her."

"You don't know a thing about her. Not a thing. She's fooled you from the start."

"Don't tell me you've had another fight? Really, Alasdair. You should—"

"I can't discuss this now. First I have to—oh, what does it matter?" He opened the door of his bedroom. "I can confront her anytime. Come in, Mary. It's time I confessed the whole truth to you, unpalatable as it is."

Before she could sit on the settee, he said, "She's a whore." He tightened his face, feeling the heat of his words sear his throat.

"I beg your pardon," Mary said stiffly. "No matter how cross with her you are, I won't allow you to—"

"I found her working in my shop, but she'd come there from the Star Inn. You don't know it, but the lowlife of Adelaide does. I wanted to use her to stop your matchmaking. I had no idea you'd have Lavender with you, no idea. From the start, my plan backfired. And now the little tart is out there rutting with the gardener behind the stables."

Mary's mouth opened and shut. Her eyes widened but not a word did she say about her brother's language. "Are you sure?" She seated herself. Her fingers pleated her skirt, but her face stayed turned toward Alasdair's.

He twisted his expression into a grimace. "I agreed to pay her to pretend to be my wife. No one could know more about her than I do after sharing a bed with her for two weeks."

Mary stood. "Was I supposed to find this amusing? I don't, you know. Perhaps your 'friend' fooled me and perhaps she hurt me, but you've done more than that. I don't think that I can forgive you, Alasdair. Paying a woman for this sort of service," she said, waving her hand at his bed, "makes me feel ill. No wonder she had so many disdainful things to say about men who use whores. I can't blame her for any of this, can I? It's you. Excuse me." With a hand over her eyes, she pushed past him.

"Mary," he began, but she made a sound of fury, which stopped him.

"Don't speak to me, please. Somehow my sense of humor has completely deserted me." Very carefully, she shut his bedroom door.

He gazed unseeingly at the window, neither reprimanded nor embarrassed. He could only picture Starling with Derry, lying under him with her legs around his hips, encouraging him by her soft whispers. He thumped his fist on the mantel, making one of his Meissen pieces leap. "Lying bitch," he said in a snarl to the porcelain goddess as he grabbed her by the waist and dashed her and her horn of plenty into the fireplace.

He swung on his heel, slammed out of his room, and strode outside to Derry's little room off the stables, certain he could force Starling to return with him and very certain that he could kill her if she refused. On this last night, when she opened her legs, *he* would be between them, he or no one. As he passed Derry's small window, he glanced in...and stood, transfixed.

Tableau-like, two figures faced each other by Derry's cot, Derry tall and implacable with his arms crossed and a female with a beseeching hand on his forearm. Alasdair couldn't mistake either the blond hair or the lilac wrap. Although she had her back turned, he knew he saw Lavender.

Now in the appalling position of eavesdropper rather than righteous employer, he froze. "But you can't prefer her to me," Lavender said, sounding not only shocked but also annoyed.

Alasdair's breathing halted. Any man would rather have Starling than Lavender, given an equal position in the world. His mind tangled and he flattened himself against the wall, determined to hear every word.

"Told you a hundred times I love her. Can't imagine why you think I'd lie. Decided last night that I don't want to be like you, and got my reward today. Ellen came to me and told me she loved me. She told me she'd marry me. I didn't have to make one promise neither, but I wouldn't be unfaithful, not now."

"Don't be stupid. She won't know."

"Reckon you're sick. The only thing that gives you pleasure is makin' people do what they don't want to do. You don't even like ruttin'. Don't know why you do it when you get no pleasure out of it. Mebbe one day you'll fall in love and—"

"You great uncultured lout," Lavender said in a tone just below a shriek. "You are nothing to me. I love Alasdair, and I have since the moment I met him. You don't measure up to him in any way, and I can tell you now that tool of yours doesn't compare with his."

Suddenly the door was wrenched open. Caught, Alasdair pushed away from the wall. He cleared his throat and glanced into Lavender's wide, frightened eyes. He drew a deep breath. "Perhaps you would like my escort back to the house?" he said in a voice of absolute calm.

She held his gaze for a moment. "Derry is arranging some camellia cuttings for me." Suddenly her eyes filled with tears, and she covered her face with both palms. "You heard, didn't you?"

"Nothing unflattering." Alasdair gathered her into his arms. "Shh. None of this matters." Not only could Alasdair hear how ridiculous his soothing was following the scene he had overheard, but he also could feel a helpless smile splitting his face.

Starling had not betrayed him.

"It does, it does." Lavender sobbed onto his neck.

Derry appeared in the doorway. When he said nothing, Alasdair nodded his head in greeting. "Good evening. I believe that congratulations are in order. I don't want to lose Ellen, but I think she'll be happy with you."

He grinned and patted Lavender's back, unable to credit that the woman he'd craved for the past six years clung to him while he could only think about Starling, a determined, loyal wretch who had now been vindicated.

Derry stared open-mouthed.

Relief making his insides shake, Alasdair steered Lavender in the direction of his house. Starling had told the truth.

While Lavender sniffed forlornly, he patted her back. "You'll grow ugly, my dear, if you don't stop this."

"I slept with Derry." She stood, dabbing beneath her pale blue, tear-drenched eyes.

Her beauty could no longer melt him, not now that he could admit she lacked humor and wit. "There, there," he said, adjusting her shawl to cover her shoulders.

"I wanted you, but since I couldn't have you, I had him, and it's all such a hollow sham."

With a thump, reality hit him. His marriage was a hollow sham. Starling was not now, and never could be, his priority. He nodded, knowing his needless game had caused this transgression of Lavender's. "I understand. We all need love of some sort."

"Six years ago you ruined me. You showed me the pleasures of the flesh, and now I can't manage without. Until I met you I was an innocent."

"But I wanted to marry you. You refused to have me then."

"Not I. I wanted you. I begged my father to let me marry you, but he wanted Richard's money."

"If you'd waited just a year, I would have had money enough to impress your father."

"Papa wouldn't let me wait for you." She clung to him. "I love you. Does that mean nothing?"

"Of course not."

"I know I made dreadful choices, but what could I do? You're not available, and if I can't have you, I don't have anything. I know you'll never forgive me for this." She glanced up at him, staring into his eyes until he dropped his gaze.

His damnable deception had caused Lavender's misbehavior. If, on the first day she had arrived, he had said that Starling was an actress and revealed why he had hired her, none of this would have happened. Lavender wouldn't have gone to Derry, and he wouldn't be standing here relieved she, rather than Starling, had.

He had to accept his punishment. "I promised I'd take care of you." Heaving a sigh, he set her back on the path to the house. "I meant it."

He walked her to the door of her room, a painful smile on his lips. His lifetime goal, marriage with Lavender, was but a step away. Even a better man that he would see this empty victory as well deserved.

Chapter 20

Having relegated herself to the position of paid employee rather than mock wife, Starling knocked carefully on Alasdair's bedroom door. Before she could lose her courage, she entered.

Alasdair sat, elbows on his knees, staring at the empty fire grate. Tall, strong, handsome, and totally expressionless, he rose to his feet. His eyebrows lifted.

She cleared the lump in her throat with a faked cough. "Early tomorrow," she said in a husky voice, "as soon as we've waved goodbye to Paul and Mary, I will leave. You'll return to work straight after, I imagine, and so I thought it might be better if you paid me tonight, rather than be held up in the morning."

Without a word, he went to the desk and took out a wallet of money. His face pallid, he counted out forty pounds and put them in a small cloth bag. "Thank you," he said, handing the bag to her, his jaw tight. "You gave me more than I asked for. You earned every penny of this."

Starling smiled brightly and turned to leave.

His voice lowered. "Where will you go?"

"I'm not sure."

"That money won't last you forever." He heaved a huge breath. "You'll have to find another job."

"Yes, I plan to."

"As I recall, you have no reference. I'll write one for you, if you'll wait for a few minutes."

Finding it impossible to hold her pasted smile any longer, she inclined her head. "Thank you."

He settled at the desk, taking out paper, a pen, and a screw-top bottle of ink. She moved over to stand behind his shoulder, watching as he headed the paper with his address and the date, her heartbeat almost audible. Being so close to him without being able to touch him...having to leave him to Lavender... She clenched her hands together.

He wrote, in beautifully formed copperplate:

To whom it may concern,

During the time Miss Smith was in my employ, she proved herself to be loyal and trustworthy. I would recommend her for any position requiring honesty, efficiency, and initiative. She takes with her when she leaves my very best wishes for her future.

Alasdair Seymour, Seymour Emporiums.

He waved the letter to dry the ink and when satisfied, swung around in his chair and passed the paper to her. "I hope it helps."

Her lips stretched and she blinked hard. "Efficiency?"

"First out of bed in the morning," he said in a sardonic voice.

"Initiative?"

"Repelling my advances."

"I won't ask about honesty." Her voice cracked.

"Free character readings." His smile flickered and died. "Most of them completely accurate. Well, now, I suppose—"

Wanting to halt any further speech, or unable to resist the urge to touch him one last time, she reached out and traced the outline of his thick hair. Time stood still as the silky edge of one curl brushed her forefinger. Her heart expanded and her emotions tangled, and she saw an expression of stark need on his handsome face. With a sound of inevitability, he lifted his hands to her waist. She dropped her mouth to his. The moment their lips met, she knew she'd kissed him with love. Only on this final night in his house could she give herself, when she would never see him again.

He settled her onto his knee and encircled his arms right around her, pressing his shaven cheek against hers. In the time they'd been together, she'd learned he appreciated any caress. With a need to give more than she took, she put her palm on his other cheek. His hand flattened on the center of her back, holding her even closer to him. His beating heart thudded against her. She moved her hands to the fabric covering his solid chest, to his broad shoulders, to the hard biceps that flexed as she helped him slide off his jacket.

In the giving, she experienced the receiving, the way his hand spanned from her rib cage to her breast, which he cupped and stroked with his thumb. She arched, pressing closer.

The soft touch of his lips heightened her fractured breathing. He took his hand from her breast, and with no change in the pressure of his mouth, he unbuttoned her gown. As he'd done so many times, he slid the material over her shoulders. He lifted down her chemise as well, baring her breasts completely. He made a sound like a shattered groan.

Shaky pleasure filled her. She trembled clumsily over his buttons in an attempt to remove his shirt. While she worked there, he ripped off his cravat. His wonderful mouth stayed on hers until, finally, his bare flesh heated her. His urgency sped her heart into pounding excitement. Her pulse thudded while his palms on her back arched her into him. One of her hands clutched his shoulder, and the other splayed across his broad chest.

His muscles bunched under her fingers. He stood, sliding her from his lap, ripping the tie on her underdrawers. Her garments dropped to the floor, leaving her in stockings and shoes. His hand rounded her buttocks and, half urging, half carrying, he took her to the bed. Only then did his lips leave hers. He leaned over, flipping the covers to the end of the bed. She found herself sitting while he peeled off her stockings and shoes.

For the first time, her nakedness embarrassed her, but only until he gazed at her with stark, shining desire. She blushed, not ever imagining she would see him spellbound by the sight of *her*. His face could have been carved from marble, and his eyes heated by the blacksmith's forge. His intensity stopped her breath.

He kicked off his shoes, unbuttoned his flap, and took his trousers and socks off so quickly that she could almost have believed that he hadn't worn them. Except she did, because she saw something then that she hadn't seen before: his naked, full arousal.

Her mouth dried. She'd touched him in that state, but she hadn't looked. Although she couldn't back out at this late stage, the sight of his huge pecker tempted her to do so. She would surely be ripped apart.

"You *have* done this before?" she asked nervously.

He gave a spurt of husky laughter. Before she could take another breath, he landed on the bed beside her and lifted her on top of him. "I'm nervous enough to *think* this is a first time." He cupped her face and brought her mouth down on his.

His beautiful mouth, his deep kisses, and the gentle caresses of his hands stilled her fears. The warmth of his nakedness along the full length of her body, the faint scent of his shaving soap, and his erratic breathing were only parts of the full glory of him. A slight movement of his hips put his hardened flesh between her legs. The slide thrilled her. Thudding with excitement, she widened her legs around him, pressing her inner thighs against his hips.

He angled his mouth and, firmly holding her bottom, he rolled her onto his side of the bed and lifted to his elbows to either side of her head. She felt protected. When he smiled at her, she ached with love. His buttocks clenched and he thrust a little way inside her. Her face tightened with discomfort, but he withdrew and moved a hand down to touch where their wet flesh met. He closed his eyes as he enticed his arousal against her. Tingling with anticipation and pounding with a kind of fear, she spread her hands over the small of his back.

He took this for encouragement, and perhaps she meant her touch for encouragement. Without further ado, and with an expression she couldn't read, he slid into her and again withdrew. Tensing, he thrust again, harder. Instead of again spurning the tight fit, he tensed his buttocks and gave one last forceful and deliberate thrust.

In a reflex action of pain, her knees slapped against his hips. He seemed to slump on top of her. His breathing sounded forced. In a tone nothing like his normal voice, he said, "I've made an irretrievable mistake."

Her eyes filled with hot tears. She turned her head to one side. Her mind raced over her inadequacy. Not for a moment had she imagined that she would not have a natural aptitude for making love. To be rejected at this stage seemed to be the ultimate humiliation. Her throat closed over.

He lifted again and searched her expression. "I've hurt you," he said softly. "I'm sorry. I didn't know."

"Don't worry," she answered in a strangely normal voice. "I'll go now."

"I can't let you go. Starling, I can't let you go, not after I've done this. I've given you the pain but none of the pleasure."

"It doesn't matter." She wound her hands into fists.

"You'll never forgive me. As it is, *I'll* never forgive me. Let me try."

"I want to go."

He drew a deep breath, stared her straight in the eye, and said, "No." Very carefully, he moved inside her, at first abrasively. With a suddenness she hadn't expected, his gliding soothed and then became stimulating.

"Ah, love, that's better, isn't it?"

"Yes," she whispered, lifting her calves over the back of his thighs.

He went deeper and harder inside her. She judged his enjoyment by the expression on his face until he made a sound like "Ahh" and jerked out of her.

She gasped. "Is that all?"

"I got a little ahead of myself. I promised you pleasure and instead I got carried away with my own." His head dipped to her breast and he began suckling.

She would have liked to tell him she'd enjoyed the other just as well, but she didn't want to hurt his feelings. Within seconds she couldn't have said those words with any truth. Not only did he tease at both breasts with equal enjoyment, but he also built in her a desire for something she couldn't find. The sensation tingling through her nipples and tightening her abdomen felt like tickles compared to the gasping pleasure he gave her when he used his marvelous fingers between her legs.

At one stage, he put his mouth there, too, and teased her with his tongue, but fortunately, he didn't continue that past her writhing attempt to stop breathing. She thought he spoke occasionally, but she couldn't hear him over the rushing of her blood and her confused, anxious pleading. Suddenly, the huge build-up throughout her body ended. The urgency disappeared. She felt completed, languorous, and sated, and she had no idea why. Trumpets hadn't blasted and the heavenly choir of angels had closed their mouths. Puzzled, she stared at Alasdair.

"It'll be better next time, my love," he said with an odd tone in his voice. "It gets quicker and easier with experience."

He entered her again with slow enjoyment. She'd forgotten her worry about his size because they seemed to have been made for each other. And she forgot her feelings of languor and satiation. Both disappeared with his lovemaking, and she could see that making love was a tender cooperation on both sides, using words and touches that no one else could share. Had Alasdair said he loved her while he glided inside her, she would have believed him. However, he didn't lie to her. Leaving him would be difficult enough without having false promises to cling to.

She had a "next time," probably what he called a climax, but she wished she hadn't when she let herself go in a very embarrassing way. However, he seemed pleased, and because he'd made her beg with his fingers again, she imagined she'd done nothing out of the ordinary. Soon after that, he lifted her buttocks in his hands and plunged into her with a desperation he hadn't used before. When he groaned and stilled, she knew she had given him the same pleasure he had given her.

He lay on her and stroked her hair for a very long time. In this aftermath, she had to restrain her urge to cry for Meg who had never had this. Had she, she could never have said belittling things about men. Starling couldn't imagine anything in the world as beautiful as coupling with the man she loved and then lying peacefully in his arms while he said nothing but expressed everything with the sleepy contentment of his hands. Eventually, he turned down the lamp and pulled up the bed covers, but he continued to hold her, resting his chin on her hair.

Starling breathed evenly, glad she had given herself this reward after two weeks of self-denial. She might have to leave Alasdair, but at least she'd loved him first.

Sometime after dawn, she awoke. Alasdair still held her. His thumb slowly and gently caressed the nape of her neck. She smiled with happiness, leaving her fingers on the curve of his biceps muscle.

"You're awake?" His voice contained no sound of sleepiness.

"Mm." She eased her position, letting her breasts rest comfortably against his chest.

"We didn't settle anything last night. I can't let you leave me. You're mine now, and you've never belonged to anyone but me. I like that thought. We had a conversation before about the difference between comfort and luxury. I can promise you luxury, love, and I want to give you luxury. You'll accept me, won't you?"

Stunned, she could do no more than cling to the big, safe body beside hers. A proposal of marriage was truly a dream ending for a perfect night of love. Her voice cracked as she asked, "You want to keep me?"

He pressed his lips against her forehead. "I can't lose you."

Arching into the only man she would ever love, she kissed his shoulder as he eased his hardened arousal deeply inside her. Now she'd heard his proposal, she abandoned herself to the full pleasure of coupling, with no thought of sin and no sense of anguish at having to leave him. Loving him more than she had thought she could love anyone, she melted into his every gliding stroke, realizing that for her, he was the perfect husband.

She could marry him and still go ahead with her plan. He approved of woman in the workplace, and he had no objection to strays. Her money would be his, but he wouldn't begrudge a penny to a group of unfortunates. No other man would understand and support her as he would, as he did right then when he brought her to another shattering climax with his fingers before he spilled his seed. "I don't want you ever to leave me." His tender words stirred in her hair.

Her hands caressed the smooth skin of his back.

"We'll have to think about preventing babies."

Why prevent babies? Would a married couple want to prevent babies? Realization dawned. She took her hands from him and dropped them on the bed. Her head tilted back. She hadn't understood. He had offered her *not* the security of his name, but the luxury of his body in a physical relationship. "Keep" as in being his mistress.

"Have you told Lavender about me?" she asked, trying to cool her face with her frozen hands.

"I had nothing to tell until last night."

"I mean that you hired me? That you're free."

"I made a commitment to her. I can't go back on my word. She's not like you. She's weak, and she needs someone to care for her. She is my responsibility because long ago I took..." He stopped. Almost absently, one of his fingers combed her hair behind her ear. "You were a virgin. She... Perhaps she isn't my responsibility. I need to think." His hand dropped from her hair and he sat up, palms behind his head, massaging his neck with his thumbs.

She rolled out of bed, numb, cold, and smiling politely. "No need to say more. I enjoyed my first experience. And you, you gave me a reference. What more could I want?"

"You couldn't want more because I gave you a reference?"

"A reference is more important to me than anything else."

Smiling faintly, he stared at her. "You can't be that unemotional."

"I'm a realist. Surely you've seen that? You don't owe me anything. You kept your promise to give me pleasure. You certainly gave me pleasure," she said, searching for her clothes while he stepped out of bed and into his trousers and dressing robe.

He turned a worried face to her. "We need to talk, but we don't have time now. I have to see Paul and Mary off, and then I want to talk to Lavender. After that, you and I will settle everything." With that he left the room.

She stepped into her chemise, her underdrawers, and her petticoat. She pulled her gown over her head, her heart shrinking. An anguished sob burst out of her throat, a torrent she needed to empty before she could face the world again. She could no more be the mistress of the man she loved than she could earn her money by immorality. Her place had been preordained years ago, when she realized she could help others in the same position as she.

She had no right to think she could die easier than leave a man whose smiles made her sing inside, whose laughter made her join in, whose interests she shared, whose humor she enjoyed, and whose body she craved.

Her shoulders shaking and breathing in wet gasps, she stepped into her shoes, her cheeks hot. One icy hand, and then two, wiped her face. She cooled her cheeks, staring in the mirror, gulping until she finally breathed evenly. Her mind unclear, and seeing her swollen eyes, her pale face, and the tangled mess of her hair, she took her brush from the set he had bought for her and began to tidy herself. When her face looked comparatively normal, her hair was tidy, and she had dressed neatly, she made her way along the passage, meaning to say farewell to Mary and Paul.

Ellen came out of their room.

"Is Mrs. Elliot in there or downstairs?" Starling asked, her voice coming from a completely lifeless chest.

Ellen nodded. "In here. Mr. Elliot is seeing to their luggage downstairs."

Starling knocked on the door and entered. "I came to say goodbye," she said to Mary's back.

Mary turned. "Oh. Goodbye. It was an interesting experience to meet you." She stared at Starling with raised eyebrows and an expression of cynical indifference on her face, reminding Starling of Alasdair when she'd first met him.

Starling insides dropped.

"Alasdair explained everything," Mary said, her eyes hooded. She dropped her brush and comb into her traveling case. "I liked you very much. I certainly believed and trusted you. You fooled me completely, and that hurts. You can stop acting now. I know who and what you are. You've been sleeping with my brother for money and I'm afraid I just don't associate with your type of woman."

Starling's face turned to marble. She'd not expected such a base betrayal from Alasdair. To be described as nothing more than a whore after their night of lovemaking seemed so needlessly cruel that for some moments she could only stand despairing and alone.

With no dignity whatsoever, she turned and ran.

* * * *

Alasdair sat in his library for fifteen minutes, trying to clear the tangle that was his mind. Even now, he couldn't believe what a fool he had been. He had continually misheard Starling's words and continually misread her motives while at the same time he treated Lavender with a respect she hadn't ever earned. With his head screwed back on the right way, he returned upstairs and knocked on Lavender's door. When she didn't answer, he entered.

For some moments he watched her sleeping, noting her perfect bone structure and her splendid coloring; then he sat on her bed. Her eyes opened. Cold blue couldn't measure up to warm brown.

"What's the time?" She sat up, automatically primping her hair with a gesture than showed she cared more about how she looked than why he would be in her bedroom before seven in the morning.

"Do you love me?"

She drew her delicate eyebrows together. "Of course. I've always loved you."

"You let me think that I had taken your virginity all those years ago. Those sorts of lies seem more manipulative than loving."

"If you've been talking to Derry—"

"He knows more than I do, does he? Tell me the truth, Lavender. Don't I deserve it?"

She turned her face away. "Men never want the truth," she said in a sulky voice. "They like to believe their own fantasies."

"I haven't passed judgment on anything you've done, and I still want to be your friend, but if you won't take responsibility for your actions, I won't feel obliged to help you."

"What do you mean 'help me'?"

He drew a breath. "Help you start a new life in Adelaide."

"You said you'd take care of me." Her mouth thinned.

"The best way to take care of you is to help you take care of yourself."

"You're trying to punish me because you caught me with Derry."

He shook his head. "Did I act as if I cared?"

"Starling must be an exceptional bed partner," she said, watching his face.

"She's exactly the sort of wife I need." Having at last admitted that, he focused on Starling's qualities, uncolored now by thoughts of the profession she'd never pursued. Until that moment, he'd seen her only through lustful eyes. Until last night, he hadn't realized how much he loved her. Now he knew, he could admit to her strength of character, independence, and quiet perception, attributes Lavender did not possess.

Lavender's mouth drooped. Her eyes filled with tears. "What you can see in a woman who can't spell, bites her nails, dresses like a schoolteacher, and trains the servants to—"

"She's soft and warm, and she's incapable of hurting anyone. The servants act out of loyalty to her. She's inspired that same loyalty in me. I wish you could see her the way I do."

"No one's ever said I'm warm and soft." Two perfect tears overflowed from Lavender's eyes. "They stare at me because I'm beautiful, and they take me to bed as a prize, but they go back to their warm and soft women. You're the same. You don't care for me. If you'd known I wasn't a virgin when we first met, you would have used me and left me all the sooner."

"I probably always knew. As you said, men like their own fantasies. We both made a mistake, but I think our ages excused us. You can make a new start as I did."

Lavender blotted her eyes. Somehow she stopped her tears while she considered him. "I don't understand love. Men have always loved me more than I love them. I've been wondering if perhaps Hamilton... What's so amusing?" she said accusingly.

He laughed. "I never realized how truly practical you are. And tough, much tougher than I thought. You'll manage very well without too much of my help." He patted her hand, relieved to know that she loved him no more than he loved her, and he left to bid farewell to Mary.

As he walked through the doorway, he saw Ellen with her cleaning bucket and rags.

"You left Mrs. Frost's door open." She made a line of her lips. "No one needs to tell Mrs. Seymour that you've been in Mrs. Frost's bedroom because she would have heard you both. You'll be luckier than you deserve if she didn't hear you carrying on."

"I wasn't carrying on," Alasdair said indignantly. "I was saying goodbye."

"Too bad you couldn't say goodbye to your sister. She's gone." With a hard smile, Ellen stalked into the Elliot's room to begin cleaning.

Alasdair stood, fists on his hips, then he shrugged. He could explain the situation to his sister by letter. Starling wouldn't take his behavior amiss. He'd told her he meant to speak with Lavender. He strolled back to his own room, but Starling was nowhere to be seen. Her gold wedding ring sat on the tallboy. For a moment, he stood, rubbing the back of his neck. Then he swore aloud. If she'd been near Lavender's room, she would have seen Mary. If she had... He had told Mary last night that Starling was a whore.

His head thudding, he ripped open the chest where Starling's gowns were stored. Nothing other than the blue evening gown remained, her wedding present from Mary. She had taken her dressing set, the holdall and every last piece of brown paper wrapping, all of which she had earned, more than earned. Thinking she might have moved these articles to the spare room she had used for a few nights, he checked there, too. Nothing; not a hair. Apparently, she'd simply had enough of his inability to express a sane thought.

Trying not to look frantic, he searched the house and the grounds and realized that during the two weeks he had known her, he had discovered not a thing about her. He didn't know her friends, her interests, where she might go, or what she planned to do with the money.

Finally, he went back to his bedroom and sat on his bed, staring at the dent in the pillow where her head had rested. He raised his gaze to the restless gray sky outside, his chest empty.

With her, she had taken one last, clearly useless article. His aching heart.

Chapter 21

After pondering for some thirty minutes in his library, head in his palms, Alasdair rose to his feet and ordered his carriage. He scarcely noticed the sway of his journey to the emporium, and he barely remembered calling Mr. Porter, the manager of the fabric department, into his office. However, he heard the small man with dainty white hands say he wished Miss Smith hadn't walked out two weeks ago. Customers had returned, wanting her advice.

The man hadn't realized the unassuming woman would be so determinedly remembered. He only recalled her as quick and neat, and until she'd gone, he hadn't thought he might miss her. "Well, not her, because I barely spoke to her, but she worked harder than her replacement does. She never thought about walking past an untidy roll without fixing it."

Alasdair found the same when he spoke to each of the other nine shopgirls who had known her in the boardinghouse. She'd been quiet, self-contained, neat, and polite, and, without being superior, she was thought of as a lady.

"She talked like a toff," one of them said. "And she made her bed real neat."

Assuming that before Starling had taken employment at the Star Inn she had lived close by, he visited the nearest of the city foundling homes. Few people moved too far out of their area. When he discovered where Starling had spent her younger days, he would find a clue, he hoped, as to where she would hide.

At the third home he tried, the heavy-browed, arthritic nun in charge, Mother Sarah, told him Smith was a common name and, in fact, any of the orphans with no known parentage were deemed Smiths. And yes, they'd had a Starling.

"A good girl, in the main. Good with the younger ones. I recommended her as a nursery maid some months ago, when she left."

A sticklike nun, Sister Berenice, introduced as a teacher, said in rather an apologetic voice, "She could have been a teacher, but the orphanage has a reputation for training servants."

Mother Sarah's mouth thinned, and she leaned heavily on her walking stick. "That's how we get our sponsorship. If we let these girls, whose parents could have come from the gutter, rise above themselves, we would be overreaching our grasp."

Sister Berenice nodded. Her mild eyes gleamed. "The class system makes servants of us all. Starling was an unusual lass, perhaps what you might call a blue stocking. She soaked up information. Unfortunately, she thought people could rise above themselves if they chose. Perhaps you found the same at your emporium?"

Alasdair had represented himself as Miss Smith's former employer who had mistakenly dismissed her. "Not at all. I'm anxious to find her so that I can promote her," he said, staring at the sparse furnishings in the place, unpadded bench seats, bare wooden floors, and uncurtained windows; it was a cold area containing no creature comforts. He would have been surprised to see a fireplace other than in Mother Sarah's rooms. "I found she was everything I needed." True, if not too true. "Could you let me know if she contacts you?" He left a sizeable donation.

Failing a trail to follow there, he drove to the Star Inn, a seedy, whitewashed building smelling of damp and hops two streets away from his emporium. The slack-faced owner pushed his thumbs into his waistcoat pockets and patted his overstretched belly with his fingers when he heard the name Starling Smith. "I took over here a couple of weeks ago. Hey, you," he called to one of the whores propping an elbow on the bar. "Do you know a female named Starling?"

"That would be the girl what done the laundry," said a towheaded creature with a missing front tooth. Alasdair had looked over this one when he'd wanted to hire his fake wife.

"Pretty little thing," said the other, whom he also recognized by the sight of her extensive cleavage. She scratched her armpit, and the jelly of her bosom wobbled. "She only stayed a few weeks, but she and Meg was real thick."

"Where could I find Meg?"

"Dunno." The female smirked. "She walked out just like that yesterday."

Alasdair didn't prolong the conversation. The smell in the inn curled his nose. He didn't want to imagine Starling in the low, dirty dive. His investigations had led nowhere. Perhaps he would have to face up to the fact that unless she wanted to be found, she wouldn't be. He fingered the gold wedding ring he kept in his pocket, the ring she had left in his bedroom, the ring he'd bought for her. Until he had offered the circlet to her again in a proposal of marriage, he would continue his search.

His servants, initially censorious because they assumed Starling had left because of his "carrying on" with Lavender, relented. Although he didn't ask, he discovered how well Starling had run his house and how often she smoothed over the problems Lavender caused. He didn't ask because he didn't want to know how blinded he had been by Lavender's face, how stupid he had been to assume that beauty had any relationship to worth, and how deaf he had been to Starling's needs.

In the meantime, he employed a man to search Adelaide for Starling Smith, who had disappeared without a trace. Thus far, two leads that caused great excitement among the servants proved to be false.

During the following two months, he saw the bottom of a bottle too often, and he followed women in the streets, thinking he had seen the woman he couldn't forget. After more than one gazing at him and reacting, not with the interested smile he was accustomed to but with alarm, he assessed himself. He had become a dead bore.

And so he stopped finding his life in a bottle. A woman as spotless as Starling wouldn't marry a sot and didn't deserve one. She deserved a husband who put an effort into his business and who scrupulously earned his money, as she had earned hers. When he found her, he would give her the best of himself, not the worst.

After facing up to his faults, he corresponded with Mary, telling her the full truth about Starling, that she had wanted him to reveal their deception and had once begun, only to be stopped by him. He told Mary he stopped Starling because he didn't want her to leave and he admitted his despair after he'd lost her.

His sister not only forgave him but also expressed her sympathy. She and Paul planned to make their next visit in August, but before they arrived, he wanted to see his Kapunda emporium. The new manager there had suggested a few changes about which Alasdair didn't quite approve.

In July, he left to attend to his newest acquisition.

* * * *

The wearisome and dusty train journey to the mining town took a day. Alasdair had seen no need to warn anyone of his arrival and consequently took the offer of a trap ride to the Clare Castle, a smallish hotel built from the locally gathered stone. He accepted a back room with a plank ceiling, furnished with a bed, a washstand, and two hooks. The windows measured a hand span but overlooked miles of rolling green hills on one side and red-dust diggings on the other. The mining boom was evident from the smokestacks and the dust-laden air.

After a hot bath and a good meal in the noisy taproom, he dropped onto his bed and slept like a drover's dog until morning. The day dawned slowly with white clouds floating in the early sky. Dressed in dark trousers and a high-crowned hat, he strode down the rutted, pit-holed street, nodding to the early morning shoppers. He would have been less conspicuous in thick trousers and a hardwearing shirt.

His emporium dominated the main street, taking up two titles. Although also built from the local stone, large front windows had been fitted, and his surname had been painted on a plaque along the top. A quick stroll through the various areas to the office at the back found him the shop's manager.

John Brand, a man in his early thirties with lank, fair hair and a pleasant face, rose to his feet. He bowed, but Alasdair offered his hand as he reintroduced himself to the slow-speaking man.

"You'll want to see the accounts," Brand said, dragging books from the shelves.

"I want to see how much money we're losing." Alasdair gazed out of the window, watching men unloading terracotta pots from a cart. One dray, pulled by four horses, held rough wooden tables and chairs, shelves, planks, and boxes marked as fragile.

"As to that, none. We're in profit."

Alasdair quickly perused the pages. "Ah, but you told me we're not making money in the women's department. I want to find out why."

Brand stared at his feet, his cheeks pinking painfully. His shoes shone; his trousers, although certainly not made of a superfine weave, were neat; and he wore a patterned green and gold waistcoat. His dark cravat was neatly tied. He looked somewhat smarter than when Alasdair had hired him. Then, he had dressed like a tradesman. Now he dressed for his position as a shop manager. "We're trying to sell quality gowns for high prices." He raised his gaze.

"You think we should sell quality for low prices?"

"We sell ready-mades. We can have the gowns altered to fit, but in my opinion," Brand cleared his throat, "those who can afford quality don't buy ready-made. The cheaper gowns will do for our customers who can't afford more than one garment per year, if that."

"At one garment per year, we still make a profit."

"We have stocked more of the better quality."

Alasdair examined Brand's face. "I don't object to holding back there for a while if you think it best."

Brand took out his handkerchief and wiped his forehead. "And the men. We only stock working clothes. Perhaps we could offer better quality to the men instead, sir."

Again, Alasdair noted Brand's outfit. "Where do you buy your clothes?"

"I had to buy everything in Adelaide. Here, we have the tailor shops for wealthy gentlemen and Seymour's for the workers."

"I can agree to expanding our options for the men, but I don't agree we should give up presenting better quality gowns to the women. In my other stores, we sell as many of the higher priced garments as we do the lower. Combining the two encourages those who have a few extra pennies to aim higher than they might otherwise."

Brand nodded but didn't look convinced. Alasdair leaned back in the chair, contemplating. His manager had a point he hadn't fully explained and Alasdair needed to see for himself whatever Brand saw. "Perhaps I'll take a walk around the town to get the feel of the place." He pulled on his gloves, tilted his hat at a businesslike angle, and nodded at Brand, who looked relieved.

He walked the one main street to the end, noting the noisy vegetable market with the vendors calling out their prices, the butchers' shop with bloody carcasses swinging from hooks, and a baker selling his warm yeasty loaves as fast as he could pack them into his customers' baskets. Alasdair smelled the wax at the chandler and the leather at the cobbler's shop. The variety of smells and goods was as large as the new population, and the competition was fierce.

The street reeked of cooking food and raw sweat and had an exciting atmosphere for a merchandiser. He noted a Lutheran church, a Bible Christian church, and flower stalls. If he hadn't already known, he would have seen by the new constructions that the population was in the process of expanding. For a demographic like this, he had stocked his emporium the same way as his Ballarat business, with tools, homewares, and basic working clothes. He didn't want to stop selling quality garments for women. In a hard-working community like this, women needed frills.

He crossed the road, deciding to walk back on the sunny side. Past his emporium, almost at the other end of the street, he spotted a board sign. *Quality Ladies' Wear.* Competition for his ladies' department, perhaps? He gave a satisfied smile. Unlikely. No town could have a finer ladies' department than he.

As he approached the shop, in the large window he saw a headless dummy dressed in a plain white gown, severely and elegantly cut, draped with lace across one shoulder. At the side stood a rack of tiny hats, decorated extravagantly with flowers, ribbons, or lace. One had a bird nestled in a bunch of silk leaves. He stopped and peered through the glass-paneled door.

Along one wall of the shop lolled an orderly selection of fabric rolls, arranged like the colors of the rainbow. A cutting counter with chained scissors ranged in front. Near the opposite wall stood three long racks of ready-made gowns. Behind were drawers, probably containing ladies' intimate apparel. A row of green velvet curtains hung along the back wall. By a pine table in front, three young females plied needles. Each wore a dark blue gown with lace frills at the shoulders and, around the waist, token aprons.

Not a regular visitor to ladies' dress shops, Alasdair entered, startling the doorbell and trying to look like a customer. Muffled conversations and giggles came from behind the curtains. No doubt a customer was trying on clothes. Two carefully dressed women hovered over the rack of gowns. "She said warm colors for me," said one, "and cool colors for you."

Alasdair glanced at the shoppers. Until Starling had entered his life, he'd thought most women bought gowns as fashion or practicality dictated, not purely by choosing a particular range of colors, as Lavender did. He removed his hat, tapping the brim against his leg.

A curtain at the back swished aside. A woman with fading hennaed hair smiled at him. She also wore the dark blue uniform and lace apron. "A gentleman. 'Ow nice. 'Ow can I help you, sir?"

"Perhaps..." With no woman in his life, he couldn't think of a thing to buy. "A gift for a lady."

She assessed him, sharp green eyes scanning from his head to his toes. A dimple appeared in her cheek. "Over here." She took him to the drawers behind the racks. "Something lacy or something racy?" she said with a naughty wink.

"You would be the owner?"

"Miss Smith is the owner. I'm her sister, Meg." She fluttered her lashes.

"Alasdair Seymour. I own the emporium in the middle of town. And I see I have some competition."

He'd not thought of himself as unimportant, but he'd never thought of his name as a conversation ender. Meg Smith's mouth made a perfect O, which she held for a full half minute. "I don't know what to say. It's good

to meetcha...meet you. But for your training, we wouldn't have all this."
She swung her hand, indicating the shop.

He smiled politely. "My training?"

"Starling, my sister, trained in your fabric department."

Alasdair dropped his hat and possibly his jaw.

"We've had great success because of that." She stooped and picked up his hat. "Ladies come from Eudunda, Tanunda, and Angaston just to buy from us. Over there are three more of our sisters, Robin, Dove, and Lizzy." The sewing girls, one fair and slightly plump, the next tall and angular, and the last long-faced, smiled at him.

"I thought Starling was an orphan. No, that's wrong. There are eighteen of you."

"More'n thirty, but eighteen old enough to work. Eleven of those work here, five in the front, and six more out the back. I had no idea you knew that about 'er. I thought she was simply one of your shopgirls."

"Oh, we were great friends, as I'm sure she would tell you...if she were here," he said, almost holding his breath.

"She's been keeping secrets." Meg grinned. She turned to the curtain and called, "Starling."

Alasdair froze. The conversation in the back area ceased.

"Yes," trilled a happy, pleasant tone, a familiar voice that made his heart leap in his chest. "I won't be much longer. We're just making sure the hat's just right." With that, a fluttering white hand pulled the curtain aside.

Apparently not the owner of the hand, out stepped a matron of forty or so, wearing a flattering blue gown, the bodice seams picked out with pale green piping. She adjusted a green pillbox hat on her mousy, neatly styled hair. Clearly of the middle class, the woman looked very smart.

"Presenting..." Starling appeared, loose curls floating around her face, with the majority caught back, and her soft eyelashes feathering her cheeks. She wore the same as the other workers, dark blue with a white lace apron. Her gaze met Alasdair's. A look of stark horror paled her face. She glanced away and finished with "...the transformation of the century," in a hollow voice.

The customer began to gush her thanks. Alasdair didn't hear a word. He wanted to breathe. He wanted to snatch Starling into his arms and ride away with her. Instead, he stood like a fish on a fence, gaping, waiting to fall on his face.

She gave him time to gather his senses; she totally ignored him.

"When she's finished with the customer, she'll speak to you," Meg said, sounding puzzled. "We can get on with choosing your gift while we wait."

"I've changed my mind. I'll let the lady choose her own gift. In the meantime..." He moved over to the rolls of fabrics and inspected them. The range was extensive and consisted of moderately priced, medium-quality materials. Silks, cottons, muslins, nets, and laces but nothing a middle-class family couldn't afford. The ribbon box was the same. The hat shapes were fashionable rather than outrageous. The young seamstresses whispered to each other while they worked on the ready-made gowns. He noticed that the young, plump seamstress had red, chapped hands with ragged fingernails.

Finally, Starling's customer left and Meg sold a gown to one of the other ladies after each had consulted with Starling as to the fit and the color. The two customers left, satisfied. Another woman entered the shop. As Starling, seeming entirely unaware of Alasdair, moved past him to greet her, he murmured, "Perhaps you ought to speak to me before my annoyance over you stealing my ideas forces me to take you to court."

Starling rounded on him, face aghast. "Your ideas? Never. This shop is mine and every merchandising idea I am using is my own."

"How about the fabrics kept in their color groups rather than their fabric groups. It's the same way in my city store, I recall."

The new customer looked interested, so Starling included her in the conversation. "It was my idea. I did it for him."

Alasdair took her arm. "I think we should take a walk and discuss this. Don't you?"

Her mouth mutinied. Then her gaze lowered and she sighed and nodded. She went behind the curtains and came out wearing a pelisse of pale blue with a burgundy hat and gloves. He stared, wondering how he had overlooked her quiet beauty. Perhaps in noticing her more important assets—her strength of character and her sweetness—he hadn't needed more.

With an ache of pure pleasure, he took her elbow and moved her into the street. "You make that color elegant. I always thought it was rather girlish."

"Only on the wrong person," she said, tilting her head away from him. The pink bloom on her cheeks was adorable. She began to walk in the direction of his emporium.

"These days Lavender wears pale yellows or peach colors," he said as he caught up. He joined his fingers together and rounded them over an imaginary stomach.

She lifted her chin and glanced at him. "She's with child?"

"In an interesting condition. Her baby is due in six months or so."

"I wish you would go away. We really have nothing to say to each other."

"We didn't finish our last conversation five months ago." He scooped his arm around her waist.

She peeled his hand from her. "I heard all I needed to hear."

"But I have more to say. I made you a proposal which I thought might keep you in my bed at least until I returned. I had the idea that you wanted to be with me, too." He held his breath.

"I didn't tell you that."

"Which is why I'm on uncertain ground now. There is much you didn't tell me. You didn't tell me that you knew what you were talking about when it came to colors. You didn't tell me that my servants would blame me for the fact that you left, and you didn't tell me that my house would never run as well without you. You didn't tell me how lonely an unshared bed is."

"I'm sure you've rectified the last. Lavender surely wouldn't insist on her own bedroom."

"I can't say. Lavender married Hamilton. I'd like to think she will find happiness, but I doubt it. Time will affect her beauty, and I'm not sure she has anything else. I wish I didn't feel sorry for her, but I do."

"It's been interesting catching up on your life. Now I have to get back to my sisters. At this time of day, the shop is very busy. Robin has only been with us a week, and she's quite unsure as yet." Starling backed, staring challengingly at Alasdair.

He smiled into her lovely, warm brown eyes. "These sisters of yours... Did Meg work at the inn?"

"Don't you dare tell anyone."

"And the others. Where did they come from? The same place?"

"They came from their various jobs, like me, and they learnt menial jobs in the home, like me. We had a pact that when one could help the others, she would. Perhaps we're not related by blood, but we are sisters. I won't let anyone interfere with our opportunity to make a new start. If you tell anyone we're not respectable women, if you say a word about how I earned that money, I'll... I'll..."

"Kiss me," he said in a low voice, unable to keep the yearning out of his tone.

"Of course I won't kiss you," she replied, indignantly. "You don't see women's kisses as a punishment."

"I can't remember. No one's kissed me for a very long time. Maybe I've always hated being kissed. Come on. See if I can take my punishment." He took her hands in his.

She lifted her fingers out of his grip, tilting her chin at an offended angle. "You've done this before—tried to trick me into doing what you want me to do by pretending you don't. It won't work. I learned my lesson from a master. You won't tell. You're not so petty."

"I might be." He pushed his hands into his pockets. "You've run my Kapunda store out of business."

"Not so, just the women's department, but it was at a standstill when Meg and I arrived here. The women bought cheap ready-made gowns from you. If they could afford higher prices, they needed to be offered special outfits, not just those made from more expensive materials."

"Which you have provided by including your advice."

"By including my interest in the garments they would like to have," she said, firmly. "I told Mr. Brand what he should do in the emporium. You should sell men's clothes and add higher quality there instead. Quite a few men here would like jackets like yours, but most can't afford a tailor. They have more money in this town than they had, but not as much as gentlemen have."

He nodded slowly. "You may be right. What made you come to that conclusion?"

"I studied. While I was in your house, I found everything I needed to know about merchandising by reading various books in your library. I learnt about accounts and how to display articles to their best advantage. And with no one to stop me, I've shown my customers that wearing the right colors makes them look like beauties."

"I suppose you'll make your fortune. Then how will I afford you?" She stiffened. "You can't buy me."

"Not for a hundred pounds a year?" he asked, ruefully.

"No."

"Two hundred."

"I can earn my own way."

"Three hundred. You could help a lot of orphans with three hundred pounds. I want you, Starling. I can't get you out of my mind. Only Paul and Mary know we weren't married, so if you come back with me, we can go on as before."

Her eyes flashed. "I want to keep my good opinion of myself."

"Would five hundred pounds elevate that opinion?"

"Indeed. Please, Alasdair. Find some other woman to impress with your money."

Chapter 22

Starling outpaced him, but she knew he wouldn't follow. Although her words had been final, her eyes ached and a constricted band around her chest caused her to gasp as she reached the door of the shop.

Meg stood just inside, hands on hips, eyes wide. "Mr. Seymour's a flash one. A gentleman like him can have anything he wants. What *does* he want?"

"The same as he's always wanted," Starling replied, rolling up the fabric on the counter.

"Which is?"

Starling shook her head. "He hasn't changed. Nothing's changed, and that includes me."

"I'm glad to hear it, if you mean you won't let him tup you," Meg said severely. "The lecher wanted to buy a gift for a lady."

"His favorite lady married someone else, a man richer than he is."

The doorbell tinkled. Alasdair re-entered the shop. "I still want...something."

Starling had believed he wouldn't follow her. Seeing him after she'd said her last goodbye was a shock. "We won't refuse your custom, of course, but circumstances between us being as they are, Meg will assist you."

"I want you. Strange. I think we've been through this before. You cost me close to sixty pounds the first time, but this time the budget is limited."

She made a sound of disgust and began rearranging the rolls of fabric.

"Meg, can you help me with a woman who'll snuggle into me in bed at night? One who'll bear my children, who'll love them and tell them all about men, religion, and politics? A brown-haired beauty who treats my staff with respect and me with honesty? Show me what you have in medium-height and slim."

Meg glanced at Starling's set face and said, "I think we ought to close for lunch. Lizzy, Dove, Robin, come with me."

Starling didn't watch the girls collect their hats and coats. Trembling, she clasped her hands behind her back and breathed in deeply, willing the thundering inside her chest to cease. The doorbell tinkled. When Starling glanced around, she saw Meg had turned the sign to *Closed*.

"I didn't think we had any more to say to each other," she said in a voice she hoped sounded firm.

"When I go through my list of needs in a woman, you're the only one who suits. When I met you five months ago, I didn't know that. I know better now. Then, I made the arrangement businesslike but that's not the arrangement I want now. I can't give you up, Starling, not until I'm sure there's no hope."

"Miss Smith. And there's no hope." She glanced away from his slate-etched eyes. How she had managed to withstand him for those two weeks was a mystery to her. The expression on his face, a combination of optimism and contrition, was a lure she could scarcely resist. She wished she could trust him, but after she had given him her body, he had betrayed her in the cruelest way, describing her as a whore while planning to marry the devious Lavender.

He took her hand in his, brushed his thumb over her palm, then lifted her fingers to his mouth. Not only her hand but also her whole body experienced the same melting sensation. She wanted to bury her fingers in his fashionably brushed hair, snuggle into his magnificent tailored jacket, and love every manly inch of him. However, she couldn't be his mistress any more than she could run away from her obligations when she had so many unfulfilled hopes, so many sisters in adversity, and so many more ideas to put to the test. She took her hand back.

He shook his head with regret. "I think you love me, Miss Smith." Angling his head, he leaned forward, touching her lips with his. "But unless you tell me you do, I won't ever know for sure."

"Please. Don't humiliate me any more than you have," she said, her eyes prickling with suppressed tears.

"If I ever have, then I'm sorry, for I've never meant to," he said in a gentle voice. He gave a wry laugh. "I must be knuckleheaded to think that a proposal of marriage to the woman I love is more flattering than shaming."

"Marriage?" She covered her mouth and nose with a palm. "When did you propose marriage?"

"Five minutes ago. One minute ago. And I'll do it again if only you'll tell me you love me."

A tear raced down to her chin and she wiped at the streak. "Did you say 'the woman I love?'"

"Did I? Didn't I? You *are* the woman I love. You can't doubt that. Why else would I be here?"

"To put me out of business."

"I'm here because I love you and I want to marry you. If I do, I won't *have* to put you out of business. I'll get your shop, too." A faint smile curved his mouth.

Her head reeled. She looked at her racks of lovely gowns, possibly none worth the price of his cravat. This rich and handsome man wanted to marry her! He loved her! Using a palm on each cheek to dry her tears, she took a deep breath, tightened her mouth, took two steps forward, and shoved him hard with both hands. "I thought you were asking me to be your fancy-piece, and I won't be any man's paid woman." She left her hands on his hard chest.

He covered them with his. "In that case, I take back the offer of an allowance of five hundred pounds a year."

She slid her hands to his neck, pressing right against him. "And so you should," she said severely, her lips nuzzling his cheek. "A woman likes to give freely where she loves."

"Ah. You do love me, Miss Smith. I don't doubt you'll be buying and selling me before I know it if I let you keep this business of yours."

"I must warn you." Her thumbs caressed his jaw. "I love you, but you won't find I'm a duke's illegitimate daughter. I'm a foundling, never placed in an orphanage but found on a doorstep. I'm probably a bastard child of no one who cares, and I have worked as a menial since I was twelve."

"That's a 'yes' to my marriage proposal, I believe."

She made a considering face, smiling as he circled his arms around her waist and dropped on her lips an earth-shattering, word-stealing kiss. Tightening her arms around him, she felt the needy flare of her body and the familiar yearning of her blood. Had they not been in full view of anyone who passed, she would be pulling at his clothes.

As if he had read her mind, he lifted his purposeful mouth from hers. "We'll do it quickly and quietly. I don't want anyone to know we didn't marry five months ago." He set her at arm's length.

"In that case, we'll have to do it quietly. That is, if I agree." She blushed. "But I don't ever want to do it quickly."

He laughed and hugged her again. "Not the bedding. I meant the wedding, my love. I'll have to send to Adelaide for a license, and I suspect that will take a couple of days. If you insist, I'll wait until we're wedded for the other."

"I should hope so," she said, trying to sound shocked. "But I can't consider marrying you until I know the truth."

"What truth?"

"Did you make your money mining gold?"

"I want to know the truth about your dealings with John Brand."

"What dealings?" She made an innocent face.

"You told him how to run my emporium. Was that to take my business away?"

"Not at all. I took your quality gowns' business on my second day. But I can't manage men's tailoring, not unless I find the rest of the Birds and convince them that the new middle class will want better clothes." She tilted her head, watching him hide his expression.

"So you suggested to him that I might want your idea?" he said, his bland tone giving her no satisfaction whatsoever.

"Actually, no." She pursed her lips. "I saw no reason to give you more than you have. It was Meg. She has an eye on Mr. Brand. She wanted to help him look efficient."

"Are you telling me he isn't?"

"Could we return to the original subject?"

"What original subject?"

"The mining."

"Ah, the mining." He hesitated. "I can see you are very interested in details. You will make a very fine business partner if I take you on as such."

She raised her chin. "I couldn't marry a man who didn't see me as his equal."

He sighed, his expression quietly indulgent. "I seem to be hearing a list of conditions."

"Isn't that the way you strike a bargain?"

"My love, you are not my equal. You are superior to me in every way." He reached out to take her back into his arms.

She balked. "I'm better than you at staying on the subject. You haven't convinced me about making your fortune with your emporium in Ballarat. You had an interest in a mine, Mrs. Trelevan says. What sort of interest?"

He rubbed his fingers across his chin. "You do realize, don't you, that gentlemen do not work as miners?"

She planted her hands on her hips. "Is it more important to be a gentleman than truthful?"

He chewed at the inside of his cheek. "More expedient, let's say. I don't mind if you know I am not a gentleman and that I was a miner, a very lucky one."

She leaned back, grinning in triumph. "I knew it was a Ballarat story from the beginning."

He lifted his brows in query. She smiled and shrugged.

With his amused gaze on her, he said, "And, while I'm telling the whole truth and almost nothing but, I have to say I want to make love to you sooner rather than later. Tonight is not *quickly* when you consider that we met each other at the beginning of January."

She laughed. "I didn't mean that sort of *quickly*. I meant rushed. Not enjoyable."

A smile lit his face. "Now you're *really* putting pressure on."

"I expect you to wait until after we are wed." She tapped a finger on her cheek. "Or, if I have a word with Meg, she can let the story slip that we married months ago. But before I completely burn my bridges, I do want five hundred pounds a year."

"Then the money is yours."

"Don't you want to know why I want it?"

"You like money. You like to bargain about making love."

"I don't," she said with a gasp. "You know I'm—"

"You want to run your shop and others like it for your fellow orphans. You want them to learn a trade so that they don't have to rub their hands raw, work as servants, or prostitute themselves."

"You know all that?"

"I found out a lot about you after you left. I'm agreeable. Very agreeable." He took her into his arms.

Absolutely, totally, and completely in love, she forgot the months they had been apart and concentrated on the moment. "I love you," she said into his cravat. "And I agree to marry you as soon as we have the license."

His palm flattened onto her back and he laughed softly. "Perhaps you haven't thought this out, but marrying you will do more to make me socially acceptable than marrying almost any other woman. I can't believe I was clever enough to find you."

"Clever? You were just plain lucky."

"Clever. Your charities will make you, and thus me, a very influential person."

She kissed him. "If you are saying you're marrying me for my money, that is yet another Ballarat story."

He shook his head, still laughing. "We'll discuss business later."

Meet the Author

From art student to stylist, to nurse and midwife, Virginia's life has been one illogical step to the next, each step leading to the final goal of being an author. When she can tear herself away from the computer and the waiting blank page, she immerses herself in arts and crafts or gardening or, of course, cooking.